D1554208

OUR TIME

BAYTOWN BOYS

MARYANN JORDAN

Our Time (Baytown Boys) Copyright 2020

All rights reserved. No part of this book may be reproduced or transmitted in any form or by any means, electronic or mechanical, including photocopying, recording, or by any information storage and retrieval system without the written permission of the author, except where permitted by law.

If you are reading this book and did not purchase it, then you are reading an illegal pirated copy. Make sure that you are only reading a copy that has been officially released by the author.

This book is a work of fiction. Names, characters, places, and incidents either are products of the author's imagination or are used fictitiously. Any resemblance to actual persons, living or dead, events, or locales is entirely coincidental.

Cover Design by: Graphics by Stacy

Cover and model photography: Eric McKinney

ISBN ebook: 978-1-947214-48-4

ISBN print: 978-1-947214-49-1

❀ Created with Vellum

Author's Note

Please remember that this is a work of fiction. I have lived in numerous states as well as overseas, but for the last twenty years have called Virginia my home. I often choose to use fictional city names with some geographical accuracies.

These fictionally named cities allow me to use my creativity and not feel constricted by attempting to accurately portray the areas.

It is my hope that my readers will allow me this creative license and understand my fictional world.

I also do quite a bit of research on my books and try to write on subjects with accuracy. There will always be points where creative license will be used in order to create scenes or plots.

1

"Morning, Sheriff."

Colt Hudson barely walked into Joe's Place in Easton before the greetings were called out from all directions. Maybe it was because he ate there every morning. Maybe it was because he was so easily recognized in his sheriff's uniform. Maybe it was just because he grew up in the area and had known many of the patrons since he was a boy.

The diner had been in the same location for fifty years, and it had looked exactly the same for as long as he could remember, with very few upgrades. Several years ago, the owners, Joe and Mavis Crouch, finally had to replace the old linoleum flooring when a few spots had worn so thin the concrete floor below could almost be seen. He vaguely remembered as a young teenager that new seats and tables and barstools had been put in, but considering he was almost thirty-five, that meant they were twenty years old.

The light green table tops were still Formica, worn

pale from cleanings. The booth seats were green vinyl, the chairs and barstools were metal with green vinyl seats. Occasionally, Mavis would use green tape to repair a split in the vinyl when needed. Any time someone suggested to Joe or Mavis that they should upgrade to new seating, they were quickly told that if Joe and Mavis had to keep buying new furniture, then they would pass that cost on to their customers.

The customers liked getting good food at a good value, so they kept their mouths shut, sat on the repaired vinyl chairs, and enjoyed their meal.

Colt offered a few chin lifts to some of the patrons as he walked over to the counter, smiling at one of the servers. "Morning, BettyJo." She had been working at Joe's Place for years, always taking the breakfast shift. Her bleached blonde hair was teased up in the front and twisted into a bun in the back. No matter how early in the morning it was, BettyJo would have her lipstick on, always matching her fingernails, usually dark red or bright pink.

He remembered when Mavis used to make the servers wear uniforms, and BettyJo would always be in a pink or blue dress with a little black apron tied around her waist. Now, Mavis had given in to more modern times, having the servers wear blue jeans with a pink or blue blouse, a black apron still tied around their waists.

Continuing down the counter until he came to the last stool, he hefted himself onto the seat, nodding his thanks as BettyJo set a cup of coffee in front of him. He fixed his coffee the way he liked, looked through the passageway into the kitchen, and offered a nod to Joe, who was in the back scrambling eggs and frying bacon.

Joe had been a cook in the Navy many years ago and started Joe's Place as soon as he got out. His bald, shiny head was easily visible, and he wore his typical uniform of a white T-shirt that used to strain across his chest but now strained a bit across his stomach. Mavis, his high school sweetheart who'd waited for him until he got home from the Navy, was at the stove stirring a pot that Colt knew would hold grits, while keeping an eye on the biscuits in the oven. Her hair was gray, but he had no idea how long it was since he never saw it down. She had worn it twisted in a bun on top of her head for as long as he could remember. Joe and Mavis ran a tight ship, but the servers who worked for them usually stayed a long time. That was a testament to the diner's longevity and how well the owners treated their employees.

He slowly turned on the stool, letting his gaze drift over the morning breakfast crowd, always noticing new faces, those traveling through, as well as the regulars. And, just like every morning, his gaze finally landed on what he had been seeking.

Carrie Beaumont.

Her arms were currently full of plates as she made her way from the kitchen to the far side of the restaurant. Greeting the patrons warmly, she sat each of the platters down, made sure everyone had what they needed and then started back through the room, checking on her tables.

Her dark brown hair, thick and shiny, was pulled

into a low ponytail, the waves hanging down her back. Her lush curves were unmistakable. Her jeans clung to her shapely ass, her blouse pulled slightly over her full breasts, and the tied apron accentuated her narrow waist.

He continued to observe as she stopped at a corner booth, one hand resting on the back of the older man sitting alone. She bent forward and whispered something into the man's ear, and Colt watched as his lips turned upward into a smile. Carrie took the man's knife and fork, cutting the pancakes into smaller bites before refilling his cup with coffee. Colt knew the older man had been finishing chemo treatments and came in every day that he could for something to eat. He also knew Joe and Mavis had not been charging the man, knowing his treatments had to punish his resources. And he also knew that Carrie would never get a tip from the man but always went above and beyond to make sure he ate and was able to handle his food.

She continued her rounds, then, as usual, her gaze moved to the last stool at the counter, landed on his, and her smile widened. And just like every morning, the sight of her blue eyes made crawling out of bed worth it. He also figured if he had those blue eyes in his bed he would never leave it.

Squashing that thought, he watched as she headed behind the counter, walking until she got to the end and stopped right in front of him. She leaned her elbows on the counter, propped her chin on her hands. "Good morning, Sheriff Hudson."

Her voice hit him in the gut every morning. A little

deep. A little husky. More than a little sexy. Something else he knew he should not be thinking about.

Colt may have grown up on the Eastern Shore of Virginia, but Carrie transplanted here while he was serving in the military. And he had noticed her the first day he was back.

"Morning, Ms. Beaumont."

She planted her fist on her cocked hip. "Are you ever going to call me Carrie?"

"Not until I know you better." It was his standard answer, the one he had given for the past year.

She tossed her head back and laughed, and it was not the first time he thought her smile would brighten anyone's day, 'cause it sure as hell brightened his.

She winked. "I can't wait to get to know you better then." With that, she reached behind her to grab the coffee pot, topped him off, then headed back through the restaurant to check on the other customers.

He wished her laughter was just for him. Same with her flirty smile and banter. And he certainly wished her wink was only for him. But no…he watched as she moved around the diner, smiling and joking as she weaved between the tables. *Fuck. Never mind...I've got no time for anything more anyway.*

"Here you go, Sheriff." BettyJo set a plate filled with sausage gravy and biscuits, scrambled eggs, and hashbrown potatoes. "I reckon it's a good thing you work as hard as you do to burn through these calories or you'd be so wide you couldn't get through the door."

He picked up his fork, shoveling food into his

mouth, looking up only when he heard Carrie call out, "Good morning, Detective Simmons."

He offered another chin lift as Hunter Simmons came walking over, taking the stool next to him. Right behind Detective Simmons were a couple of Colt's deputies. Hunter wore the easy uniform of blue jeans and a dark blue shirt, while the deputies wore the traditional uniform of khaki pants and brown shirts, their patches and deputy badges in place. He figured one of the reasons Joe liked being near the Sheriff's Office was that with so many law enforcement personnel in his restaurant, he never had to worry about problems.

It only took a few minutes for Carrie to get their orders and coffees poured. "Trevon, how's that wife of yours? I haven't seen her in here recently and didn't know if she had had that baby yet."

He shook his head. "She's due any day. Honest to God, though, she's ready. Looks like she's about to pop!"

"Well, I can't wait to see the little one, so you'll have to let us know when she has it." Glancing down the counter, she said, "Of course, you'll be busy. So perhaps Sheriff Hudson will let me know."

"If he doesn't, I'll be sure to come in and give you all the updates."

Colt glanced up as one of his deputies, Mark Robbins, flirted with Carrie, and he rolled his eyes. As Carrie smiled at all of them, Colt felt a bolt of jealousy, tamping it down as he shoveled in more breakfast.

"Oh, you don't have to worry about that. I see Sheriff Hudson almost every day," she replied.

Colt swallowed a grin at her reply to Mark. Glad

when she moved away to take care of a few more customers, he felt Hunter's gaze boring into the side of his head.

Refusing to take the bait, he heard Hunter chuckle before mumbling, "Don't know why you don't go for that, Colt."

Ignoring him, Colt continued eating before reminding the others of the staff meeting that morning. Finishing his breakfast, he threw money onto the counter, making sure to add a good tip for Carrie and BettyJo.

Offering more chin lifts to Joe, Mavis, BettyJo, and a few of the patrons, he could not help but look for Carrie as he was walking toward the door. She came from the kitchen, delivered a plate to a table nearby, and he watched as her gaze moved to the counter where he had been sitting and then quickly jerked around toward the door.

She walked toward him, smiled and reached to lay her hand on his arm, saying, "Have a good day, Sheriff Hudson."

"You too, Ms. Beaumont." He tried not to look at her hand on him, feeling the burn of her light touch.

Her laughter followed him as he walked outside, moving directly to his SUV. He sat in his vehicle for just a moment, easily able to see her through the windows of the diner as she made her rounds among the tables. Inwardly rolling his eyes, he started his SUV and backed out of the parking lot before anyone could catch the Sheriff pining over a woman.

In his rearview mirror he saw Hunter, Trevon, and

Mark leaving Joe's Place, and he was glad, knowing that Mark was no longer inside flirting with Carrie.

It only took a couple of moments to pull into his reserved parking spot in front of the North Heron Sheriff's Office in Easton. Just a few miles north of Baytown, Easton was a tiny town of only two hundred people. But, as the county seat, many people worked there since it held all of the county government offices, including the jail for both North Heron and Accawmacke Counties.

Energized from a full breakfast and coffee served by the one person that could make his day brighter, he headed straight to his desk, ready to get to work.

Carrie felt his eyes still on her even after the Sheriff had walked out of the diner. As she filled the coffee mugs at one of her tables, she looked through the window and observed him staring inside, and she could have sworn he was staring at her.

She had worked for Joe and Mavis for almost ten years, the last five of those acutely aware of the handsome new sheriff. She still remembered the first time she saw him. She had heard that a local boy who had served in the Army was moving back to the Eastern Shore and running for the Office of Sheriff.

She had never thought much about law enforcement other than she knew to stay on the good side of it. But everybody coming into and working at Joe's Place had been excited when he returned, saying that it was time they had new blood in the county.

According to BettyJo, the old sheriff who was retiring had been slow to modernize the office, slow to try new techniques, and slow to do anything except just arrest a few drunks and catch speeders.

According to Joe, the county was becoming a major drug-running area, some gang activity had been discovered, and the sheriff's department was outdated.

According to Mavis, the outgoing sheriff was just a 'lazy fuck'.

The first time Carrie had seen Colt Hudson drive up in his big, shiny SUV with the word 'Sheriff' emblazoned on the side, she could not help but to laugh, thinking of an old western movie where someone would say, *'Boys, there's a new sheriff in town.'* But, when he climbed down from the driver's seat, her laughter had died in her throat.

Tall, easily topping six feet four inches, with thick, black hair. She did not know what she had expected, but the musclebound man who looked as though he could make a living as a fitness model was not what she imagined a sheriff would look like.

It was not hard to find out more about him considering the gossip mill was running full time, and he was the talk of the county. Joe, Mavis, and BettyJo remembered him as a kid. Brenda, another server, had gone to high school with him.

Good kid, never in trouble. A star athlete with the Baytown Boys. Supposedly, he could have gotten a sports scholarship to college but left the Shore to join the Army. He was gone for twelve years, then left the Army to return five years ago to run for sheriff, which he easily won.

For five years he had been coming into Joe's Place most mornings for breakfast, occasionally a lunch, and rarely for dinner. And every single time, Carrie found herself honing in on him like an invisible tractor beam was pulling. They seemed such opposites, but maybe that was part of the attraction. He was stoic, and she made her living chatting up the customers, both wanting them to be happy and hoping the tips would be decent. Colt appeared to have secrets, and she figured most people knew all her business.

It was not hard to imagine herself a little bit in love with him, but she was a smart woman. Life had taught her self-preservation. She was not putting herself down when she knew that her feelings would be unrequited. A woman like her would just not be the right person for him. At least, that was what she figured everyone else would think. Considering he kept her at arm's length, he must think the same thing.

"Carrie."

She startled as she looked up, seeing Joe walking toward her.

"Are you going to keep staring out the window even though he's long gone?"

Blushing, she threw a narrowed-eyed glare at him. "I was just checking the weather."

"Well, unless it's gonna start raining men, I don't think there's anything out there worth looking at anymore."

She cocked her hip, adopting an attitude. "Did you want something, or did you just come over here to bust my chops?" Not many people would talk to Joe that way, but she knew he was gruff on the outside and a teddy bear on the inside.

He and Mavis had taken a chance almost ten years ago on a scared twenty-year-old, giving her a job when she was desperate. Joe learned how to cook when he was in the Navy many years ago. He moved to the Eastern Shore, bought Joe's Place from Mavis' father who wanted to retire and had continued to sling hash ever since. Tall and wide, with a shiny bald head and a dark goatee shot with silver, he looked a little bit like a pirate.

He glared in return. "Ellen called and said she was going to be running late today and won't get here until just before the dinner shift. Will you be able to cover until she gets in?"

Carrie held his gaze and nodded. She needed the overtime, and he always threw it her way. Working a ten-hour day was no big deal, considering she often worked double shifts of sixteen hours at a time.

Pushing thoughts of Colt from her mind, she hurried back over to check her tables, making sure the customers were happy.

2

Standing in his office, Colt looked out the second-floor window, another cup of coffee in his hand. One of the things that he was proud of was the new Sheriff's Office that was part of the government building complex in Easton. Set back off the main road, the buildings formed a large square with a parking lot in the middle. One side held the county offices and the Courthouse. Opposite was the Sheriff's Office, and on the back was the new Regional Jail.

He walked down the steps to the first floor to the large meeting room where the morning report would be given. His sergeant, Bud Sinton, was in charge of the meeting, but Colt always made sure to be there if possible. He hated that so much of his job was administrative, but he refused to be tied to his desk. Standing with his back against the wall, he looked out over the men and women in the room. North Heron County was one of the poorest in Virginia, but with grants, he had been able to upgrade the sheriff's department.

Now, besides just deputies in the room, there were two canine units, a drug task force, one deputy who specialized in the older population, and another deputy who worked hand-in-hand with the social services department. Besides the deputies, several more detective positions had now been filled.

Bud was currently reviewing the information the deputies would need for the day. "Pearl's Pawn Shop reported a break-in early this morning. Detective Simmons is over there now and will be compiling a list of what Jonas Pearl says is missing. Once we have that list, we'll get it out to everyone so you can be on the lookout for any of these items. Some of you may have your suspicions of who might be involved, and if so, please talk to Detective Simmons. The school rotation list is on the board outside. Please check to see when it's your day and times to rotate through the schools."

"Sergeant, do you have any idea when that might become a permanent position?"

Colt looked over as one of the new deputies asked the question.

Bud answered, "Not at this time." He looked over at Colt and lifted an eyebrow.

Pushing off the wall, Colt drew the deputies' attention to him. "We can't fill that right now. There isn't money to have full-time deputies in the elementary, middle, and high schools. That's in the budget for next year, and I've got someone pushing at the state level for that funding. As you probably know, studies are proving that having an assigned deputy on a full-time basis in each school can reduce teen crimes, gang activity, and give the younger students another person to turn to with their problems at home. It's important, and I promise that I'm working on the funding."

Bud continued down the list, and he listened with interest. There had been a small building set on fire, which made everyone nervous, considering they had recently had an arsonist in the county. It'd turned out to be the owner who wanted to save on the demolition costs to get rid of an outbuilding, so he set it on fire. Eye rolls and chuckles made their way through the room, and he dropped his head, a grin pulling at his lips as well.

Bud finished with the assignments, giving several of the deputies traffic duty. The main road cutting from one end of the Eastern Shore of Virginia to the other was a four-lane, straight highway, the speed limit clearly marked at fifty-five miles per hour, slower near towns. But many drivers who were used to using the road to get from New England to the southern states by bypassing the busy Washington D.C. area tended to fly down the road. Many of them grew angry when they were pulled over for speeding, but the deputies did not care, ticketing them anyway. It was a source of revenue for the county, but more importantly, with so many stores and houses on the road, speeding was dangerous.

Bud dismissed the meeting, and Colt watched as the gathering of deputies stood and left the room, prepared for their day. He and Bud walked out together, Bud following him up to his office. They had formed a habit of talking after the morning briefing.

He finished his cup of coffee and decided a third cup

would make him too jittery, but his secretary, Loretta, got a cup for Bud.

Settling into the chairs, Bud asked, "What's on your mind?"

"Who reported the theft at Pearl's Pawn Shop? Harvey or his son Mickey?"

"Mickey, but Harvey was there this morning when Hunter got there. Why?"

"Mickey's always been careful to stay clean, but I wonder. This makes two thefts in two years. Maybe for a pawn shop that's not too much, but I thought Harvey put in a better security system."

Bud nodded. "It seems the new person working there didn't follow all the procedures."

He lifted an eyebrow, stating, "That seems kind of suspicious."

Bud chuckled and said, "It'll be interesting to see what Hunter reports when he gets back in." Finishing his coffee, Bud left, and Colt spent the next two hours completing paperwork and reading over the reports from his detectives and deputies.

Glancing back out his window, he saw Hunter's pickup truck pulling into the parking lot. Needing some exercise, he left his office and headed downstairs. Meeting Hunter, the two of them walked toward the back where a large room held several detectives' desks. Organized chaos was the best way to describe the room, with files, papers, and two whiteboards on the walls, filled with information from open cases. Hunter sat at his desk and Colt settled in the chair next to it.

Hunter, like him, was a big guy, but kept his light

brown hair long, almost brushing his shoulders. Having been an undercover officer with the Virginia State Police, Hunter had come to the North Heron Sheriff's Department a year ago. A natural leader, he assisted the gang task force as well as taking charge of the other detectives.

"What did you get this morning?"

"Supposedly, the new girl they hired followed almost all the security procedures, except she forgot to pull down the metal shades on the front windows. She said she was so busy setting the alarm correctly that she completely forgot about it. She was in tears, a total mess, terrified she was going to lose her job. Someone busted one of the windows, and of course, the alarm went off, but not before they had cleaned out what was in the front display area."

"Kids?"

Shaking his head, Hunter said, "I don't think so. Whoever it was parked just outside the range of the security camera. They wore black clothes and ski masks, making it premeditated unless people just happen to have a ski mask in their cars during the summer."

"You checking out the girl?"

Nodding, Hunter said, "Yeah, that's my first line of inquiry. I'll find out exactly who she is and who she knows."

Colt cast his eyes up at the whiteboard, thinking about the new rounds of theft in the county. The men and women of the sheriff's department had a large area to patrol. Unlike the police force of a much smaller town, sheriffs had an entire county to be responsible for. In North Heron this included a lot of farmland, back roads, several towns, and neighborhoods that had million-dollar homes as well as those that were below the poverty level. *Many homes below the poverty level.*

Feeling Hunter's burning gaze, he turned and looked back at the grin on his friend's face. "You want to tell me what that shit-eating grin is for?"

Chuckling, Hunter said, "You go into Joe's Place every single morning for breakfast. Half the time you pop in to get a sandwich for lunch. And I don't have any doubt that you occasionally stay for dinner, especially if Carrie is pulling an evening shift. What I want to know is when are you finally going to get your head outta your ass and ask her out?"

"What makes you think I want to ask her out?"

Eyebrows raised, Hunter said, "She's a nice girl. Why wouldn't you want to ask her out?"

He grimaced as he replied, "I went down that road once before, and it didn't turn out too good. Figure now, I'm just best going out of the county when I have an itch that needs to be scratched."

"Just because you had a bad marriage years ago when you were younger doesn't mean you can't ask a nice woman out on a date. Hell, I'm not saying you need to marry her, nor use her to scratch an itch, but I hate to see anybody pining as hard as you do for her."

"I don't pine for her," he huffed, hating the peevish sound in his voice. "I just like looking at a pretty woman, that's all."

"Well, if that's true, then I don't guess you'd mind if

anyone else takes a look at her either, do you? Although I could have sworn you wanted to choke Mark this morning when he was flirting with her."

"Carrie is not the type of woman who needs somebody making a mistake with her," Colt said. "I figure life's been hard enough on her, and she doesn't need anyone else's baggage. As busy as we both are, it's just not the right time."

Hunter was quiet for a moment. "There's something about her that reminds me of my wife, Belle. You know, the kind that's had it rough, but they don't go under. They get up every day fighting to make life better for them and those around them. That's a damn fine trait in anyone, but you wrap that in the package of a pretty woman, and it's something to be able to claim that for yourself."

He did not have a response to that sentiment, knowing that Hunter's wife was exactly as he described. Hunter was lucky to have Belle and knew it, but then, Colt figured, Belle felt the same about her husband.

Not wanting to continue down the road of discussing Carrie anymore, he stood and said, "Keep me up on the theft case." He glanced at the clock on the wall as he walked out of the room and saw that it was almost lunchtime. He hesitated for just a moment and then thought, *Fuck it. There's no reason why I have to avoid Carrie, and anyway...I'm hungry.*

The lunch rush had started, and with spring getting

ready to roll into summer, the seasonal crowd had picked up. There were not a lot of vacationers on the Eastern Shore, although the quaint town of Baytown, just south of Easton, had a public beach and lovely inns. But Joe's Place sat right off the main road that ran through the Eastern Shore, making it a perfect stop for families who needed to get something to eat and have a bathroom break for their kids. The fact that there was a gas station just down the road did not hurt.

Carrie could not help but look up every time the bell over the door rang, secretly hoping that Colt would walk in. He came in often for lunch, although not as regularly as he did for breakfast. Sometimes he just ordered a sandwich to go, and other times he would have a seat and eat in. Regardless, Joe and Mavis always kept the last stool at the counter next to the wall free in case he wanted it.

Already today she had had to make sure that two different groups had not taken that seat, one of them grumbling mightily, and she felt sure it would cut into her tip. But no matter, it always made her feel better to know that with the heavy weight of the sheriff's job on his shoulders he would always have a place to sit down when he came in.

The bell over the door rang again, and she looked up, seeing Colt walk in. A smile lit her face, and she walked up to him, patted his shoulder. "Welcome back, Sheriff. Are you in a hurry today or can you visit a bit?"

He looked down at her and smiled widely, and she hoped her knees were locked so that she would not go down on the floor. His smile was just that beautiful. His teeth were straight and white, his jaw square, with a touch of dark shadow forming even though he had shaved that morning. His nose was almost perfect, except she could tell at some point it had been broken, but she only thought that made his face more interesting. She noticed he always smiled at her, and it made her feel special, even though she knew he was just being friendly.

"I got some time to sit down."

She blinked for a second, forgetting what she had asked. "Well, good, because we kept your place open. Have a seat, and I'll be right there." Her gaze stayed on the back of him as he walked away, heading toward the far stool at the counter. He was the only man that she thought the back view of him was almost as good as the front, and she sucked in a quick breath before letting it out slowly.

"You'd better stop drooling," BettyJo said as she walked by, a sparkle in her eyes.

Wondering what on earth was wrong with her, she gave a mental shake, fetched a few more plates to deliver to tables, and headed behind the counter. Giving Joe the order for Colt, she caught sight of the big yellow school bus pulling into the parking lot.

Colt must have seen her staring because he swiveled on his stool and looked out the window as well. "Already?"

Nodding, she replied, "The kids have some half days here at the end of the school year."

They both watched as the door to the school bus opened, and a dark-haired boy hopped down. He shifted his backpack around, then waved to the bus driver and his friends. He then turned and hustled to the front door of the diner, and she could not help but grin as the bell rang and the boy walked in.

He looked around, met her gaze, and grinned widely as well. He walked straight over to the counter and called out, "Hi, Mom!" The boy hopped up on the stool next to Colt and said, "Hey, Sheriff Hudson."

"Hey, Jack. You're out of school awfully early."

"It's almost the end of the school year! Yesterday we had a field day. Today we had a party. And tomorrow, we help our teacher get the room ready for the summer cleaning."

"When are you going to get any learning done?" Colt asked, lifting an eyebrow, pretending to scowl.

Carrie watched as Jack threw his head back and laughed. "We've already had our state assessments, and I passed them with flying colors. I think I've had enough learning for one year, don't you think?"

She rolled her eyes. "If you're so smart, how come you haven't given me a hug since coming in?"

Jack got up on his knees, balancing on the stool, and leaned over the counter, and she bent forward. She felt his arms wrap around her neck, and she closed her eyes, knowing that was the best feeling in the world. She also knew that the day when he would want to hug his mom in public was soon coming to an end.

With his arms still around her, she opened her eyes and was surprised to see Colt's face so close, his gaze penetrating as he stared at the two of them. Not being able to read that look, she pulled back after giving Jack a quick kiss on his forehead. That must have pushed the limit because he wiped his forehead and complained, "Mom!"

Soon, she delivered Colt's lunch to him, also setting a plate in front of Jack. Mavis and Joe had called out to him from the back, and he waved with excitement.

"Just so you know, Jack, Grandma is taking her neighbor to the library this afternoon, and she'll come by and pick you up when she's finished. Until then, you're stuck with me."

Jack cut his eyes toward Colt and said, "There are worse places I could be stuck. At least here, I get to have some of Mavis' apple pie when I want to."

Colt chuckled. "Sounds like you've got quite a deal going on here."

"It's great! I get as much food as I want, and they love me here."

Placing her fists on her hips, Carrie said, "Boy, you might get Mavis' apple pie, but you're going to work for it. As soon as the lunch crowd thins, you're going to help wipe down tables and see what else you can do."

Jack shook his head and looked at his mom before cutting his eyes back over to Colt. "Sheriff, isn't there something about making kids work for their food?"

Colt adopted a serious expression and said, "I think we can trust your mother to make sure you're not overworked." Leaning in closer, he whispered loudly, "But, Jack, if you ever think I need to investigate your mom, you let me know."

Rolling her eyes again, she tried to ignore the thrill that shot through her at the idea of Colt investigating her. Deciding to walk away before she did something foolish like ask him to frisk her and pull out his handcuffs, she headed around the room, checking on her customers, determined to get her mind back on her job. The only problem was that she kept looking back over to the corner of the counter, seeing the best man she had ever met, laughing and talking with her son, who was her favorite person in the whole world. And she smiled.

3

A little later, after waving goodbye to Colt, she sent Jack around with a spray bottle of cleanser and a cloth, letting him wipe down some of the tables and seats. She moved into the kitchen where she gathered trays of washed and dried silverware and headed to a booth where she sat down and began to roll the silverware into napkins.

After a few minutes, she was joined by BettyJo and Mavis, who slid into the booth opposite her. BettyJo's hands automatically moved to the silverware tray and napkins, starting to roll them like she had done for so many years.

Mavis, on the other hand, glanced around to see where Jack was before softly asking, "When are you going to let Colt know that you've got your eye on him?"

Her gaze shot up to Mavis. "I've known the man for five years since he first rolled back into town. If he hasn't shown any interest in me by now, I hardly think he's going to."

"He might show interest in you if you gave him any encouragement. But you treat him just like you do everyone else."

"What's wrong with how I treat him?"

"I didn't say there was anything wrong with it. You're friendly with everybody. Everyone who meets you likes you. You're easy to talk to, and you're easy on the eyes. But you also give off a vibe that says you're busy, your life is busy, so no one even asks you out."

Huffing, she glanced around to make sure Jack was out of earshot. "I am busy. I'm a mom. I'm a working mom. A full-time mom and a full-time waitress. I don't have time to get gussied up and go trolling for a man in the local bar."

Throwing her hands in the air, Mavis said, "Who's talking about going to a bar? Most of the single deputies come in here just hoping they can get a look at you. Hell, that's why the sheriff comes in so much!"

Carrie laughed. "Colt comes in because he lives by himself and doesn't want to fix breakfast or lunch."

"Are we the only place around here to eat?" BettyJo interjected, lifting a perfectly plucked eyebrow.

Sucking in her lips, she realized there was no way she was going to win this argument. Finally deciding to shut it down, she said, "Look, I appreciate what you're trying to do. But the reality is I'm a waitress who barely finished getting my high school diploma. I also come with a ten-year-old boy who's never met his father and likely never will because we weren't good enough for him. I'm not blind...I look in the mirror and know I've got the looks that can make a man interested for a night or maybe a little more. But I also know I'm not the kind of woman that most men would want to become involved with. I'm not about to bring a man into Jack's life who only wants a tiny piece of me and that's mostly the piece he can get between the sheets. I'm just not the kind of woman they want to take home, not with my baggage."

"I'm not sure what that says about you, but I think it says you don't think very much about Colt," Mavis threw out.

Holding her friend's gaze, she sighed. "I think it says exactly what I know about Colt. He's a good guy who has a heavy job, and the last thing he needs is something else hanging around his neck."

"You see yourself as one more thing Colt would have to worry about when I know a good woman like yourself could make his life better," Mavis said.

BettyJo added, "Are you sure that you're not just waiting to see if Colt will make the first move?"

Her heart hurt just a bit. "There're very few things in life I'm sure about. I know I love my son, and I can't give him much, but I give him everything I can. I also love my friends. I was lucky eight years ago to land in this job, and I figure I'll keep serving tables as long as you keep having me around. Other than that, it's just not the time for something else."

Mavis placed her hands on the top of the table and

pushed herself up. Leaning over, she kissed the top of Carrie's head.

Tears pricked Carrie's eyes, but she gave herself a quick shake, holding them back. Crying was something she rarely allowed herself to indulge in. Tears did not seem to help, and it seemed more of a waste than anything else.

BettyJo looked up at the clock on the wall and said, "Well, I'm off. I'll see you tomorrow, darling." She called to Jack, who ran over to give her a hug before she walked out of the diner.

Mavis and Joe's son, Joe Junior, and his wife, Cindy, came in to work the kitchen for the dinner shift. Everyone called out their greetings, and the bell rang over the door once more. Carrie's mom, Della, came in, greeting Jack with exuberance.

"Jack," his grandmother said, "tomorrow is your last day of elementary school!"

Standing with the tray of rolled silverware in her arms, Carrie said, "Please, don't remind me. He's growing up too fast as it is!"

He puffed out his chest. "I'm going to be eleven years old in a few weeks, Mom. That's practically a teenager."

Making big eyes at him, she said, "How did we go from ten years old to suddenly being a teenager? I don't think so."

Della ruffled his hair. "Go get your backpack, and I'll take you home since your mom's gonna be a little late today."

They both watched Jack scamper off, and the

thought hit Carrie once again how much longer he would scamper instead of trying to walk with a swagger.

Della turned to her. "You okay, baby?"

Smiling, she hugged her mom. "I'm good."

"Did Colt come in today?"

"Yes, but Mavis and BettyJo have already been after me. It's the same as every other day. I'm just Carrie, the friendly waitress from Joe's Place. And he's Colt, the man everyone looks up to…the one who's got the weight of the whole county on his shoulders."

Sighing, her mom nodded, and Carrie knew that she understood. Life did not always turn out the way we thought it would, but you have to get up each day determined to make that day as good as it could be.

Giving Jack a goodbye hug, she stood at the door and watched him and her mother heading out to the car, grinning as Jack talked nonstop. Feeling someone come close, she glanced to the side to see Joe looking out the door as well.

"You got a mighty fine boy there, Carrie," he said. "You've done a good job."

Wrapping her arms around her waist, she admitted, "I didn't do it by myself. I couldn't have done it without Mom and Dad. And God knows, I couldn't have done it without you, and Mavis, and everyone else around here. Between Dad before he passed away, you, Joe Junior, and recently, the American Legion coaches, Jack's had some wonderful male role models."

"That might be true, but you're the one who put

those people in his life. So, I'd say it still comes down to you doing a good job."

She smiled up at him, loving the fact that she had found her way to his diner when she and her mom first moved to the Eastern Shore eight years ago after her dad died.

An hour later, Ellen hurried through the door, apologizing for being late, and Joe looked over. "Okay, Carrie, you head on home now. I'll see you tomorrow."

Driving home, she headed south toward Baytown but turned onto a little street before getting into town. It was not a neighborhood but had several houses and duplexes spread out before the road wound its way back to the highway. She was proud of her duplex, being able to afford the rent although the owner did not do a lot of the maintenance.

Parking out front, she pulled next to her mother's car. Walking in the front door, she called out, "I'm home!"

Her mom came out from the kitchen, wiping her hands on a dishtowel. "I've got some beef stew started in your crockpot. Jack is out in the yard practicing his baseball pitches."

"Do you want to stay for dinner, Mom?"

"Sure, sweetie. I'd love to. By the way, do you need me to get Jack tomorrow?"

Shaking her head, Carrie said, "It's the last day of school so I'll have the bus drop him off at the diner again, and I promised him that Joe would make him a famous ice cream sundae. I only have the breakfast and lunch shift tomorrow so he can hang with me and then we'll come home."

She walked through her narrow living room, which took up the entire front of her house, down the short hall to the eat-in kitchen. The duplex was not large, the downstairs consisting of the living room, eat-in kitchen that held a stacked washer and dryer behind louvered doors in a closet, and a small half bathroom underneath the stairs leading to the second floor.

The owner had renovated the duplex years ago, but it was hardly top-of-the-line. The countertops were a cheap composite, but the color was dark green, and she liked that. The appliances were black, certainly not stainless, but Carrie could not have cared less, just thrilled that there was a dishwasher.

The kitchen was U-shaped, opening to space for the table and chairs that were next to the sliding glass door overlooking the back patio.

She walked to the counter, lifted the lid on the crockpot and sniffed appreciatively, stirring it before turning the heat down. She heard the whack of the baseball hitting the cinderblock wall that ran along the back of their small yard, and she walked to the sliding glass door. Peering out, she smiled as Jack picked up the baseball and threw it toward the wall. He had hit another growth spurt, and she realized she would need to buy him more clothes soon.

Ever since she had taken him to the first American Legion baseball practice, her son had been hooked. She had met most of the coaches, knowing many of them lived and worked in Baytown, and would occasionally see them come into Joe's Place. Sometimes her mom would take him to the practices when she had to work, but she tried not to miss any of his games. But then, she and Jack needed to eat and have a place to live, so she did not ask for much time off. Even when there was a game on Saturday mornings, she could come in early to the diner, getting there about six o'clock in the morning, and still make it to the game by ten o'clock. As soon as the game was over, she headed back to Joe's Place in time to work the lunch crowd.

Tapping on the glass, she captured Jack's attention, and he grinned widely as he waved at her. She watched as he picked up the ball and headed toward the house. She turned to see her mother setting the bowls on the table and said, "I'm going to check to see if George wants to eat with us."

She kissed the top of Jack's head as he came in. "Wash up and then help Grandma set the table. I'm gonna run next door to see if George wants to eat with us."

Jack grinned and nodded. "Cool! I hope he does. I'm getting to the age where I feel like I need another man around to balance out you and grandma."

"Lord, save me!" she said, watching her son grin and her mother roll her eyes. She moved through her living room, out onto the front porch, to the door leading to the other duplex. Knocking loudly, she called out, "George! It's Carrie!"

It took a moment, but she could hear the lock being flipped before the door swung open, and her gaze landed on the older man standing there. His white hair was wispy about his head, but his blue eyes twinkled, and his smile widened. "Hey, Carrie darlin'." He unlatched the screen door.

"Mom is over, and we're having stew tonight. We've got plenty and wanted to know if you'd like to come to eat with us."

She could have sworn his eyes brightened as he exclaimed, "Now, isn't that nice of you. I'd love to come."

He stepped out onto the porch, pulling his front door closed behind them. Sticking his hand in his pocket, he pulled out his key ring, locking the front door along with the deadbolt. Shoving his keys back into his pocket, he followed her across the front porch and into her house.

"George!" Jack yelled from the kitchen before running down the hall to greet their neighbor.

George patted Jack affectionately. "I saw you out there pitching that ball, boy. I think you're getting better and better."

Grinning, Jack puffed out his chest. "At our last practice, Coach Hudson said he'd help me this summer with my pitching."

Carrie startled, giving her son her full attention, glad to hear that Colt was encouraging Jack. "You never told me that."

"He said I was really good. He said I was the best pitcher that we had at my level. He even suggested that I could improve if I had a pitching net."

She had no idea what a pitching net was or how much it would cost but pinched her lips in frustration that Colt would have said that to Jack without checking with her first.

"Stew's on," her mother called out, and Carrie recognized the attempt to wade in and keep the peace. Before she had a chance to say anything else, her mother had greeted George and began dishing out the stew into bowls before getting the biscuits.

Seeing her son's excited face, Carrie figured she would get on the computer tonight and look up pitching nets. She had not decided what to get Jack for his birthday anyway, so, hopefully, a pitching net would fit into her budget.

Soon the four of them were laughing and talking, enjoying each other's company. George was like the grandfather she never knew, and she loved that she could give Jack a chance to have four generations at the table.

Jack regaled them with tales of his last days in elementary school, his plans for becoming the king of baseball during the summer months, and how much he looked forward to starting middle school in the fall. "I know kids can be jerks, but I'm not scared about middle school. I've got lots of friends that will be there, and I plan on being on the baseball team as well."

George seemed to come alive as he told of some of the baseball games he had been to in his younger years. "I remember watching Brooks Robinson play for the Baltimore Orioles in nineteen fifty-nine. He was nicknamed The Human Vacuum Cleaner."

Jack, eyes wide, breathed, "You are kidding! Why?"

"He was considered one of the greatest defensive

third basemen in major league history," George said. "He won sixteen consecutive Gold Glove Awards. The other thing that was special about him was that he played his entire twenty-three-year major league career for the Baltimore Orioles. That still stands as the record for the longest career spent with a single team in major league history."

Carrie enjoyed seeing the awe and excitement on her son's face. As soon as the dinner was over, George gave her a hug, thanked Della, patted Jack on the back, and headed over to his side of the duplex. After helping her wash dishes, her mom said goodbye to Jack before grabbing her purse by the front door and offering a hug to Carrie.

Reveling in the embrace, Carrie knew that besides Jack's hugs, the arms of her mom around her were the next best feeling in the world.

That night, as she went into Jack's room to say good night, knowing he was too old to be tucked in, she sat on the edge of his bed. He had a few baseball posters that he had bought at the dollar store and thumbtacked to his walls. The only furniture in his room was his bed and dresser, but she had decorated with a thick, navy rug on the wooden floor and a comforter with stripes of navy and light blue. He told her that he liked the room because it had *guy* colors. Looking over at him, she asked, "Are you really cool about tomorrow being the last day of elementary school?"

Jack was often exuberant, but ever since he had been a small child, she would watch him carefully consider certain things. And right now was one of those times.

He drew his knees up and clasped his arms around his legs, resting his chin on his knees. "Yeah, I really am. My teachers in elementary school have been good, but I'm ready to learn more. I'm ready to have a science teacher who really knows science and an English teacher who let us get into stories. And I'm ready for pre-algebra next year."

It was hard for her to believe that he was growing up so fast. She was so glad that Jack enjoyed school and learning, wanting him to have the opportunities in life that she had not had. Looking at her son, she knew there was no way she would have traded him for any college experience, but nonetheless, wanted him to be able to do anything he chose to do.

"Grandma asked me what I wanted for my birthday," he said, drawing her attention away from thinking about her son in college.

"What did you say?"

His forehead crinkled. "I told her I'd think about it. Hearing George talk tonight, I was wondering..."

He hesitated, and she prodded, "Wondering what?

"Well, how much do you think tickets for the Baltimore Orioles would be?"

Carrie hoped her poker face was holding because she was afraid that tickets for a professional baseball game would be far out of their means, and she hated that. She hated that no matter how many hours she worked, she still had to pinch pennies to make their budget each month. She hated that no matter how much her mother loved watching Jack, her mother had always done it for free, allowing Carrie to save on childcare.

Staring into Jack's eyes, she maintained the honesty that she always told him she would give him.

"I don't know how much those tickets cost, baby, but they would probably be more than what your grandma could afford to get you for your birthday."

He nodded, his expression still serious. "If I get any money for my birthday, we can see if there's enough to buy two tickets. I'd really like to take George to a Baltimore Orioles game."

For a woman who swore she did not like to cry, she felt the tears hit her eyes for the second time that day. Not caring if Jack felt like he was too old for hugs, she threw her arms around him and pulled him in tight.

"Have I told you lately that I think you're a phenomenal kid?"

He looked up and grinned. "Not today, but you're more than welcome to let me know now."

Throwing her head back in laughter, she said, "Okay, fine. You're a phenomenal kid."

He laughed along with her, then slid under the covers. She bent and kissed the top of his head. "Starting tomorrow, when I kiss you good night, I'll be kissing a middle schooler. I can't believe it." His grin warmed her heart as she walked out of the room, turning off the light.

There were only the two bedrooms and one bathroom upstairs. She walked across the hall to her bedroom, which was definitely decorated in *girl* colors of peach and green, and soon got ready for bed. She read until her eyes were tired, and, knowing they had to get up early the next morning, she flipped off the lamp by her bed and slid under the covers.

As she lay caught between awake and asleep, her mind drifted as it always did to Colt. Sighing, she rolled over and closed her eyes. Some dreams, she knew, would not come true.

4

Colt pulled into his driveway, looking up at his house as he approached. It was a few miles outside of Easton, close to Baytown, and had belonged to his grandparents. The property contained a large, two-story brick house with several acres of land around it. He remembered playing in the wide yard when he was a child, and the house was often a refuge from his own home.

He drove into the garage, pressed the button to close the garage door behind him, then alighted from his SUV. Entering his house, he walked through a tiled room that his grandmother always referred to as the sunroom because of its floor-to-ceiling windows on two sides, letting in a flood of light. His grandmother used to keep a small table and chairs in the room, often serving breakfast here instead of the dining room. There had been a small settee and matching chair in one corner, where she would knit or read. His grandfather did not spend a lot of time in this room, using it as a path to get from the garage to the kitchen, but it was a particular favorite room of his grandmother's. Now, it sat empty.

As he walked into the kitchen, he tossed his keys onto the counter, moved to the refrigerator, and pulled out a beer. He popped the top off, tossed it into the trash, and leaned his hip against the U-shaped counter. The kitchen was large, with lots of cabinets and counter space, which for him was wasted. Many of the cabinets were empty, and the counter only held a coffee maker, a toaster, and a microwave. He could cook but hated to for just one person. But if he ate breakfast, lunch, and dinner at Joe's Place, he might as well turn his paycheck over to Joe.

Searching in the freezer, he found leftover chicken casserole from one of the women in the county who figured a single man was a good catch and would sometimes come by to offer him a cooked dish. Often it appeared they were offering more than the food so he generally turned them down, but this time it was left at the station for him so he did not have a chance to refuse. Now, he was glad. Nuking it, he carried it and his beer into the dining room.

Unlike the sunroom, this room still held his grandmother's table, complete with six chairs and her now-empty china cabinet. He ate quickly, glad that the casserole was in a plastic container that did not need to be returned to its owner. Rinsing it out along with his utensils, he left them in the sink and grabbed another beer, deciding to watch the ballgame on TV.

He walked through the foyer, past the half-bathroom and the door leading into the study, making his way into the family room. Hardwood floors covered the entire first floor of the house with the exception of the kitchen that had ceramic tile. His grandmother had had a full rug that covered the center of the family room, but it was also long gone.

The family room only contained a sofa, a recliner and end table where he could set his beer, and an entertainment table with a flat-screen TV perched on top. No more lamps, knickknacks, or pictures on the wall were present.

After an hour of TV, he clicked it off, walked back into the kitchen to toss the empty bottle into the recycle bin, and double-checked the security of the house. Climbing the wooden stairs, he walked to the master bedroom, ignoring the three other bedrooms that were completely empty.

The master bedroom contained a king-sized bed, matching dresser and chest of drawers, and two nightstands with matching lamps. A dark blue and grey patterned comforter was on the bed, along with a dark blue rug on the floor. It was the only room in the house that looked complete. It was not that he spent a lot of time in the master bedroom, but sleep was often elusive, and he found that having the room comfortable seemed to bring him a modicum of peace.

He walked through the bedroom into the master bathroom. After a shower, he wrapped the towel around his hips and stared for a moment into the mirror, not seeing his reflection, but looking at the bathroom.

Full soaking tub, wide shower, double sink, separate

toilet, walk-in closet, and a separate linen closet. It had not looked like this when his grandparents lived in the house, but his grandfather had the foresight and his grandmother had the dream that Colt would one day be able to bring his bride to this house and live here. That had been their dream, and honestly, his too.

Well, that dream was shot all to hell. His grandparents died before they ever had a chance to meet his wife, but, in his opinion, that was a good thing. If she hated being a military wife, she sure as fuck would have hated being the wife of a rural sheriff, living in the middle of nowhere.

Frustrated with where his thoughts were going, he brushed his teeth, whipped off the towel and pulled on boxers. Climbing into bed, he read for several minutes before flipping off the light and sliding under the covers.

Closing his eyes, he saw the image of Carrie, with her friendly smile and sexy curves, and how she made every room come alive. A flash of her in his house hit him, and he squeezed his eyes tight. Thinking of what would never be was a surefire way to spend a restless night, and Lord knows he had had enough of those.

Colt looked around the room, proud to be part of this close group. Once a month, the heads of the other law enforcement departments on the Eastern Shore of Virginia met to discuss concerns, share information, and simply enjoy the camaraderie. The group consisted of him, Mitch Evans, the Police Chief of Baytown, Hannah Freeman, the Police Chief of Easton, Liam Sullivan, the Sheriff of Accawmacke County, Wyatt Newman, the Police Chief of Manteague, and Dylan Hunt, the Police Chief of Seaside.

Today, the topic of conversation centered around a string of robberies in the two counties.

"I've had one break-in recently," Mitch reported. "It was mostly small electronics, some cash, and some jewelry that were taken."

Hannah nodded and said, "I've only had one in the town limits, but I heard some people in town talking about friends that live in the county."

Wyatt shook his head and said, "I've had no reports in Manteague, but honest to God, don't know that anybody in my town has much worth stealing."

Colt looked over at Dylan and Liam, his eyebrow lifted in silent question.

Dylan also shook his head but said, "No reports so far. But the couple of hotels we've got will soon be filled with vacationers and weekend fishermen. I've already talked to the two hotel managers to make sure they increase security."

Liam, the sheriff of the county just north of North Heron, had a much larger area to police like Colt did. "The reports I'm getting are from the southern area of the county, which may mean that it's someone in North Heron who's crossing the county line to do their robberies."

Colt added, "It concerns me because there is a directness and purposefulness to it. They're too similar to be unrelated, and yet dissimilar enough not to point to the same person doing the robberies."

"Are we looking at gang activity?" Mitch asked.

"What are you thinking?" Hannah asked.

"Well," Mitch continued, "it seems random and yet organized. What's being taken is something that younger people could take, but maybe they have someone who's behind it all."

"You all know that we've got several Blood gangs in my county that we're dealing with. It's only a matter time before it moves into North Heron if it hasn't already," Liam noted.

Colt nodded. "I suggest we all send some of our officers out to start questioning anyone who might have an idea of what's going on. We've got to do some digging on this. I've got Hunter on the pawn shop robbery, and I'll go out there this afternoon with him. I want to stay on top of this."

Their conversation moved into discussing budgets and upcoming events as well as the local politics that affected their jobs and districts. As the meeting came to an end, the gathering left the Sheriff's Office, deciding where to go for lunch, since that was their tradition.

"It's no debate for me," Mitch said. "It's got to be Joe's Place."

Liam agreed, saying, "You can't beat Joe's cooking."

"I wouldn't want to miss the pretty smile of Carrie," Dylan said, grinning.

Colt scowled at Dylan's comment, jealously shooting through him, then cast a quick glance toward Hannah. Her smile was tight, not reaching her eyes. He wondered how Dylan could be so blind, not seeing Hannah's subtle interest. Hell, considering he had been interested in Carrie for years, he had no business trying to analyze anyone else's love life…or lack thereof.

He pushed through the door first, the bell ringing over his head, immediately drawing Carrie's eyes. Her smile lit her face as it always did, then her eyes moved to the side as she watched the others walk-in.

She exclaimed, "Joe and Mavis! You'd better watch out, it's not only the long arm of the law, but a whole lotta arms walking in!"

Joe and Mavis called out their greetings from the kitchen, BettyJo waved from behind the counter, and once everyone had greeted Carrie, she showed them to a table. Colt found that he hated not being able to take his single seat at the end of the bar, instead having to be at a big roundtable in the middle of the restaurant. Taking their drink orders, he felt Carrie's presence standing right next to him. The others gave their orders first, then her hand landed on his shoulder as she asked, "Sheriff Hudson? What would you like?"

All he could think of was, *'You. I want you.'* Instead, he coughed to clear his throat and ordered sweet tea. She turned to leave, and he looked up, seeing the others smiling at him.

"What?" he all but growled.

Dylan shook his head and said, "If you don't get in there, you're a fool…and Colt, I know you're no fool."

"I'm not the only one," he muttered. Scowling at the others, he hoped it would shut them up. The last thing he wanted was for Carrie to hear them joking about the two of them. Soon, she and BettyJo brought over their plates. Carrie held on to his until last, once again placing her hand on his shoulder as she set the plate in front of him. Her fingers gave a little squeeze, and she said, "Hope you all enjoy."

As she came back around later to check on them, Hannah asked, "How's Jack?"

Carrie's face lit as it always did when she talked about her son. "It's the last day of school, and he's excited. I can't believe he's starting middle school next year."

"He's a fine ballplayer," Mitch said.

Colt could have sworn a concerned look crossed her face, quickly hidden behind another bright smile. The group finished eating, and Hannah, Dylan, Wyatt, and Liam said their goodbyes first. As he and Mitch stood, Mitch shook his hand, lowered his voice, and said, "Colt, we've been friends for years. I wouldn't blow smoke up your ass. Carrie is a good woman, worthy of a good man."

"Mitch, she's friendly to everyone. She's never given me any reason to think I'm different."

Mitch cocked his head to the side. "And why do you think that is?"

"Probably because she doesn't care anything about a man with a heavy job, an empty house, and baggage."

Shaking his head slowly, Mitch said, "You're a better detective than that, Colt. I'd say it's probably because *she* thinks she doesn't deserve *you*."

"Why would she think a fool thing like that?"

"Asking *why* about a woman is a dumbass thing to

ask, Colt. You ought to know that." Mitch paused for a second, his eyes darting over Colt's shoulder to see Carrie in the back with Joe and Mavis. "All I know is you could be missing out on the greatest thing that could ever happen to you if you don't get in there and let her know that she's worthy."

Mitch walked out the door, and Colt stood rooted to the floor, watching him leave. Still stunned from Mitch's words, he gave himself a shake and headed for the door, but a hand on his arm stopped him. He turned around, looking down into Carrie's face.

"I need to talk to you, Sheriff Hudson...um...as a coach."

"Sure. What can I do for you?"

"I know everyone is saying that Jack is a good baseball player for his age, but he mentioned that you said he should have a pitching net. I don't know if that's something that I can afford—"

"I already looked into them, and I can get one for about twenty dollars at Walmart."

He watched as she blinked, her mouth opening slightly, a blush hitting her cheeks. "Oh, I thought they were much more expensive than that. I'm sorry. I should have checked into it first. That'll be easy for me to—"

"Don't worry about it. I'm getting him one for his birthday."

Her brows lowered in confusion, and she repeated, "His birthday?"

"He's got one in a few weeks, right?"

Nodding, she said, "Yes, but you don't have to get him anything. I can get—"

"I wouldn't have mentioned it to him if I hadn't planned on getting it for him. I just figured his birthday was a good time since it's near the start of summer vacation."

She finally seemed to come out of her shocked stupor. "Seriously, Sheriff Hudson, you don't have to get him anything—"

"Aren't I invited to his party?"

This seemed to shock her once again, and her eyes widened. He discovered he loved the fact that he had her off balance.

"Well, he's just having a small party. Some friends and a few others."

Grinning, he said, "Okay. I count as both a friend and an *other*." He looked down and saw her hand was still on his arm, and she snatched it back as though burned.

"Um...okay. If you want to come, that's fine. I'll let you know when it's going to be, but you don't have to bring a present—"

"Don't worry about it, Carrie. I'm coming to the party, and I'll bring him the pitching net as my gift to him." With that, he walked out, a smile on his face, deciding that his friends were right. Maybe it was time to let her know that he wanted to be in her life.

5

Carrie stood behind the counter at the diner, still trying to process how she went from questioning Colt about the net, concerned about its cost, to him informing her that he was not only going to buy it for Jack but planned on showing up to Jack's birthday party. She was so caught up in her own thoughts, she did not notice Belle walk in until she slid onto the stool right in front of her.

Carrie had met her when Belle came into Joe's Place with Hunter one day and they struck up a conversation. Belle was extraordinarily pretty, her dark hair pulled back from her face, tied with a colorful ribbon that matched the nursing scrubs that she wore. She was also extraordinarily sweet, with a soft voice, caring manner, and it was not hard to imagine her excelling in her chosen profession of working with the aged.

Since Belle worked at a nursing home not too far from Joe's Place, Carrie saw her often, and they had become friends. Through their many conversations, she discovered that Belle had not had an easy upbringing, growing up desperately poor in a mobile home park in Baytown. During the previous summer, Belle had met Hunter, their romance had moved fast, and they had married last fall.

Belle waved her hand in front of Carrie and laughed. "Hello? Are you in there?"

Blinking, she greeted, "Hey! Sorry…I was lost in thought."

The afternoon crowd had thinned out, and Mavis and BettyJo sidled up to either side of Carrie. "What were you and the Sheriff talking about?"

Sighing, she said, "I needed to talk to him about a pitching net."

Obviously not what the other women were expecting, she caught their scrunched-nose questioning gazes and chuckled. "Jack loves going to the AL baseball practices and games, and the coaches tell him that he's really good. He goes outside almost every afternoon after school and practices throwing an old baseball against our fence. Last night, he mentioned that Sheriff Hudson told him that he should get a pitching net."

"What on earth is that?" BettyJo asked.

"I didn't have time to look it up last night, but according to Jack, it's a special kind of net that you can pitch into. It gives someone a chance to practice their pitches, is soft enough to not mess up the ball, and has a target on it so they can practice their accuracy." Her gaze held no acrimony when she said, "I had no idea how much was going to cost and seeing Sheriff Hudson today reminded me that I wanted to check with him. If it was going to be expensive, then I was going to need to let Jack down easy so that he wouldn't expect it."

"God, pinching pennies is so hard, isn't it?" Belle asked, sighing heavily.

Carrie knew that Belle understood and nodded.

"What did Colt say?" Mavis asked.

"He told me that I can get one at Walmart for only about twenty dollars. That was much less than I thought, so I breathed a sigh of relief thinking that I can get it for Jack's birthday, but then Colt told me he was getting it for Jack's birthday."

"Well, good," BettyJo said. "That way you'll know he'll get a good one."

"I don't know why he'd get it for us at all," she said, throwing her hands up to the side. "I know he's a coach, but he doesn't buy all the kids something like that. On top of that, he informed me that he's coming to Jack's party." The other three women shared a smile and glances. "What?"

Mavis nodded. "I knew that boy had been interested in you for a long time. I just can't believe it's taken him this long to do something about it."

Rolling her eyes, she said, "It's hardly like he asked me out on a date. He likes my son and knows I can't afford a lot for baseball. He's just helping out, which I admit makes me feel weird. But since I know the nets don't cost that much, I won't worry about it."

"If he's just helping out, why is he coming to Jack's party?" BettyJo asked, tapping her red painted fingernail on the counter.

"Do you like him?" Belle asked, her voice soft, and her eyes kind.

She looked down at the counter for a moment, pulling all the thoughts slamming into her together. "What's not to like? He's handsome. Has a good job. Works with kids."

Just then, the front door opened with a bang and Jack came running in, having just gotten off the school bus. Throwing his hands into the air, he yelled, "That's it! I'm done with elementary school! I am officially a middle school student!"

Laughing, she walked around the counter as Joe, Mavis, and BettyJo clapped for Jack. She was thrilled that, given the occasion, even her son did not mind a huge hug in public on his last day of elementary school.

"Remember what you promised, Mom. Joe is supposed to fix me the greatest ice cream sundae of all time to celebrate."

"Already working on it, boy!" Joe called from the back.

BettyJo ruffled Jack's hair before moving on to serve a few of the afternoon customers, and Mavis went into the kitchen, saying she had some apple pies to bake.

Jack climbed up onto a stool where he could see Joe working on the sundae in the back. In a moment, Carrie set a gigantic bowl in front of her son, wondering if he would be able to finish it all. Chocolate, vanilla, and strawberry ice cream. Strawberry syrup, chocolate syrup, and whipped cream with a cherry on top. He immediately dove in, and she smiled before walking back down the counter toward Belle.

"Carrie, I asked you earlier if you like Colt, and you gave me a litany of some of the things about him that anyone would like. What do you really see?"

Keeping her voice low, she glanced toward Jack. "There's something about him, Belle. He's smart and educated. Hard-working and caring. Let's face it, I'm just a small-town girl who's got little to offer and a lot of my own responsibilities."

"Are you talking about Jack?"

Whispering, she said, "I would never in a million years call my son baggage because he is *not* that. Jack is my world. And because of that, there's not a lot of men that I would let in to get close. But from what I've seen, Sheriff Hudson is one that I would. But then, that's also scary."

Belle nodded her understanding, reaching out and placing her hand on Carrie's. "I don't know a lot about him either, but I know Hunter has nothing but respect for him. I also get the feeling, though, when I see Colt, that he's very lonely. I mean, think about it…as sheriff, everyone wants a piece of him. But I think what he needs is someone who's giving, not taking. I think you and Jack fit that perfectly."

Before she had a chance to respond, Hunter walked in. Carrie watched as Belle twisted on her stool, watched her husband walking toward her, and beamed her smile upon him. Hunter was muscular, his hair hanging to his collar. She watched as the two greeted each other, as though the entire world fell away and it was only Belle and Hunter in the center of their universe. Her heart was glad that Belle had that and was slightly envious at the same time.

"Hey, Coach Simmons!" Jack called out, barely swallowing his bite of ice cream before greeting Hunter exuberantly. "It's my last day of elementary school. I'm now officially a middle schooler."

Hunter walked over and congratulated Jack before moving down the counter and sitting next to Belle.

Carrie observed as he kissed his wife lightly, having no difficulty imagining that he would have liked to have taken it much deeper. When he looked back at her, she asked, "What can I get you, Hunter?"

"Just a cup of coffee and maybe a piece of Mavis' pie. I knew I might be working late tonight, so I wanted to have a chance to see Belle."

As she set the slice of pie in front of Hunter, she jolted when Belle said, "I was just telling Carrie that I thought she and Colt would be perfect together."

The coffee cup in Carrie's hand rattled as she set it down harder than she meant. Eyes wide, she said, "Belle!"

Hunter chuckled. "You have to forgive my wife, Carrie. I think she's on a mission to pair up all of our single friends."

Belle pretend-huffed, then smiled sweetly. "Don't you think they would be good together, honey?"

Carrie felt the heat of blush on her cheeks and had no problem imagining that her face was as red as BettyJo's fingernails.

Hunter held her gaze and said, "I've only known Colt for less than a year. But in that year, I can tell you that he throws himself into his work, partially because he's dedicated and firmly believes in what he's doing."

Carrie's gaze did not leave Hunter as she listened to what he was saying, having the feeling that Hunter was giving her more than she was understanding. Biting her lip, she waited to see if he would say more.

"I said *partially*," Hunter repeated. "You can think about a reason why a man would throw himself into his job, besides just the job."

Hunter turned his attention back to his pie, quickly scraping the saucer clean. Looking toward Belle, he said, "I've got to get back to work. Colt and I are going out to do more investigation into the pawn shop robbery. You can walk me out, babe?"

Belle nodded, and Hunter threw his arm around her, waved toward Carrie, and they walked out together. She watched the two of them go, wondering if she would ever see the day when Colt would throw his arm around her.

Thinking back to Hunter's cryptic words, she thought, *If there's nothing else in your life, then you throw yourself into your job.* Sucking her lips between her teeth, she thought about everything she had heard and knew about Colt, and she realized she had never heard much about his personal life.

Blinking out of her musings, she looked over at Jack, and saw the bowl was almost empty. "All right, kiddo, finish that up, and I'll clock out. No working late today."

Colt looked around the inside of Pearl's Pawn Shop. It was not the first time he had been in the shop, but it had been a while. Of the several pawn shops in the area, they had never had a problem with Pearl's before.

Jonas Pearl came from the back, a small, wizened older man, unassuming in appearance but sharp as a tack. His white hair was thick, except for the very top where he was shiny bald.

Jonas greeted, "Detective Simmons, Sheriff Hudson."

The front window had the metal blinds pulled down, the broken glass had been swept away, but the display cases were still in disarray. Colt knew that it had been dusted for fingerprints and initial statements taken as to what had been stolen.

Hunter, cutting to the chase, asked, "Do you have any reason to suspect the new girl you hired as having done this on purpose?"

Jonas rubbed his whiskers and chin. "As upset as she was, I can't see it. I'm a pretty good judge of character, and she was really shaken." Sighing, he said, "I got all over Tom for leaving her alone when he left last night."

Tom was Jonas' son, had practically been raised in the pawn shop business, and Jonas was in the slow process of turning everything over to Tom as he prepared for retirement.

"We've circulated the list of what was taken, but as you know, a lot of it can't be traced," Hunter said.

Colt's gaze moved over the room. "You've checked everything? There was nothing else missing except what was in the window display?" Jonas nodded, and Colt looked over as Tom walked in from the back.

Walking up to the counter, Tom said, "I did an inventory this morning after the police came in and did their fingerprinting. Everything that was grabbed was right there in the front. Problem was, we have a lot of good stuff there."

"Did it seem like anything was picked through? Anything that was left behind?"

Tom shook his head emphatically. "No."

Nodding, Hunter said, "We'll keep you up on the investigation and may be back for some identification if we find things."

Colt and Hunter moved back to the SUV, climbed in, and headed back to the station. "I'm going to talk to Liam again about the Bloods gang that has shown up in Accawmacke. I know they have initiation rites that their new members have to go through. This kind of hit would be right up their alley."

Scrubbing his hand over his face, Hunter sighed. "God, I hope we don't have to start dealing with that here."

Colt agreed but wondered how long the sleepy rural county would stay safe from the influxes of the much larger city's problems.

6

Colt walked into the American Legion meeting, held in Baytown once a month, and greeted his friends and fellow legionnaires. Mitch had brought the charter to Baytown when he and several of his childhood friends came back to live on the Eastern Shore after having served in the military. Mitch served as the commander, and when he stepped down, Grant Wilder, another Baytown Police officer, took his place.

The original Baytown Boys had gone to the same high school that Colt had gone to, and the title Baytown Boys was also used for their baseball team. Colt was a year older than Mitch but played sports with them until he graduated and left for the Army. Not raised in the town, outside of school he did not spend much time with them until he got his driver's license, and they had bonded as teenagers.

Aiden and Brogan McFarlane ran Finn's Pub in Baytown, a popular place for locals and visitors alike. Brogan was married to Ginny, another police officer for

Baytown. Colt had also worked with Zac Hamilton when Zac was the fire chief of Baytown, now the Rescue Captain. Another original Baytown Boy, Callan Ward, had served with the Coast Guard and now worked with the Virginia Marine Police.

Colt may have been friends with them as teens, but now, with many of the men working as first responders and all of them in the American Legion, they had formed adult friendships.

The meeting hall was filled with men and women who had served in the military. As Colt looked around, he saw the diverse group of all ages and races brought together by their experiences. His gaze snagged on someone sitting next to Jason. A rough-looking man, Colt remembered seeing him volunteering with the Baytown Fire Department, and Zac had also mentioned he was working in the tattoo shop with Jason. *Joseph… that was his name.*

His gaze continued to scan the room. There were a few of the older members that he did not see at this meeting, and he made a note to check on them the next day.

One of the responsibilities of the Sheriff's Department was their senior outreach program. It gave seniors who were living in the county peace of mind. When a senior was enrolled in the program, they received a phone call each morning. If there was no answer, a deputy was dispatched to check on the person's well-being. He could not remember if the older AL members were part of the outreach program but decided that was something he wanted to make sure happened.

The meeting only lasted an hour, with the various subcommittees giving reports and information about the youth ball teams' successful program being lauded in the community. Zac also mentioned the fishing contest from the Baytown pier that the AL was sponsoring with the Legion Auxiliary. "If you know of any kids who would like to participate, the cost for them is free," Zac mentioned, and Jack ran through Colt's mind.

At the end, Grant, as the Commander, announced that it would soon be time for new officer elections. He asked the members who had put their names forward to please stand. Ginny was interested in becoming the Commander, and Colt wondered how she managed to be a police officer, mom of a newborn, and command the American Legion all at the same time. *Hell, I feel like all I do is my job and that sucks up all my time.* Observing her smiling face, he could not help but smile himself. If anyone can do it, Ginny could.

Scott Redding stood up as a nominee for the Post Service Officer. Colt had only met Scott a few times but knew the former soldier was a good runner in spite of his prosthetic leg. In fact, Scott had proposed a 5K run as a fundraiser for the American Legion.

Colt continued to nod as the other candidates stood, and by the time they voted everyone in, he was sure that the AL would be served by dedicated officers for the next year.

At the end of the meeting, he walked several blocks to Finn's Pub, a group of the members often gathering informally after an AL meeting.

Walking out of the dark night into the warmly lit

pub, he smiled. Aiden and Brogan had already moved behind the bar, beginning to pull beers. He made his way through the crowd to a group of tables near the back. At one time, most of the men had their women there. But in the last couple of years, several of his friends had had children, their lives and habits now changing.

He grabbed his beer and slid into a seat, Belle and Hunter on one side, Mitch and Grant on the other side of Hunter. With a conversation about the robberies in the area between the four of them in law enforcement, he was surprised when Belle touched his arm softly. Turning to her, she smiled, leaning closer so that she could keep her voice low over the din of the crowd.

"You know, I've had the chance to get to know Carrie Beaumont in the last year," she began.

He continued to stare, fascinated as a blush moved over her face.

Shaking her head, she said, "I'm not very good at this, Colt."

"Not good at what, Belle?" His curiosity was piqued.

She cleared her throat, her nerves obvious. "Trying to be coy. The truth of the matter, Colt, is that I think you should ask Carrie out. She's such a nice woman and such a caring mom."

Nodding, he agreed. "I can't argue with that at all. But what makes you think she'd want to go out with me?" He cringed as soon as the words left his mouth, feeling like he was in middle school, checking with the girl's friend to see if he was going to get shot down if he asked her out. He started to back away when she turned her wide eyes up to him.

"I think Carrie doesn't realize what a wonderful catch she is," Belle said.

He leaned back in his seat, startled by Belle's statement. Tilting his head to the side, he asked, "You're kidding, right?"

She shook her head. "No, I'm not. But I think it's going to take somebody very special, and somebody very strong, to let her know just how wonderful she is."

He wanted to ask more, no longer worried about sounding like an adolescent, but just then, Hunter turned around and said, "Hey, babe. Are you about ready to go home?"

Belle's pretty face went soft as she looked at Hunter. Nodding, she said, "Yeah, honey. I'm ready whenever you are."

Colt watched badass Hunter's face, having seen that soft look on his other friends when they found the woman they loved. Hunter leaned forward and kissed Belle's forehead, saying, "It's been a long day, babe. Let me get you home."

Belle stood, saying her goodbyes to everyone, then turned and looked back down at Colt. Leaning down so that she did not have to shout over the noise, she said, "I probably shouldn't have said anything, but I just hate seeing two wonderful people who could be so good for each other not give it a shot."

He watched Belle and Hunter walk away, Hunter's arm casually draped around his wife's shoulders, noting how Hunter threw his hand out to keep anyone from bumping into her as they left the crowded bar. It was a simple gesture and one that he had certainly never seen his own father use. Where the thought of his father came from he did not know but had no desire to continue down that path of thought. Draining the last of his beer, he stood and began his round of goodbyes.

Making his own way toward the front, he looked over and saw Mitch talking to one of the older men from the AL meeting. As the man turned slightly to the side, he recognized him. *George... Hell, George somebody.* Just then, Mitch caught his eye and waved him over.

"George, Mitch," he greeted. "Is everything okay?"

"George got a ride here tonight with one of the men who lives near him, but he's already left and forgot to take George with him."

"Dang fool. Stanley can't remember a thing. I told him don't forget me. In fact, that's why I'm here, because he said he was going to come to the pub after the meeting. I told him that was fine with me. Then I get here, have myself a beer, start looking around, and someone said they saw him get in his car and drive off."

Colt's lips twitched as he held back a smile at George's tirade. "I'll be more than happy to take you home, George."

George turned his blue eyes up toward him, and Colt could have sworn they twinkled.

"Well now, Sheriff, that's real neighborly of you. I hope it won't be too much outta your way."

He did not know where George lived but was willing to take him wherever he needed to go. "Are you ready? I was just about to leave."

"Yes, sir. I'm as ready as I'll ever be."

Mitch clapped George on the shoulder as he said goodbye, then turned and shook hands with Colt.

Stepping out of the pub, the quiet of the night immediately descended over the pair as soon as the door shut behind them. "I'm parked just up the road."

He shortened his stride to match the older man's, and they soon reached his SUV. Clicking the locks, he hesitated to see if George needed any assistance, but the wiry older man quickly climbed into the passenger seat.

"Whoowee, I ain't never ridden in a police car before. No, sir, not my whole life. Proud to say I've never been in trouble with the law."

Grinning, Colt walked around the front and settled behind the steering wheel. It only took a moment to leave Baytown behind and get back out to the main highway. "Where do you live, George?"

"Head to the north a little ways, Sheriff. I live on Brush Road. Got me a sweet little duplex out there. Don't own it. I rent it, but I've been there for years. Got nice neighbors, and we don't have any problems. I like it like that. I'm too damn old for problems."

Chuckling again, he nodded his agreement but barely had a chance to respond with George keeping up a running monologue. It only took ten minutes to turn onto Brush Road, but in that time he had been made aware of George's opinion of politics, religion, and even some of the history of North Heron.

The rural road was dark, no streetlights for illumination. He had been on this road before, but it was several years earlier. As George mentioned, with nice neighbors he would not have been called to patrol here. As his headlights beamed, he could see that they passed several small but fairly neat houses before they came to a duplex. Even in the dark, when his headlights hit them, he could see that they were older but also neatly kept.

"Right here. This is mine," George called out, pointing the way. "I'm the one on the left."

Colt turned into the drive, his headlights now facing the duplex, and he was glad to see that the front porch lights were on. George turned toward him, sticking out his thin hand, and said, "I appreciate this, Sheriff. I guarantee you that I'm going to give Stanley a piece of my mind when I talk to him tomorrow!"

Before he had a chance to let George know that the drive home had been no problem, the front door of the duplex on the right opened, and he was stunned to see Carrie step outside. She lifted up her hand and placed it over her eyes since his headlights were facing straight toward her.

He shut the lights off quickly as George opened his door and hopped down from the SUV. He saw a head peek around from behind Carrie and realized that Jack was still awake.

"George! Are you okay?" she called out, concern evident in her voice.

"Stanley left me in town and forgot to bring me home."

She hurried down the front porch steps and placed her hand on George's arm. "You could have called me. I would've come and gotten you."

He had gotten George home safely, but now that he saw Carrie, he quickly shut down the engine and threw open his door. Her head swung around at the sound, and her eyes narrowed as though she was trying to see in the dark.

"Sheriff Hudson!" Jack called out, darting off the porch.

Colt grinned down as Jack came skidding to a halt right in front of him, his face turned up.

"What are you doing here at our house?"

Placing his hand on Jack's shoulder, he turned him slightly, and they walked toward the porch. He caught Carrie's wide-eyed face, her lips slightly parted as though she was going to speak, then her attention was recaptured by George.

"I told you. Stanley left me in town after the meeting, and Sheriff Hudson was good enough to give me a ride home."

Jack's smile had not faded as he stared up at Colt. Poking his chest with his thumb, he pronounced, "Today was the last day of elementary school for me, so I'm now officially in middle school. And, since summer vacation has officially started, Mom was letting me sit up late, and we were having a popcorn party."

Colt glanced at Carrie, seeing her open her mouth to speak, but Jack was not finished.

"Hey! I've got an idea! You and George need to come in and join our popcorn party. There's tons for us to share!"

"Jack! I'm sure that Sheriff Hudson has other things to—"

"I'd love to." Colt smiled at Carrie, watching her blink in surprise. "George, what do you say?"

George swung his gaze from Colt to Carrie and then back to Colt again, his lips curving slightly and the crinkles at his eyes deepening. "I think I'll pass and let you young people enjoy the popcorn. The dang hulls get stuck in my false teeth." George patted Carrie on the shoulder, and she walked with him to his front door, making sure that he got in and his door was locked.

While she saw to George, Colt allowed Jack to lead him inside their home. He was immediately struck with two thoughts: one, their house was tiny, and two, their house was a home. The front door opened to the living room, which took up the entire front of their duplex. The back wall held a small cabinet with a television, and facing that, along the front wall, was a dark green sofa. It was worn but clean and brightened with pillows in a blue, green, and yellow pattern. The outside wall had a dark blue comfy chair next to a small bookcase that appeared to be filled with a mixture of paperbacks and children's books. A coffee table sat in front of the sofa, a variety of popcorn-filled bowls covering it.

The inside wall that was next to George's duplex was covered in framed pictures, and at a quick glance, Colt could see that they were family pictures depicting the years of Jack's life. Directly in front of him were the stairs leading to the second floor. A large blue and green rug covered the wooden floor, also worn but clean.

Hearing the door shut behind him, he turned, seeing Carrie step into her house. Her hair, normally pulled up for work at the diner, was loose and much longer than he imagined. She always caught his attention when she was dressed in jeans and work polo, but seeing her in black yoga pants that clung to her generous ass and a pale green T-shirt worn thin with many washings hanging off her lush breasts, and he knew he would always remember her the way she looked right now.

7

Colt and Carrie stood staring at each other for a moment, neither saying anything. Finally, he tilted his head down toward the coffee table and asked, "Popcorn party?"

Not giving her a chance to speak, Jack answered, "Yeah! It's the best! Mom fixes a bunch of popcorn, and we mix a whole lotta different stuff with it and put it in different bowls. That one over there has peanuts and M&Ms mixed with popcorn. That one over there has Chex mix in it as well. That one over there has raisins and dried cranberries. And that one over there is cheesy—"

"Jack!" Carrie admonished, "I think Sheriff Hudson gets it." She looked up at Colt and asked, "Would you like something to drink? Soda? Beer?"

"I'll take a soda, thanks."

She sucked in her lips, almost as though she wanted to say something but was holding it in. She gave a quick nod before walking down the short hall into the kitchen. In a moment she walked back with a soda in one hand and what looked like lemonade in the other. Handing the soda to him, she said, "Jack, this is your last drink for the night, or you'll be jumping up all night long."

He watched Jack roll his eyes before plopping back on the chair. Looking up, Jack encouraged, "Have a seat and dig in!"

Carrie laughed and rolled her eyes, and it hit him how much mother and son were alike. "Please, make yourself at home." She handed him an empty bowl and indicated for him to grab whatever popcorn flavors he wanted.

He sat on the sofa, choosing a position that left plenty of room for Carrie while making sure they would be close together. She hesitated, then sat next to him, leaning forward to refill her bowl. The TV was showing a west coast college baseball game, and in between shoving popcorn into his mouth, Jack began chattering about the game. Carrie would smile indulgently at her son, occasionally offering gentle reminders about his manners.

After a few minutes, Colt settled back into the comfortable cushions of the sofa. The game was interesting, but his attention was focused on the warm room, the laughter between mother and son, the tasty popcorn treats—a snack he had not had in years—and the realization that Carrie had not only created a home for her son but was giving Jack great memories as well. Neither of which Colt had had, and both of which he had craved.

"So which is your favorite?" Jack asked, shoving a handful of popcorn and M&Ms into his mouth.

"I gotta tell you, boy, it's been a long time since I've had plain, boring popcorn. Right now, I love all of this." He glanced to the side, seeing Carrie staring at him, and he hoped she understood his double meaning. She looked away quickly, her gaze going back to the television, but he noted two spots of red high on her cheeks.

Thirty minutes later, the ball game was over, the popcorn bowls were empty, the drinks were sipped dry, and Jack was still bouncing, although whispering instead of his usual exuberant shout.

"She gets like this late at night. Of course, I'm usually in bed by now, but if we have a late night, then Mom crashes."

Carrie had slowly been slipping further down against the cushions until her head rested on a pillow and her feet were tucked tightly against Colt's thighs. Colt had never had a chance to see Carrie when she was not bustling around the diner or rushing to and from the AL baseball games. She always seemed to be in motion, but now, sleeping on the sofa next to him, he had the opportunity to stare at her features, soft in slumber.

Her hair was thick and glossy, and his fingers itched to slide through the tresses to see if they were as soft as he imagined. Her eyelashes lay in dark crescents on top of her cheeks, and as pretty as she was with a little bit of makeup on, he could now see a sprinkle of freckles across her nose.

Not wanting to disturb her, he looked toward Jack

and said, "How about we clean up this mess for your mom?"

Jack readily agreed, and Colt could easily tell that Jack was not only a good kid who would do that for his mom, but he seemed to suck up male attention, and Colt was more than glad to give it to him.

Standing, he and Jack stacked the empty popcorn bowls on top of each other and carried them into the kitchen. He could easily see that the downstairs was essentially two large rooms, the living room in the front and eat-in kitchen in the back. A staircase with a tiny half bathroom was in the middle. Squirting some detergent in the sink, it did not take long to get the bowls washed and rinsed and placed in the drying rack.

"Are you going to be at practice tomorrow, Sheriff Hudson?"

Nodding, he said, "Yep. I try never to miss unless there's something I'm doing that can't wait."

"Like catching bad guys?"

He could see Jack's eager excitement over the idea of Colt catching bad guys. He remembered what it was like being a young boy and thinking that wearing a badge and a gun would be the greatest job ever. He also remembered that his own father put down that idea every chance he got. "I'll admit that sometimes my job is doing a lot of paperwork, and some of the investigations aren't very exciting. But, yeah, when we get to catch a bad guy, it's a great feeling."

Jack nodded his agreement with all the wisdom that an almost-eleven-year-old could have. The sugar rush that Jack had exhibited earlier was beginning to fade, and Colt knew it was getting late, and he should leave. "Why don't you go wake your mom, and once she's up and I'm sure she's not going to face-plant on the stairs, then I'll leave."

Jack grinned, and they walked back into the living room. He wanted to stand and stare at her some more but hated for her to wake up to his unabashed perusal. Instead, he walked to the wall next to George's duplex and looked at the pictures hanging there. Framed photographs of a younger Carrie, her mom, and a man Colt assumed was her dad. Photographs of a young exhausted-but-smiling Carrie holding a newborn. Pictures of the last eleven years, showcasing Jack with his mom, his grandparents, Joe and Mavis, even George...but no father.

When he first saw Carrie at Joe's Place five years ago, he noted right away that she did not wear a wedding ring, and he was interested. When he found out she was a mom, he assumed she was married and just did not wear a ring. When he found out she was a single mom, he assumed she was divorced. Now, it appeared that Jack's father had never been in his life.

Turning around, he watched Jack bend over Carrie and shake her gently. "Mom. Mom," Jack whispered. "Sheriff Hudson is ready to leave, Mom."

As though the words suddenly hit her brain, Carrie bolted up, her eyes flew open, and she muttered, "I'm awake. I'm awake."

Jack giggled, and Colt was unable to keep the chuckle from slipping out. Carrie rubbed her eyes and scowled at both of them.

"It's rude to stare at somebody who's been sleeping," she groused.

"Well, you were snoring like a—" Jack began, his grin still wide.

Standing quickly, Carrie wobbled, and Colt took a step forward with his hands out, but she regained her balance. "I did not snore," she announced. "I never snore."

Jack and Colt laughed, and he watched as she was unable to keep her lips from curving into a smile as well. She looked at the clock on the TV and said, "Oh, my goodness. Jack, you need to get to bed. Say good-night to Sheriff Hudson, go on up and get ready, and I'll be up in just a few minutes." She leaned over and kissed the top of Jack's head, and Colt heard her whisper, "Thanks for cleaning up, Bud."

Jack hugged his mom, then bounced over and threw his hand up to high-five Colt. "Thanks for coming and having a popcorn party with us, Sheriff Hudson. It was a blast!" With that, he turned and ran up the stairs, leaving Colt and Carrie staring at each other.

They both walked to the front door at the same time, and as she placed her hand on the doorknob, she looked up, smiling. "It was really nice of you to bring George home tonight. I'm sure you probably have lots of things to do besides hang with us and eat popcorn…even if it was really *awesome* popcorn."

Her smile struck him straight to the heart, and he tried to remember if he had ever seen her when she did not appear happy. If he had only seen her at Joe's Place, he would have assumed it was all an act to keep her tips high. But the times he had seen her away from work, she generally had a smile on her face.

"You're wrong, and you're right," he said. Before she had a chance to question him, he continued, "You're wrong that I had lots of other things to do tonight, but you're right about the popcorn. It was *awesome*."

They stood smiling at each other for a moment, then she startled as though realizing her hand was still on the doorknob. Pulling it open, she stepped back and allowed him to walk through. He turned around, towering over her, very much in her space, but she did not move back. Instead, she looked up at him, her lips parted slightly, and he battled the desire to kiss her.

"Good night, Sheriff Hudson." Her voice was soft as she held his gaze.

She had not stepped back, and he hoped he was reading the signals right, not wanting to fuck things up with her. He placed his hand on the curve of her waist, bent, and whispered, "I think we're getting to the time where you can call me Colt," just before he barely brushed his lips across hers before leaning back again. "Good night, Carrie. Make sure to lock up behind me."

He turned and headed to his SUV, and as he pulled himself up into the driver's seat, he looked toward the house and saw her still standing there, one hand resting on the doorframe, and the other hand lifted, her fingers touching her lips. She startled, then tossed a wave toward him, and stepped back inside the house. He watched as the downstairs light flipped off, and the light upstairs turned on.

It only took a little over ten minutes for him to pull

into his own driveway. As his headlights hit the front of his house, he was struck with how much larger it was than her small duplex. Walking inside, he was struck once again with how warm and inviting her home was. Compared to his cold, empty house, she had created a haven from very little.

What the hell was that? Carrie jolted out of her Colt-kiss stupor, closed the door quickly, flipped the lock, then turned around and pressed her back against it. Her lips still tingled, and yet the kiss had lasted no more than two seconds and had been so light that she could have imagined it.

Before she had a chance to consider Colt's actions further, Jack called from upstairs. "Mom! I'm ready!"

Sucking in a deep breath, she let it out slowly before she said, "I'm coming." She flipped off the living room lights and walked up the stairs. Going into Jack's room, she looked at him already in bed. "Wash your face?"

"Yep."

"Brush your teeth?"

"Yep."

"Well, I can see you're in your pajamas, so I guess you're all ready." She grinned, sitting on the side of his bed.

"Wasn't that cool for Colt to stay for a party?" Jack asked. "Do you think he'll come again?"

She thought about how Colt said he would come to Jack's birthday party and how he was going to buy him the pitching net. Then she thought of the surprise visit tonight. Sucking in her lips, she was not sure how to answer her son. She wanted to say *'Yes, Colt is interested in us, and he'll come around more'.* But she tried to never make a promise to Jack that she could not keep. She knew that if Jack got used to Colt and then Colt moved on, it would devastate him. Of course, it would not do her any good either, but she figured she could handle it.

"I don't know, baby. Tonight, he just happened to find us living next door to the man he brought home. I think he likes hanging with you, and he's one of your coaches, and so he probably felt comfortable coming over and hanging with us a bit. As far as coming back, I don't know."

Jack was silent for a moment, and she felt his contemplative perusal. Tilting her head, she waited to see what he was going to say.

"He was watching you."

That was not what she was expecting, and her eyes widened in surprise. "Huh? He was watching me?"

"We carried the bowls into the kitchen and then he went back to grab some more. I wondered where he went when he didn't come back right away. He was just standing and stared at you for a moment. When he came back into the kitchen, he had a smile on his face."

Uncertain how she felt about Colt staring at her while she slept, and even more uncertain about how she felt about Jack witnessing that, she tried to joke. "He must have been listening to me snore."

Jack shook his head and said, "Nah, Mom. I was only kidding. You don't snore. He just seemed to like watching you sleep. Then, when he had me wake you up after we washed the dishes, he was looking at all the pictures on the wall downstairs. He didn't just glance at them. He was really looking at them."

She sucked in her lips, once more uncertain what to do with any of the information Jack was feeding to her. He suddenly yawned widely, and she said, "Oh, my goodness. You've got to go to sleep." She leaned over and kissed his head, and his arms came around her neck to give her a hug. Embracing him in return, she whispered, "Sleep tight."

Just as she was getting ready to flip off his light, he said, "I like Sheriff Hudson, Mom. I hope he hangs around us some more. I think he likes you."

Heading into her own bedroom, she went through her nightly routine and climbed into bed. Deciding she was too tired to read, she slid down under the covers. This time not only did thoughts of Colt move through her mind, but she could have sworn her lips were still tingling.

8

"Mom! We're going to be late!" Jack complained as Carrie pushed the speed of her old car to the exact speed limit, careful not to go over.

"We're fine, we're fine," she claimed, looking at the clock on the dashboard.

She had gone in to work the breakfast crowd at the diner, leaving Jack next door with George. She left as soon the breakfast rush was over, made it back home, ran upstairs, got out of her jeans and polo and jerked on cute capris, pulled her T-shirt over her head, and slid her feet into sandals. Without skipping a beat, she ran a brush through her hair and slid on a baseball cap. Running downstairs, she saw Jack jumping up and down at the door, raring to go.

Now, in the car, she turned onto the road to get to Baytown but knew that she had to slow down to twenty-five miles an hour as they approached.

"Mom!"

"Jack, you might as well settle down and chill out,

boy, because I'm not going to get a speeding ticket just to get you to a ballgame."

"You know Sheriff Hudson, Mom. If you get a speeding ticket, he can just tear it up for you."

She shook her head, casting a glance toward Jack. "I'm afraid it doesn't work that way in real life. And anyway, this is Baytown. If I get a speeding ticket, it would be from Chief Evans."

"Well, he's one of my coaches too, and he could tear it up for you. In fact, Coach Wilder is a policeman also, and he could tear it up."

Turning into the parking lot at the Baytown ball field, she pulled to a halt, twisted around to look at Jack, and said, "Since we're here on time and I didn't get a speeding ticket, I think you can forget all about someone having to tear one up. Now, go!"

Jack hopped out of the car, opened the back door to grab his glove and hat, and with a jaunty wave, ran toward the ballfield.

Sighing in relief, Carrie checked herself in the rearview mirror, glad that she had put on concealer since she had dark circles under her eyes. She pulled out her lip gloss, and with a quick swipe over her lips shoved it back into her purse. Rubbing her lips together as she walked, she tried not to think too hard about the reason behind putting lip gloss on to go to a youth baseball game. *It's not like I'm doing it for any special reason…or for any special person. Oh, Jesus, who am I kidding?*

The team of older kids had just finished their game as she made her way past the concession stand. Easily ignoring the scent of popcorn, she tried to ignore the scent of hotdogs grilling. Deciding that maybe some more caffeine would be good, she got in line and bought a soda. Shoving her change back into her purse, she had just taken a step forward when she almost ran into someone. Throwing her hand out to the side to keep the soda from spilling, she said, "Oh, I'm so sorry!"

Looking up, she was surprised to see Colt standing there, smiling down at her. His dimples deepened, and his voice slid over her as he said, "Good morning, Carrie."

Tilting her head in a nod, she greeted him. "Sheriff Hudson."

"And I thought we'd made it past the formal greetings," he said, lifting an eyebrow.

Her lips curved into a smile. "I'm not quite sure we're there yet."

"Well, then I'll just have to make sure we get there on time."

She glanced to the side, seeing Jack run out onto the field, getting ready for the next game. "I'm sorry if Jack got here late."

"Was there a problem?" he asked, his gaze never leaving hers.

Shaking her head, she replied, "No. I just had to go in and work the breakfast shift this morning."

"So, the popcorn party kept you up late last night and then you had to be at work early this morning?"

"You know how it is…bills to pay."

He leaned forward slightly, holding her gaze. "Listen, Carrie, if you ever need me to pick up Jack and take him somewhere, then I can do it. If you need me to bring him to a game so that you don't have to rush to get here, that's fine too."

"Oh, he would love a ride in the Sheriff's SUV. He'd be the envy of all his friends," she said, laughing.

His smile deepened. "Well, good. Then maybe we can arrange that."

They stared at each other for a moment, then he said, "I want to thank you for letting me crash your party last night."

At the mention of him crashing the party, the thought of the light kiss had her sucking in a quick breath. Instead of focusing on the kiss, she quipped, "I have a hard time believing that you didn't have anything better to do than hang with us, watch TV, and eat copious amounts of popcorn."

His penetrating gaze held her in place as he said, "I didn't have anything better to do. In fact, I thought it was a perfect evening." He twisted his head around and looked toward the field. "I've got to go. If you need to leave early, I can bring Jack home."

She shook her head. "No. I've got him." Placing her hand on his arm, she gave a little squeeze, adding, "But thanks." She watched as Colt jogged over to the field, and she began walking toward the bleachers.

"Hello, Ms. Beaumont," she heard.

Turning around, she smiled at the man who was walking toward her. "Pastor Hackett, hello." She watched as the pastor of one of the county churches walked toward her, a big smile on his face. One of Jack's friends had invited him to visit the church, and he had gone once or twice.

"I haven't seen Jack in a while but wanted to let you know that this summer, we've got a great youth program organized. It's going to be for middle and high school students, and since he's going to be in middle school, I wanted to make sure he could come."

The idea that Jack could spend some time with other youth that he would be going to school with interested her. "I'd love to hear more."

"We know a lot of parents work during the day, so we'll be getting together two mornings a week. The middle schoolers will have a program, and the high schoolers will have a separate program, then everybody will be together for certain activities." He reached into his pocket and pulled out a pamphlet, saying, "We've put all the information here, and you can just call the church office if you have any questions."

She thanked him, and as he continued on down the path toward the concession stand, she turned and looked up at the bleachers, seeing Belle, who was waving at her. Waving back, she climbed up several rows of metal bleacher seats and sat down next to her friend. She recognized a few of the women that were sitting around them, having a good eye for remembering the faces of people who had come into the diner.

"Hey, y'all, I don't know if you've met my friend, Carrie Beaumont," Belle said. "She works at Joe's Place near Easton, and her son is Jack."

"Jack, the pitcher out there?" one of the dark-haired women asked, bouncing a small boy on her lap.

Nodding, Carrie said, "That's him."

"He's really good! I can't believe he's just getting ready to turn eleven. I'm Katelyn, by the way."

Another beautiful dark-haired woman with green eyes smiled at her, and she remembered seeing her at the elementary school. "Hey, I'm Jade. I'm a first-grade teacher at Baytown Elementary, and I know Jack. I didn't have him in my class, but I know he's one smart little boy."

Carrie laughed, saying, "Thank you," unable to keep from beaming with pride. "But don't let him hear you call him a little boy. He just celebrated the end of elementary school last night."

Belle continued the introductions, and she met Mitch's wife, Tori, Grant's wife, Jillian, and the two wives of the McFarlane brothers, Lia and Ginny. She had met Zac many times when he came into Joe's Place with some of the other rescue workers, and now she had the opportunity to meet his wife, Maddie. Callan, working with the Marine Police, popped in the diner also, and his wife, Sophie, smiled up at her. And last was Rose, who owned the new ice cream shop in town. She had never been there but knew Rose's husband who owned the town's auto shop.

Greeting Rose with excitement, she said, "My son has been begging me to bring him into your shop."

Rose smiled. "Oh, yay! You must come in!"

"Maybe we can come in today after the game. He'd love that."

The game began, and soon, Carrie was cheering right along with the other women, excited for every good pitch that Jack made and glowing from the compliments she heard from all around about his talent.

Jack was on fire as a pitcher today, and Colt watched with pride as Jack was accurately and effectively shutting the other team down. As excited as he was for Jack, the AL was dedicated to giving all kids a chance to play, so he needed to get the other pitcher on the mound and give some other kids a chance to hit. So, with the signal from the other coaches, he walked over to Jack.

"You're killing it today, Bud."

Jack looked up, his smile wide, and said, "I've been practicing every chance I get."

Placing his large hand on Jack's shoulder, he nodded. "It shows."

Jack cocked his head to the side, still hearing the cheers from the crowd, and said, "It's time for me to come out though, isn't it? So someone else can have a chance to pitch."

Colt knew that he should not be surprised at Jack's maturity, considering Carrie had raised her son to be just as driven, and yet just as compassionate, as she is.

Nodding, he said, "We're gonna let you come out for a little bit, give a couple of the other kids a chance, but I wanted to make sure you understood that it's not you."

Jack also nodded. "Nah, I get it. You all are always telling us that we're here to learn the sport and the sportsmanship. It's cool."

Colt watched as Jack jogged off the field to the

dugout, glad that the parents were still cheering, knowing that whoever else came in might not be as talented.

The game continued, but after a moment, he noticed a man by the fence who had engaged Jack in a conversation. A lot of parents and townspeople hung on the fence cheering, but Colt's antenna shot up because he did not recognize the man. When he cast his eyes toward the bleachers, he saw that Carrie had honed in on her son and the man as well and was already beginning to move down the bleachers toward them. He continued to watch Carrie, glad that he was not having to actively coach on the field at the moment or his attention would have been completely diverted. Carrie had made it to the man and was smiling, along with Jack.

Convincing himself that he was just curious and not the least bit jealous, he made his way over to where they were standing. "Everything okay?"

Carrie looked up at him, and her smile hit him right in the gut, as always. He wanted to crow at the sight because that was certainly not the smile she offered the other man. He also noticed the man's eyes dropped to Carrie's chest when she was not looking at him, careful to lift his gaze back to her face when she turned toward him. It pissed Colt off, but then he could hardly call the man out, considering that Carrie had a body that would make any man notice.

"Mr. Jameson is from the middle school," Jack informed him. "He wants me to come to a middle school camp they're running this summer."

"Yeah? What kind of camp?"

The man smiled widely and said, "I'm Tad Jameson, one of the teachers at the middle school. We have a summer science camp that's for kids a couple of times a week."

Colt stared into Tad's eyes, something about the man not settling right with him, but then, he had to admit it could just be that the other man had Carrie's attention.

"Colt?"

His gaze darted over to Carrie, who was staring at him, her forehead scrunched, and her head tilted slightly to the side. Seeing her confused expression before he looked down at Jack, who was bouncing up and down on his toes in excitement, he said, "Sounds like fun."

Tad turned his attention back to Carrie. "Can I get your phone number or your email? I'm sending out texts and emails to let parents know when we meet and what our schedule will be."

Colt watched Carrie hesitate, and he almost stepped in, but then she said, "I'll give you my email."

As she rattled it off, Tad scribbled it down. "Great, great." He patted Jack on the shoulder, then added, "Good game out there. Maybe I can use you to help teach some of the others. I always have my eye out for natural-born leaders."

As Tad walked away, Colt watched Carrie squeeze Jack's shoulder, careful not to show too many signs of affection in public for her growing son.

"You're going to have quite the summer," she said.

"First, Pastor Hackett said that he's got a new youth group going, and now you'll have activities at the middle school."

Jack stood tall and looked up at Colt. "Mom always tries to find things for me to do during the summer, which is really cool, but I often also hang around Joe's Place a lot, which is cool, too. Especially when Joe teaches me how to make the perfect hamburger."

He laughed and patted Jack on the shoulder. "Never discount the ability to make a great hamburger. You'll have to show me sometime."

With a nod, Jack ran over to be with the other kids, and Colt's eyes followed Tad as he walked around chatting with the other parents.

"You weren't overly friendly to him," Carrie noted aloud.

Turning back to hold her gaze, he said, "I wasn't overly thrilled with the way he kept staring at your chest."

Carrie blinked, her mouth opening and closing several times, but nothing came out. Finally, she sputtered, "I don't even know what to say to that!"

"Nothing to say to it. You're a gorgeous woman, and you've got a great body. Men are going to notice. But that doesn't mean that I like it when they ogle you right in front of me."

Her eyebrows lifted, and she repeated, "Ogle?" Then a giggle slipped out between her lips.

Scowling, he said, "Glad you find this funny."

Her giggle slowed, and she said softly, "Thanks for all you're doing for Jack."

He stared at her for a long moment, taking the time to appreciate her up close. Her hair was flowing from her baseball cap, allowing the waves to fall down her back. Her blue eyes could change from hard to soft depending on what she was dealing with, and he was beginning to recognize those changes. Her pants cupped her ass and hips perfectly, and her T-shirt, while not tight, stretched slightly over her breasts. He was able to take in the whole package while his eyes still remained on her blue ones.

"What are you and Jack doing after the game?"

She bit her lip and said, "I thought about taking him to the new ice cream shop, Sweet Rose."

Nodding, he smiled and said, "Sounds good. I'll meet you there after the game."

Her teeth let go of her bottom lip as her smile curved once more, and she said, "Okay," then turned and walked back toward the bleachers.

His eyes followed her for a moment, then realized the women she was sitting with were smiling back at him. Turning around, he watched some of the other coaches grinning at him, and he shook his head. It had been a long time since he had played the dating game and was no longer sure if it was a game he could win...or if he even knew the rules anymore. Glancing back at Carrie's sweet ass climbing up the bleachers, then glancing back over at her son who was grinning widely and excited as he talked to his friends, he knew it was a game he was going to give his all.

9

Carrie, with her hand around Jack's shoulders, walked into Sweet Rose Ice Cream Shop. Jack could not decide which way to look, considering an auto mechanic shop was just across the street, and he was fascinated with the work being done on the cars. But then, the idea of specialty ice cream pulled his attention as well.

Laughing, she said, "I just found out that the lady who runs the shop is married to the man who owns the car shop across the street."

Jack bounced on the balls of his feet and said, "That's the best combination ever. Those are the best two jobs in the whole world!"

"And I thought you thought being a sheriff was the best job," she joked.

His face grew serious, and he nodded, saying, "You're right. Working on cars is cool, and making ice cream is even better. But being a sheriff, that's the best job in the world."

"Glad to hear it," a deep, familiar voice said.

They both startled, looking behind them to see that Colt was walking into the ice cream shop and had overheard Jack's comments.

"Coach Hudson! I didn't know you were going to be here!" Jack said.

Colt smiled, and Carrie found herself staring at his face, mesmerized by how the hard lines were softened when his lips curved.

"Your mom told me that y'all were trying this place out, so I thought I would, too."

Rose was already behind the counter and greeted Carrie, then told Jack she'd watched the game and thought he was wonderful. Rose looked up at Colt and said, "I think this is the first time you've been in."

It did not miss Carrie's attention that if this was Colt's first time in the ice cream shop that he must be there for them. Before she had time to process that, several more people were coming in behind them so they moved up to the counter. After much deliberation, Jack made his selection and then she and Colt decided. As she pulled out her wallet, Colt put his hand on hers and said, "My treat." She watched Rose smile before winking to someone at the side. Glancing over, she saw a table with Tori, holding onto a toddler. Mitch had also walked over to his wife and son.

Once they had their ice cream in hand, Mitch called over to them, and they joined them at the table. Carrie slid into a seat next to Tori, smiling at her son, Eddie, who had ice cream all over his face. Jack grinned at Eddie but moved to sit on the other side of Colt, who had taken the chair next to her. With Jack sitting in between Colt and Mitch, she knew he was thrilled to be in the middle of the Sheriff and the Police Chief.

The ice cream was delicious, and she ate while chatting with Tori. As she finished, she leaned back in her seat, startled to realize that Colt's arm was resting on the back of her chair. Glancing over, she saw that Jack's eyes were pinned on the two of them. Inwardly grimacing, she hated for her son to get an idea that might not be interpreted the right way.

So far, Colt was very good to Jack and sweet to her, but in the five years that she had known him, he had never expressed an interest in her. Looking over at Tori, it was easy to see why Mitch chose her for his wife. She was not only sweet but beautiful. There was an elegance about Tori, her clothes and makeup and demeanor screaming of class. She had found out that Tori owned the Sea Glass Inn.

Carrie was not ashamed of who she was or what she did, but she knew that a single mom, working hard to keep a roof over their heads, was not exactly going to be a catch. And if Colt was playing a game she did not want her son caught up in that. Or, even if he was not playing a game and he was interested, she hated the idea that Jack would be devastated if they started something and then it ended.

She felt a light touch of his long fingers on her shoulder, and Colt whispered in her ear, "You okay?"

Her gaze shot over, and she saw his expression, full of concern. "Yeah, I guess I'm a little more tired than I thought I was."

As soon as she said that, he turned and said, "Jack,

your mom is kind of tired. What do you say we pack it up and head home?"

Jack was in agreement, but Carrie was confused. Jack made it sound as though they had driven together, but they had not.

Before she had a chance to ask, he said, "You take your car, and Jack can ride with me in the Sheriff's SUV. We'll follow behind to make sure you get home safely, and he'll get the thrill of riding with me."

She wanted to say that was not necessary, but because the offer was already out, Jack was virtually bouncing in his chair. Tori and Mitch grinned at her, and all she could say was, "Sure." Saying goodbye to Tori and Mitch, she stood and grabbed her purse, noting that Colt had already taken her ice cream bowl away for her. As they walked out the door, Colt placed his hand on her lower back, guiding her gently down the sidewalk as Jack walked backward in front of them so that he could keep talking.

They passed several people on the sidewalk, many of the men that she knew were friends of Colt's and their wives that she had just met. Everyone seemed to notice Colt's hand on her back, and their faces were filled with smiles. The touch of his fingertips burned through her shirt as though she were being branded. That was a feeling she had never had and decided she liked. Maybe whatever this was would not last very long, but if her skin felt like that with the barest touch of his hand, she was willing to find out what more he had to offer.

She climbed into her car and watched as Jack hopped into the front seat of the Sheriff's SUV. She watched as Colt made sure that he was buckled securely before he gave her a two-finger wave and she pulled out in front of him. She always drove carefully, but with a Sheriff's vehicle behind her, she did not go one tad over the speed limit.

Looking into her rearview mirror, she could see that Jack was talking nonstop. She could also see that Colt was occasionally looking at him, smiling and nodding, talking in return.

The drive to her home was not long but filled with thoughts. From the moment she had discovered she was pregnant at seventeen, she had been scared but excited. Her boyfriend was already in college, twenty years old, and they had been inseparable for a few months. They had always used a condom, but she remembered he got very nervous one time when he pulled it off. She did not think anything about it until morning sickness struck, and she drove to another town to get a pregnancy test.

Terrified, she told him, but his reaction was not what she hoped. He demanded she have an abortion, said he would pay for it, adding that his parents would never agree to him having a child with her.

Distraught, she told her parents, who were upset, but they held her tightly, supporting her decision to keep the baby. She had only seen her boyfriend two other times after that, both times begging him to stay with her, but he refused.

He finally told her, "Don't you understand? You were a summer fling. My dad told me those were fine, and it didn't matter what kind of woman I had with a fling. But you're not the kind of woman who can take my career further or who would be good on my arm when I get where I want to go. My parents would never agree to this."

That was the last day she had seen him. His name was not even on Jack's birth certificate. Without being able to give Jack a father, she had been determined to give him everything she could, even though her family was poor. Her father had been a good role model but died too early, and Jack barely remembered him. She had been lucky when Joe and Mavis hired her, a young, unmarried, twenty-year-old mother who had just moved into the area. Joe had become like a favorite uncle. Because Joe's Place was so close to the county government buildings—including the Sheriff's Office—it was often filled with some of the good men and women of law enforcement, and when Jack was around, he made friends with everyone.

She knew she was a good mom, but she also knew it was a risk to bring someone into Jack's life that could abandon him. She figured she could take it. It had happened before. But she was not willing for it to happen to Jack. So it had been a long, somewhat lonely eleven years.

But now, looking in the rearview mirror at Colt and Jack laughing and talking, Colt giving him a ride in the Sheriff's SUV, her heart warmed. She knew Colt was not playing her, even if they had no idea how the game would turn out. She just had to figure out how far she was willing to risk her—and Jack's—hearts.

"Two more robberies last night," Hunter confirmed to Colt.

"Fuckin' hell. What did they get this time?"

Before Hunter had a chance to answer, Loretta, Colt's secretary, let him know that Chiefs Evans and Freeman were there. Colt looked up as Mitch and Hannah walked in, offering greetings before sitting down at the table with him and Hunter.

He had been expecting them before Hunter had dropped the latest news on him, and he had Hunter detailed the latest robberies.

Hunter continued, "One house had a laptop taken, and both houses had prescription drugs that were stolen as well."

Eyebrows raised, Colt barked, "You're shitting me. Prescription drugs?"

"Up to now, what's been taken has seemed random. But the one thing that's holding strong is that these are not robberies of big houses that might have a lot to steal. In other words, they're not million-dollar homes, they're not vacation homes. They are places that are easy to get to, easy to get away from. Both homes last night were on small roads, older people on subsidies. Their cell phones weren't great, but one of them had a laptop. It was an older model, and he said his son had given it to him. He used it to send emails to his grand-kids. But both homes had prescription drugs stolen."

Colt asked, "From their bedrooms? Bathrooms?"

Shaking his head, Hunter said, "A lot of people keep their prescription drugs in the kitchen. It's easy for them to remember when they get their coffee or breakfast. And if they don't have little kids running around the house, then they don't have to worry about kids getting into them."

"Are we looking at professional drug runners?" Hannah asked.

"Or someone with a drug habit that's stealing to support that?" Mitch asked.

Shaking his head, Colt replied, "I've got no fuckin' clue at this point."

Hunter added, "In both cases last night, the homeowners were asleep and didn't hear a thing. One of them doesn't even lock his doors because he says he never thinks about it and doesn't have anything worth stealing anyway. The other one locked his door, but it was a simple twist bolt and was easily jimmied."

"If this was just kids, it seems too organized," Hannah commented.

"If it's coming down from the north, how are they targeting these houses?" Mitch asked.

Rubbing his chin, Colt pondered for a moment. "Is there anything to suggest that this is tied into the pawn shop robbery?"

"Not now," Hunter said. "There's nothing that's tying any of these robberies to the pawn shop."

Sighing, Colt said, "Okay. Keep working on it and keep me up on everything. Make sure the Sergeant gets everything out to our deputies. The people in this county are going to start wondering what's happening, and I want them assured that we're doing everything we can, no matter who's being robbed."

Hunter agreed, offering a chin lift to those in the room before leaving.

"I can't believe that this is just in the county and hasn't hit anyone in Easton or Baytown yet. But I have a feeling that might come," Colt said.

Just then, Hannah got a call, and she stood, saying she was needed at the courthouse.

Colt looked at Mitch and continued, "I've pulled up the information from Liam on the gangs in his county, but I swear, I'm just not seeing a pattern down here."

Mitch nodded his head slowly, then said, "In Baytown, we have vacation homes, historical homes, and some high-end homes with good security. But also, most of our homes are close together, with very little yard space in between them. It sounds like the people being hit here are on rural roads where there are not a lot of eyes on them."

Nodding, Colt said, "Yeah, I thought about that. But this county is so fuckin' spread out there's no way that my deputies can patrol all the streets. The best I can do is get something out in the news that lets people know this is happening and that they need to lock their doors and be careful."

The two men stood and got ready to leave the conference room. Mitch turned and said, "I've got to tell you that Tori and I talked yesterday. We both agreed that you looked good in the ice cream shop with Jack and Carrie." Throwing his hands up, he rushed, "No, I'm not here to give you any shit. I'm just letting you know that there was an ease about you that I haven't seen before. Tori noticed it too. Just know that your friends want the best for you…and her."

Realizing that Mitch was not hounding him, he nodded. "I gotta admit, it did feel good." Watching Mitch leave the room, he slowly walked back to his own office, thoughts of Carrie moving through his mind as they so often did. With a grin, he hoped it was not long before he saw her again.

10

Carrie slept light, she had for years. She used to think it was because Jack was a baby, and she wanted to wake in case he stirred. Back then, she lived with her parents, and even if they might wake, she always wanted to be the one to get to Jack first. Then, when she and her mom moved to the Eastern Shore after her dad died, she rented her own place. They considered renting together, but Carrie wanted independence, and Della fell in love with a small, one-bedroom apartment that was near the store where she worked part-time.

When Carrie continued to sleep light, she thought it was because she was a single parent who needed to hear if Jack was sick or in the bathroom at night. But he slept like the dead, and at his age, if he needed her, he would come to get her. But still, she always woke easily, and tonight was no different.

Her eyes jerked open, and she could not discern what had made her wake. Climbing from the bed, she padded across the hall and looked into Jack's room, seeing him asleep. Not just under the covers asleep, but on his stomach, one knee bent with the foot kicked out to the side, one arm tucked under his pillow. She could not help but grin, thinking that when her boy slept, he *slept*!

She tiptoed quietly to Jack's window which overlooked the back yard, but it was dark outside, and there was nothing for her to see. She left his room, partially closing the door, before going downstairs. Her way was lit by a series of nightlights, one in the hall at the top of the stairs as well as one at the bottom. She never wanted Jack to wake up and be frightened in the dark, so she made sure she had nightlights around the house.

Checking the front door, she could see that it was secure, and she walked into the kitchen, finding the sliding glass door locked as well.

No noises could be heard other than a car driving down the road. That was not unusual because while she lived on a rural street, there were still some houses around. In fact, she knew one of the men who lived down the road had a job at one of the few factories on the Eastern Shore, and he worked shift work.

Deciding there was nothing amiss other than her usual light sleeping, she went back upstairs and crawled into bed. It took a little while to find sleep again, her mind now filled with Colt instead of her sleeplessness.

When he had dropped Jack off in the Sheriff's SUV that afternoon, George had been sitting on his porch, his hand up shading his eyes as he watched them approach. He had made a big deal about Jack being able to ride with the Sheriff, even joking that he thought maybe Jack was under arrest. Jack had informed George that if that was the case he would be in the back seat in handcuffs instead of sitting in the front seat.

George announced that he had gone to the grocery store and bought Jack's favorite soda and an apple pie and invited them all to share it with him on the front porch. Carrie knew that Jack had just filled up on ice cream but convinced herself that since it was a dairy product, it had to be somewhat healthy. Plus, the apple pie had fruit in it. Nodding toward Jack, she told him to go inside and help George get the snack. She looked up at Colt and thanked him for bringing Jack home, but he was already sitting down one of the chairs on the front porch.

Surprised, she realized that he was staying for George's invitation as well. George and Jack came back out, large slices of pie on saucers and four cans of soda. They enjoyed the pie, which was good but not as good as her homemade, which George pointed out to Colt. That prompted Jack to tell Colt that he needed to have some of his mom's pie sometime. She wanted to roll her eyes at the blatant attempt of George and her son to try to push Colt and her together, but she just smiled instead.

Colt looked over at her, his eyes smoldering, and said, "I can't wait to try your pie."

She sputtered in the middle of a sip of soda, and Jack jumped up to slap her on the back. Feeling as though she had entered an alternate universe with others trying to pair her up with Colt and he suddenly flirting with her, she managed to get her coughing under control and told Jack that if he killed his mom by beating on her he would be in trouble for perpetrating a crime right in front of the Sheriff.

That caused Jack to bust out laughing, and everyone eased into fun conversation again. A few minutes later, Colt's phone buzzed, and after he checked the message, he said that he needed to leave. After watching him drive away, she felt strangely adrift during the rest of the afternoon.

Now, in the middle the night, trying to settle her mind so that she could sleep, she could no longer deny that it seemed that Colt was definitely interested. Her lips curved into a secret, sleepy smile, and she closed her eyes, wondering when she might hear from him next.

"Jack, buddy, please go check with George to see if there's anything else he needs. I know he went to the grocery store yesterday, but since we're getting ready to go, I want to see if he forgot anything."

Carrie had a rare morning off from work and planned on taking advantage of it. First stop was the grocery store, then the bank, and she wanted to take Jack by the library to make sure he had some books to read. On the days that he did not have church camp or middle school camp, George was going to keep an eye on him when she was working.

Walking downstairs, she made sure she had her paycheck and her envelope filled with tips to take to the bank.

Jack came flying back through the front door, skidding to a stop in front of her, yelling, "Mom!"

"Did he need anything—" Turning, she observed the wide-eyes staring up at her and immediately asked, "What is it?"

Jack was shaking his head and said, "I don't know. George's door is open."

"Well, maybe he's doing yard work on the side of the house."

"No, Mom! It looks like it's been broken open."

Instantly alert, she said, "Here," shoving her phone into his hands. She rushed out of her front door and around to George's. Jack was right, the front door was standing open a few inches, the area around the doorknob looked like it had been forced. Pushing the door open, she called out, "George! George!" She did not hear any noises and moved to the living room and into the kitchen. George's side of the duplex was exactly like hers, only in reverse. Seeing nothing downstairs, she made it to the top of the stairs, heart pounding, still calling his name, with no response.

George kept one of his bedrooms as a spare in case his son or grandkids visited, which was not very often since they lived far away. That door was open, and it was easy to see there was nothing there. George's bedroom door was also standing open, and as she pushed it further, she instantly saw George was lying on the floor, dried blood on the side of his head.

She screamed for Jack to call 9-1-1 and dropped to her knees next to George. He was still breathing, struggling to open his eyes.

"Just stay here, just stay here. We're calling for the ambulance." She jumped up and rushed into the bathroom to get a wet cloth and saw his medicine cabinet open, some things spilled onto the sink and floor. Knowing she should not touch anything, she backed out of the bathroom and dropped to the floor next to George again. Grabbing onto his hand, she held tight.

Hearing a noise, she looked up and saw Jack's terrified face standing in the doorway. "Jack! What are you doing here? You should get back downstairs."

Her son's voice was shaky as he asked, "Is he...?"

"No, he's injured but alive, baby. Did you call 9-1-1?"

Jack looked at her and nodded but said, "I called Sheriff Hudson first."

She looked up in surprise, but he said, "He gave me his number and told me to call him if we ever needed anything."

She held George's hand after telling Jack to go back downstairs and wait for the ambulance. Looking down, she continued to assure George, holding his gnarled hand in hers, until she heard the sirens in the distance.

Carrie hated to let go of George's hand but ran to the window that overlooked the front yard so that she could keep an eye on Jack. Turning into the driveway in front of the ambulance was a Sheriff's SUV, and she had no doubt who was driving it. She watched as Colt bolted from behind the wheel, charging toward the front of the duplex. She heard Jack call out, "Colt!"

Her heart pounded a ferocious beat as Jack ran toward him, not stopping. Colt lowered himself enough to scoop Jack into his embrace. She watched Colt's mouth move but was unable to hear what he was saying. Nothing had prepared her for seeing her son clinging to a good man. A man who did not have to do what he was doing. A man who could have sent deputies and just the ambulance. A man who could have told Jack to go back into his house and stay in there. But instead, Colt was holding her shaking son, offering him comfort, while teaching him that a man, a good man, is never too busy to hug a friend.

The air in the room felt thick, and she could barely suck it in. A movement from behind her jolted her away from the window, and she ran to drop back down at George's side. "They're here. It's going to be okay," she assured.

She heard the pounding of footsteps on the stairs and cried out, "Colt! We're in here!" She looked up in time to see his large frame filling the doorway, his perceptive gaze sweeping the room.

He dropped to the floor next to her, his hand going to the back of her neck, squeezing gently before nudging her out of the way, and said, "Hey, George. We've got the ambulance here to take a look at you." George struggled to sit up, but Colt kept his hand on the older man's shoulder and said, "No, no. Let's just lay here and rest until we see how you're doing."

He looked over at Carrie when she whispered, "Jack?"

"He's at the front door telling the paramedics where to come."

She knew the paramedics did not need a child giving them directions, but she was so grateful that Colt understood that Jack was traumatized and needed something to focus on. More noise was heard on the stairway, and she looked up to see two paramedics, their hands full of cases and equipment. She let go of George's hand and moved out of the way.

"George, do you know what happened?" Colt asked as another deputy came into the already crowded room.

George winced as the paramedics were checking him for any broken bones and he said, "I heard something in the hall. It sounded like something was knocked over in my bathroom, and when I opened my door to see what it was, I got hit. I thought it was damn squirrels getting in through the attic again until I got hit. I must have been out a long time because I don't remember anything after that. When I opened my eyes, it was daylight, and Carrie was coming in." His explanation seemed to take everything out of him, and Colt told him that he was going to be taking a trip to the hospital.

"Damn nuisance," George complained, but Carrie could see on his face that he was in a lot of pain.

Because the duplex stairs were narrow, the paramedics placed George on a thin stretcher, strapped him in, and managed to get him down the stairs with little problem, considering he was slight of weight.

"There's a mess in the bathroom," Carrie said.

Colt's eyes jumped to hers, and he asked, "Did you touch anything?"

Shaking her head, she said, "No. Something didn't feel right. I just wanted to get a wet cloth for him, but I came out of there and sat with him instead."

"Good thinking," he said as two more deputies came up the stairs. Turning to her, he said, "Carrie, go downstairs and be with Jack. Take care of him and let us work here. If we need you, I'll come next door and get you."

Nodding, she started to walk out of the room when he reached out and caught her hand, giving her fingers a squeeze. As she looked at him, a comforting feeling settled in the room, and she felt that as long as Colt was there, he would take care of everything. She scooted by the other deputies, nodding at the ones she recognized, and headed down the stairs. Finding Jack on the porch, they stood together, her arm around him, and they watched as George was loaded into the ambulance. The sirens engaged again, and it pulled out of the driveway.

"Mom, is he going to be okay?" She heard his shaky voice and looked down at his pale face, nodding, "I think so, baby. I hope so. As soon as Colt lets us know that it's okay, we'll go to the hospital and check on George. Right now, let's go back into our house and just wait. We need to stay out of their way, and Colt promised that he'd let us know what was going on."

Jack sucked in a fortifying breath through his nose before letting it out slowly. He wrapped his arm around her waist, and she watched as her son's face morphed from child to young man. The sight nearly took her breath away.

He pulled gently on her arm, leading her back into their house. "You're right, Mom. Let's do as Colt says. If you want, I'll fix you a cup of tea."

At that, she blinked at the moisture gathering in her eyes.

11

Colt walked back into George's bedroom, seeing Hunter and his partner, Detective Elizabeth Perez, talking to one of the deputies, Trevon. Moving into their huddle, he asked, "What have we got?"

"Pill bottles are gone from the bathroom. I'm going to check with Stuart's Pharmacy in Baytown and Markham's Pharmacy up the road to see where he got his prescriptions filled and what was taken," Elizabeth said.

Trevon added, "Mark and I have been going through things downstairs, and we've got the fingerprint boys here. The victim isn't a pack rat, but he's got quite a bit of stuff around so it's hard to tell what's been moved and what has just been collected."

"Family?"

"He's got a son who lives in Pennsylvania. He, his wife, and kids visit a couple of times a year."

Colt stood, rubbed his chin, and Hunter asked, "What are you thinking?"

"Well, I know that George keeps an eye on Jack when Carrie's mom can't watch him, so I figure Jack has been over here a lot."

"You think he can identify what may or may not have been taken?" Elizabeth asked.

"Let me talk to him and then we'll bring him over," Colt said. He walked out of the room, down the stairs and back out the front door. Carrie was standing on the shared front porch, offering mugs of coffee to the detectives that were coming and going. Chuckling, he walked over and asked, "You always taking care of everyone?"

As soon as the words left his mouth and she turned her face up to his, he regretted the quip. Worry radiated from her eyes, creasing her brow. He pulled her in for a hug, unheeding of who might be around, and said, "Scared the fuck out of me, babe, when Jack called. I'm still trying to get my heart to stop pounding, but it's gonna be okay." He watched as she tried to smile, but it did not reach her eyes. "Let's go inside."

As soon as he entered Carrie's side of the duplex, he could see Jack on his knees on the sofa, staring out the window at the activity. Jack jumped down, hurrying over, but Carrie reached out, tagged her son, and pulled his back to her front. Bending to kiss the top of her head, she whispered, "Give Sheriff Hudson a chance to tell us what he needs to before we ask too many questions."

Jack nodded but immediately turned his face up to Colt, a mixture of boyish curiosity and adult concern crossing his young face.

Not wanting to tower over Jack, he said, "Can we sit a minute?"

Nodding, Carrie released Jack, and they walked over to the chair and sofa, Jack sitting near Colt.

"Okay, Jack, this is where we're at. Someone broke into George's house, and we can tell that they stole his medicine—"

"His medicine?" Jack asked, his face scrunched. "Why would someone want to do that?"

Colt shot a look toward Carrie, uncertain how much she wanted him to tell Jack, but he should have known that Carrie believed in honesty, even if she softened it.

She said, "Jack, the truth is that some people will steal anything. Anything that they think they can use or sell. Even though those were prescription drugs for George that he takes to keep him well, other people can use them to get high, or they can sell them to others."

Jack looked at his mom, his face still scrunched, then asked, "So prescription drugs can be used like the drugs we learned about in school?"

Nodding, she said, "Yes, all drugs are…well, drugs. Some are legal, and doctors prescribe them to make us better. Most of the drugs you learned about in school are the ones that are not used by doctors, and those are considered illegal. But then, somebody can get hold of legal drugs and actually use them in an illegal way."

Jack's breath left his lungs in a rush, and he said, "That's whacked! Stealing drugs from an old person who needs them to stay well…Mom, that's just whacked."

Carrie's lips curved slightly, and she nodded again.

"You got that right, Jack. Now that we've gotten that straight, why don't we listen to see what Colt wants to tell us."

He shot Carrie a quick grin, hoping she understood how much he admired how she was raising her son. Looking back at Jack, he said, "I know you've spent a lot of time in George's place, and you know that his place is a little full."

"George likes to keep things. He and I go through them a lot because he says he wants to save things for his grandkids and for me."

"That's good. Because this is where I'm going to need your help if it's okay with your mom. There's nothing scary going on over at George's house right now, but we need someone who knows what's there to let us know what might be stolen."

Eyes wide, Jack asked, "You need me to be like a detective?"

Nodding, Colt said, "Absolutely. As long as it's okay with your mom."

Jack jumped to his feet and said, "Oh, she won't mind. This is all to help George and you, and other than Joe, you two are Mom's favorite men."

Colt's gaze shot back over to Carrie, seeing her blue eyes widen impossibly and a blush rise over her face.

"Jack!"

Chuckling, Colt said, "Well, I'm mighty pleased that I'm on the list with Joe and George, two men I admire." Seeing Carrie beginning to sputter, he stood and said, "Come with me, Jack, and we'll go take a look at George's place."

He accompanied Jack next door, and they entered George's living room. Elizabeth was correct when she said that George was not a hoarder, but he did have a lot of things. Besides the sofa, chair, coffee table, and end tables, several bookshelves were stuffed with magazines. Jack took a quick walk around the room, looking at everything. He moved to the empty coffee table and, twisting his head to look up at Colt, said, "George had a laptop."

Colt glanced over at Elizabeth, seeing she was taking notes.

"It was kind of old, but he bought it at a pawn shop. I don't think he used it much, but he liked to play around on it. He said it made him feel more connected to his grandkids to have a computer around."

"Did he have a cell phone?" Colt asked.

Shaking his head, Jack said, "No. He hated the constant ringing of a phone, so he just had the old-fashioned kind that's in his kitchen. We helped set him up an answering machine so that he could listen to the messages without having to talk to people right away."

"That's good," Colt said. "Is there anything else you can see that might be missing? Anything else that George had that was of value?"

As soon as the word *value* left his mouth, Colt watched Jack's eyes go wide, and he cried out, "The cards!"

Jack darted past Colt and ran up the stairs, passing Hunter in his haste. Colt, Hunter, and Elizabeth looked at each other before quickly following Jack into the second bedroom.

"Jack, what is it?" Colt asked, seeing Jack opening the closet door. There were several boxes stacked inside the closet, and Jack immediately went to the second one from the top, pulling it out. He knelt on the floor and jerked off the lid, then heaved a great sigh.

Colt knelt next to him and looked inside the box. It was filled with old baseball cards, and at a quick glance, Colt could see that many of them would be quite valuable based on their age and the player that was on the card.

Jack twisted his head around and looked at Colt, saying, "George and I go through these cards sometimes. He tells me all about the players, tells me about the ones he actually saw play and told me that of all the things he has in his house, this is the only true thing of value."

He clapped Jack on the shoulder and gave a little squeeze. "Then when George gets out of the hospital, he'll be happy to know these cards are safe and sound."

"Do you think George would mind if Mom and I held onto these for him until he comes back? What if the thieves come again?"

Colt knew the odds of anyone coming back to George's house were slim to none but could see that the events of the day were taking their toll on Jack. Nodding, he said, "Yeah, I think George would like you to make sure that they're safe." The two of them stood, and Colt lifted the box, carrying it back downstairs. Once in Carrie's house again, he set it on their coffee table and said, "Jack would feel better if this was kept here until George comes home."

"Of course," Carrie agreed, her eyes scanning Jack, and Colt could tell that she was concerned for her son. Turning her gaze back on him, she asked, "I'd like to go to the hospital as soon as you think we can."

"We're almost finished here, and the deputies will lock up when they're done. I'd like to go with you, but I really need to get back to the station. Will you call me to let me know how he's doing?" He did not need Carrie to call him to fill him in on George's condition, considering that he could pick up the phone and call the hospital himself, but he would come up with any excuse to make sure she talked with him later that day.

"Of course, I'll call. Um... do you want me to call the station?"

Shaking his head, he said, "No. My personal number should be in your phone since I gave it to Jack. Use that."

Before he had a chance to say anything else, another detective called for him from outside. He placed his hand on Jack's shoulder, giving another squeeze, and said, "You did really good today, Bud. I'm proud of you."

Jack beamed, a smile that hit him straight in the heart, then he looked up at Carrie, and her smile nearly knocked him over. He wanted to pull her into his arms, but instead, simply placed his hand on her back as he walked toward the front door.

"There will probably be some activity coming and going next door for a couple of hours. I know you had errands to run and want to go see George, but I'll be back to check on you later."

Her gaze held his, and she barely nodded before her

eyes dropped to his lips. Deciding not to resist, he bent and once more placed a soft kiss on her slightly open lips. He battled the desire to pull her into his arms and take her lips in a kiss that was much more than just a light brush. But to give them the attention he wanted was going to take some time and a lot more privacy. Something he planned on doing just as soon as they could.

"Do you know how many bad scenarios could have come from last night?" the man asked, his voice vibrating with anger.

The two people he was talking to just stood, silent and stared back, their eyes wide.

"First, it was a duplex. Even if the old man had not heard anything, it was too risky that the neighbors would. Then he woke, and you hit him, which changes the situation from robbery to assault. But worst, he could possibly identify you."

The other two people in the room avoided eye contact, shuffling their feet as the uncomfortable silence continued.

"This calls for severe measures. We need to make sure the old man is taken care of. Do you understand?"

They nodded, but both began to sweat profusely at the idea of what was being proposed.

"You'll do exactly as I say. And I don't expect any more screw-ups."

12

Carrie bustled around the diner, breakfast always being a busy time. She looked up as Colt came in, throwing him a wide smile as he walked over to his stool at the counter. She poured him a cup of coffee and said, "Joe will have your food out in just a moment."

Hurrying back to her tables, she carried plates, took orders, and poured coffee. She checked on Mr. Bradley, who appeared to be eating better today. Her attention was snagged by another older man, Mr. Jones, who often came in for coffee when he had tied one on the night before. Making sure his cup was filled with strong black coffee, she felt Colt's eyes on her and turned around, seeing Colt twisted on the stool, a smile on his face as he watched her go about her job. Finally catching a moment's break, she hurried behind the counter again.

"It looks crazy in here."

Nodding, she smoothed her hand over her hair and

said, "The vacationers are already hitting the road, and we're a perfect stop for them."

Joe yelled, "Order up!" and she turned to see Colt's regular breakfast order on the shelf of the pass-through. She grabbed it and placed it in front of him, grimacing as she said, "I'll be right back." She hurried to take the check to one of her tables, did a pass through to see if anyone needed anything and then she came back. "Anything on George's house?"

Shaking his head, he said, "No. These robberies are getting frustrating." Taking a bite and chewing, he asked, "How's George?"

"Yesterday, after Jack and I got finished with going to the bank and the grocery store, we went to the hospital and checked on him. He's fine but fightin' mad."

Laughing, Colt said, "Yeah, I imagine he is."

"Anyway, because he had a concussion and needs to get his medications, they wanted to keep him for two days. Tomorrow, I'll go and pick him up and bring him home."

"How's Jack doing?" Colt asked, his gaze pinned on her.

Loving how Colt cared about her son, she said, "He's a resilient kid. He's upset for George but glad that he'll be okay. I actually think Jack's kind of excited that something happened right in our neighborhood, and he got to be involved. Yesterday he was at the middle school camp, and today he's at the church camp."

"I'm glad he's got something to do during the summer."

"Me too. When he was younger, Mom was often able

to babysit, and George has always been a big help to keep an eye on him when I needed it. But Jack really wants to be around other kids, and he loves learning stuff." Shrugging, she added, "But with the middle school camp being two afternoons a week and the church camp being on two different mornings, there's a lot of running around for me, but I'm glad I can do it for him."

She saw one of her customers walking to the cash register and turned to assist them, but BettyJo threw her hand up, winked at her and Colt, and said, "I've got it. You two keep chatting."

She could feel blush heating her face and said, "Sorry."

Chuckling, Colt said, "I think BettyJo's a romantic at heart." Holding her gaze, he added, "But I don't mind. I'll take every moment with you that I can get."

She opened her mouth to reply but could not think of anything to say, continuing to blush instead. His eyes moved about her face, and she wondered if he was thinking about a kiss the way she was. Colt's phone buzzed, and he pulled it out of his pocket.

Nodding toward his plate, she said, "Do I need to box that up for you?"

Shaking his head, he said, "No, but I have to go in a few minutes."

"Then eat up," she commanded, winking before she darted off to pour coffee for some more customers. She wanted to give him plenty of time to finish his breakfast, and when it looked like his plate was empty, she went back behind the counter.

He reached over and placed his hand on hers and said, "Before I go, I wanted to ask you. Would you like to have dinner with me sometime? Just you and me…dinner."

Sucking in her lips, she asked, "Like…a date?"

He grinned, and said, "Yeah, Carrie. Like a date."

She could not contain her smile as she nodded her agreement. "Yeah. I'd like that a lot."

Nodding, he said, "Then I'll set something up." He placed money on the counter and said, "Walk me to the door?"

She met him on the other side of the counter and walked toward the door, realizing that all eyes were on them. Leaning in, she whispered, "I think every person in this room is staring at us."

One side of his mouth curved up, and he said, "That's what I planned on." Placing his hand on her waist, he leaned in and brushed his lips lightly against hers. "I'll call you soon. Can't wait to hear about Jack's camps."

She watched him walk out toward his Sheriff's SUV then whirled around, seeing that most eyes were on her, including BettyJo, Mavis, and Joe. And they were all smiling.

That afternoon, she was grateful when Ellen showed up on time. Carrie rushed to the church, pulling into the parking lot just as it appeared other parents were picking up their children, too. Surprised at the number of kids around, she walked quickly into the vestibule, seeing Pastor Hackett waving at her.

"Hello, Ms. Beaumont. I think I can say that Jack had a wonderful time today."

Smiling, she said, "I'm sure he did."

"He's a natural-born leader. Very social and highly intelligent."

Nodding, she said, "I agree with you. That's also what Mr. Jameson from the middle school said as well."

Just then, another young man walked over, and Pastor Hackett said, "Oh, let me introduce you to the leader of our camp. Brian Jeter. The summer camp, actually, was his idea."

Carrie turned and lifted her hand to shake Brian's hand, but found the young man's eyes continually dropped to her chest as he greeted her. Giving his hand a slight squeeze, he jolted, and his eyes lifted back to her face as a pink blush hit his cheeks. She knew she should be used to it, and in many ways she was. Aware of her own curves, Carrie had developed early, and by the time she was thirteen years old she had noticed boys—and men—would often stare at her chest when they talked to her.

Strange, she thought, that she had never found Colt just staring at her boobs. He was a man—all man—and had no doubt noticed her physical attributes, but when he spoke to her, he always held her eyes.

Pastor Hackett continued the introductions, saying, "This is Jack's mother."

Brian enthused, "He's a wonderful boy. He mentioned that you work at Joe's Place. I haven't been in there yet, but I hear it has great food."

"Yes, I've worked there for years. And you should come in. Joe and Mavis are wonderful cooks."

She heard Jack call out from behind her, and she turned to walk toward him. Jack looked up and asked, "Shelley thinks she might need a ride home. Can we give her one?"

"Sure, but let me check and make sure it's okay."

She walked back toward the ministers, then stopped as she heard Brian ask, "She's a single mom?"

Pastor Hackett nodded and said, "Yes. I don't believe she's ever been married but provides a good home for Jack."

Incensed that they would be talking about her, she clapped her mouth shut, realizing that most people enjoy a bit of gossip. Jack called again, and she looked up, seeing Shelley's mom standing with Jack and Shelley. Walking back over, Shelley said, "Thanks for the offer to take me home, Ms. Beaumont. My mom is here now."

She smiled at the other mother, introduced herself, and said, "I'm more than willing to bring Shelley home anytime she needs."

Donna smiled and said, "And the same goes for Jack."

Normally she would have stayed and chatted for a few minutes but Carrie guided Jack out, saying, "We need to get home."

As they drove away, she questioned Jack about the church camp.

"They have the middle school and high school kids divided," he said, "and then we all came together at the end."

"What are some of the things you did?"

"They had time for crafts, but I thought that was lame. It was the same kind of things we did in elementary school. The music time is pretty cool, though. I liked that. They had a couple of high school guys who had guitars, and the songs we sang were fun."

"Like church songs?"

"Nah, we sang the stuff you hear on the radio. Some country songs, and one of them even broke out into some rock 'n' roll."

She was surprised, but Jack's face was so alive with enthusiasm, she kept her opinions to herself. "So, what else did you do?"

"They divided us into small groups and asked us what we like to do for fun. They asked us about what our families were like, that kind of stuff."

Glancing over, she asked, "And what did you say about your family?"

He grinned and said, "I said I had the coolest mom ever."

Laughing, she said, "Now I know you're just sucking up."

Shaking his head, Jack said, "No, I'm not. Honest mom. You wouldn't believe what some of the kids said. Some said they had great homes or big houses, or they had a swimming pool or live near the beach. But then there are a lot of others who talk about how their parents worked all the time, and they were at home alone most of the time. Or how they didn't have anything in the house. A few of them said they didn't have money for food all the time."

Brows lowered, she said, "That seems rather harsh to have the kids admitting things like that in front of a bunch of others."

Thinking, Jack said, "Well, that's when we were in small groups. Then later it seemed like they sorta divided everybody."

"Divided?"

"Yeah, I noticed the people in my group who seem to have it the worst were later sitting with some of the other kids that I knew from school that are like that. Then I saw some of the richer kids were sitting together. I was kind of in the middle group…I'm not sure what that means."

Feeling as though her head was going to explode, she worked to keep her voice steady. "Are you telling me that they actually have the kids sitting with other kids, divided by their family situations?"

"Not for everything, Mom. Just when we were in that big group. We broke up into smaller groups to go outside and play."

She glanced at Jack, his eyes on her, and she forced a smile onto her face. He seemed to have had such a good time and had a chance to play with his friends, and she did not want to trounce on his enthusiasm. *Maybe, I'm just oversensitive.*

She sighed, not liking what Jack was telling her about the church camp, deciding she wanted to keep an eye on how they did things in case she needed to stop having him attend.

Hunter, Trevon, and Elizabeth were sitting at their desks when Colt walked back through the station. Trevon was a deputy working toward becoming a detective, and Hunter was helping him. Colt caught Hunter's eye and made his way over to them. "What have you got?"

"We're starting to make a few connections," Hunter said. "We found out that in the last four robberies that involve prescription drugs, they all got their prescriptions from Stuart's Pharmacy in Baytown. That, in and of itself, is not strange because other than Stuart's Pharmacy, there's only Markham's Pharmacy that's about fifteen miles north of here. We did find out that for shut-ins, Stuart's has an employee that will deliver the medications to them on Wednesdays. Will Penland is the employee. He's been working for Stuart's Pharmacy for over ten years, exemplary employee, and has no priors. Trevon and I are going to go interview him in just a few minutes."

"Do you think Will is letting someone know where he makes his deliveries?"

"We're considering it. Since he makes home deliveries, he can scope out the place, see if the person lives alone, and he would know what drugs are in the house."

Trevon said, "It seems risky, though. If he's smart, he would have to know that if the homes that he has visited have break-ins, then we're going to look at him."

"One thing you can always count on with some criminals is that they're not always smart," Hunter responded. "I did find out that two of the four victims go to the same free clinic, and another three out of the four attend the same church. So there're several tie-ins, but I don't know that any of them are connected to the robberies."

Nodding, Colt said, "Good work. Will Penland might just be the biggest tie-in that we have so far. Anything on the fingerprints?"

Elizabeth answered, "We found George's, both neighbors, Carrie Beaumont and her son Jack. There were a few small children's fingerprints, which we're going to ask George's son if we can get his family's fingerprints to rule those out."

Shaking his head, Hunter said, "I feel like we're making baby steps, but it's still not coming together. With the various robberies going on, we're not even sure that any of them are actually tied together, with the exception of the prescription drugs."

Colt nodded and said, "Keep working the problem and let me know how it goes."

He started to turn away when he could see that Hunter wanted to ask something else. Lifting an eyebrow, he observed Hunter glance between Elizabeth and Trevon, both of them nodding and moving to another set of desks.

"I wonder how you're doing with all this...you know, it being so close to Carrie."

Not used to discussing his personal life, Colt realized that in the past he did not really have a personal life to discuss. He scrubbed his hand over his face and admitted, "I got that call from Jack, saying that something had happened next door, and all I could think about was getting to them. Once there, I just focused on the job, but later, when I thought about somebody stealing and assaulting George with Carrie and Jack sleeping right next door, I about lost it."

Nodding, Hunter said, "Yeah, when Belle was in danger, that was worse than any case I'd ever faced."

"How'd you deal?"

Grinning, Hunter said, "First, I knew that just having her in my life made everything better. And second, I kept her as close as I could." With that, Hunter clapped him on the back before heading over to the other detectives.

Spending the rest of the afternoon working on state and local reports, Colt's mind often drifted to Carrie. He could not believe how nervous he had been asking her on a date, still uncertain, even with all the signals, that she was interested in going out with him. He thought about where he wanted to take her, adding and crossing several possibilities off of his mental list. It had been a long time since he had taken a woman out to dinner and realized he might need a little help.

He stepped outside his office, seeing Loretta sitting at her desk, efficiently handling much of the paperwork that he detested. She was probably his mother's age, kept herself neat and fit, noticing that her eyes always sparkled when she talked about her grandchildren. Sucking in a fortifying breath, he walked over and said, "Loretta, I need to ask you a question."

She looked up, her brow furrowed, and said, "Of course, Sheriff Hudson."

Shaking his head, he said, "This isn't from Sheriff Hudson. This is just from Colt."

Her brow furrowed even more, and she said, “Okay,” drawing out the word.

Glancing around to make sure no one else was listening, he said, “I want to take someone to dinner. I’d like it to be a nice restaurant, but not overly fancy. Someplace where you can dress up or be a little casual. But a place that makes…uh…a statement. You know…a statement that says we’re not just having dinner, but I’m really interested in you.” As soon as the words left his mouth, he almost turned around and walked away, feeling utterly foolish.

Loretta’s smile deepened as her brow relaxed. “I see you’ve finally gotten off your duff and asked Carrie to dinner.”

Jerking in surprise, he asked, “How did you know?”

“I think everyone’s been pulling for you two for a while. You’re never together often, but anytime someone sees you in Joe’s Place, it’s obvious that you two can’t keep your eyes off each other. Anyway,” she patted his hand, “take her into Baytown. Take her to The Sunset Restaurant. It’s right on the water, has fabulous food, is nice but not pretentious.” Leaning forward, she whispered, “I promise, she’ll love it.”

The pressure in his chest released, and he smiled in return. Thanking her, he walked back into his office, looking forward to when he could take Carrie to dinner.

13

"This has gotta be better than hospital food, right, George?" Joe asked, calling back from the kitchen.

"You got that right," George said, sitting at the counter, shoveling in eggs and bacon.

"Are you going to take George home soon? He's gonna pop if he keeps eating," Mavis joked.

The breakfast crowd had eased, and the lunch crowd had not yet started. Carrie was on the schedule for the breakfast shift only and would soon be getting off. Looking up at Joe and Mavis, she nodded and said, "Yes. I wanted to make sure he had a good breakfast. I went through his house yesterday and cleaned, making sure the fingerprint dust was off of everything and straightened up. I called Stuart's Pharmacy, and they're delivering his new medication this afternoon."

"You didn't need to do all that," George fussed.

"Girl, I don't know how you take care of everything," Mavis said.

"Mom is a superwoman!" Jack called out, sitting on one of the stools at the counter. "She can do anything!"

Carrie rolled her eyes but leaned over to ruffle Jack's hair in affection. Her wide smile was filled with motherly pride even when he tried to duck her hand. Laughter greeted the pair from the others, and she managed to kiss the top of Jack's head before hearing the bell ring over the door again.

"Carrie?"

Carrie turned around and looked at a face that had aged but was one she never expected to see again. Peter Bernstein. Stunned, she stared without saying anything.

He repeated, "Carrie?"

She startled, jolting out of her statue-like state, and asked, "What are you doing here?"

"We...uh...I wanted to talk to you."

It was then that she realized he was not alone and wondered how she could have missed the statuesque blond next to him. The couple was striking, impeccably dressed, and she had no doubt that the woman's haircut probably cost as much as Carrie made a week or more in tips. The woman appeared uncomfortable, looking as though she wanted to offer a smile but was uncertain as to whether or not she should.

Carrie felt a presence nearby, and the scent of BettyJo's perfume let her know that she had moved in close. Instinctively, she realized that Mavis and Joe had circled behind her as well, and she knew the unwelcoming tone of her voice was giving her away. "This is where I work. Did you want anything to eat?"

Peter shook his head, his gaze taking in the place, and said, "No. Thank you. I need to talk to you."

Joe, as though reading her unease, said, "This is my joint. If you don't want to eat, then I'll need to ask you to move on."

Carrie watched the woman's hand reach down and clutch Peter's, and fear moved through her, knowing Jack could witness the scene. "I can only give you a minute, but we would need to step outside. As Joe said, this is his business."

Peter nodded and turned with his hand on the woman's lower back, guiding her through the front door. Carrie felt fingers on her arm and glanced down to see Mavis nearby. "You need one of us to go with you, girl?" Glancing back at Jack, who was staring at them, she whispered, "No, stay with Jack. Keep him busy." Smiling at her son, she said louder, "I'm going to step outside and talk to an old acquaintance. I'll be right back and then we can get George home." She was thankful to see that her words seemed to satisfy Jack, but his eyes were curious.

"Girl, you look like you've seen a ghost," Joe said.

Sucking in a deep breath, she let it out slowly and said, "No, not a ghost. Just someone who ghosted on me."

"Shit," Joe cursed under his breath, and she was sure he could guess who Peter was.

She broke away from her posse and headed out the door, seeing Peter and the woman were standing in the shade to the side. A silver Mercedes was nearby, and she had no doubt it was theirs. She almost laughed, seeing it parked so close to her old car. Money and the trappings of wealth had meant everything to Peter's father, and it appeared the apple had not fallen far from the tree. A rush of gratitude that Jack had not been raised with that mentality slammed into her.

Taking a deep breath, she walked over and, keeping her eyes on Peter, said, "I can't imagine what you need to see me about after eleven years." She watched as a wince crossed his face, the expression surprising her.

In many ways, Peter looked very much the same as she remembered. Handsome. Lean but muscular, and she remembered he liked to swim and play tennis. From his tan, she assumed he still did. His hair used to be a little shaggy but now was neatly trimmed and groomed. Dress pants, white long sleeve shirt, and navy tie. He now looked like a younger image of what she remembered of his father.

Turning to the woman, she stuck her hand out and said, "We haven't been introduced. I'm Carrie Beaumont."

The woman took her hand and smiled nervously. "Hello, I'm Abigail Bernstein…Peter's wife," she said, her voice soft and delicate.

A strange thought crossed Carrie's mind, and that was she could not imagine Abigail ever at a youth ball game, screaming and cheering. Giving herself a mental shake, she turned her attention back to Peter. "I was serious when I said I only have a few minutes. I'm afraid you've interrupted my workday, and I'm paid by the hour."

Peter nodded and said, "I'm sorry. I thought this might be better than trying to come to your house."

Visibly startling, she reared back. "You know where I live?"

Shaking his head quickly from side to side, he said, "No, but I did have someone let me know where you are working."

"I can't imagine after all these years why you would feel the need to pay someone to find out where I am. Probably a Google search would've done the same." Her stomach began to knot, and she wondered what Peter wanted.

Just as he opened his mouth, her attention was snagged by a large vehicle pulling into the diner parking lot. Her eyes bugged when she realized it was the Sheriff's SUV, and Colt was climbing from behind the wheel, making his way directly to her. She noted his eyes did a head to toe scan of her, going back up as though he were checking to see how she was. *Joe must have called him!* She wanted to smile at him, but since Peter had not explained the reason for the impromptu visit, she had no clue what silent message to send to Colt.

"Hey, Carrie," he said, walking over and casually putting his arm around her shoulders, leaning down to kiss her forehead. "Are you already off work?"

Shaking her head, she said, "No. An old acquaintance came by and wanted to speak to me. I thought it was best to take it outside instead of in the diner."

Colt's gaze shot to the window, and she knew it landed on Jack sitting at the counter. He turned, a wide smile on his face that did not reach his eyes and said,

"I'm Sheriff Hudson. I'm a good friend of Carrie's. And you are?"

Peter had always been tall, but he was easily three or four inches shorter than Colt, and Colt outweighed him by quite a few muscles. All this ran through Carrie's mind, and she wondered how the conversation was going to play out.

Shaking Colt's hand, Peter said, "Peter Bernstein. This is my wife, Abigail. We came because we had some private business we wanted to talk to Carrie about."

Carrie smiled at Peter and said, "You can discuss anything you want to in front of Colt."

Peter's eyebrows lifted slightly at her calling the sheriff by his first name, but he plunged ahead. "I wanted to talk to you about our son."

The bottom fell out of her stomach as her worst fears were realized, and if Colt had not put his arm around her, she would have dropped to the pavement.

Colt felt Carrie's knees buckle, and he tightened his grip around her waist. Uncertain what to do or say, he glanced at her pale face, understanding that all of this was coming as a shock. Her body stiffened in his arms, and she locked her knees in place, straightened her spine, and threw her shoulders back. He felt rage burning through her and wanted to cheer but stood silently, offering his support.

"Our…" she croaked, then cleared her voice and began again. "*Our* son? I believe the correct terminology would be *my* son, considering that you were no more than a sperm donor."

Peter's lips tightened as he sucked in a quick breath. "Carrie, I'd like to help out."

"Help out?" she asked, her voice abnormally high. "The last time I laid eyes on you was when I was pregnant. You told me to get an abortion because your parents would never allow their son to have a baby with a girl who had no family connections."

Colt's fingers flexed as anger curled through him. Abigail gasped as though that news surprised her, and Colt observed Carrie shifting her gaze to the other woman.

"I can only assume since you are married to Peter, you must fit the profile of what his parents considered to be acceptable. I congratulate you on that because I certainly didn't. My parents didn't have a lot of money, but what we did have was love. I was seventeen years old, refused to have an abortion, and thank God I had parents that made sure that my pregnancy went well. I had money for doctor's appointments, and my mom held my hand when I pushed out *my* child."

Her gaze moved back to Peter, and she continued, "You, on the other hand, were not there for any of that. I know we were young, but you were twenty years old, and I was almost eighteen. Things could have gotten very ugly for you, but I didn't want that. We didn't have to get married, but you could certainly have helped out then and in the past eleven years that my son has been with me."

Peter nodded, his head jerking, and said, "You're

right. I was young, but I should've stood up to my father and done what was right. But I didn't. I've had to live with that, and I'm sorry."

Colt's profession called for him to read people, and what he read from Peter was only half-truths. There was some reason why Peter decided now was the time to make an approach, but he would bet his paycheck it had nothing to do with guilt. Deciding to wade in, he asked, "I'm curious as to why you're making the approach all these years later. What is it exactly that you want to do?"

"I would like to make sure that our…um…her…son is taken care of," Peter said, looking at Carrie. "I know you've managed for all these years, but I'd like to set up a bank account for him and make sure that I assist with child support payments."

Colt felt Carrie's body jerk again, and he tightened his grip on her. Her arms crossed in front of her, probably both in defense and to hold herself back from doing something she might regret, like slap Peter.

"Child support? You want to start giving us money? Guilt money, I presume?" Snorting, she said, "There's no way this idea came from you after all these years, so what's really behind this?"

"Don't be obstinate, Carrie," Peter bit out. "You work in a diner. You can probably hardly afford to pay for anything, and I have the ability to do so—"

Carrie leaned forward, her face twisted in anger, and said, "You sanctimonious prick. Don't you dare act like I haven't been able to provide for my son!"

Abigail stepped forward, placing her hand on Peter's

arm, and said quietly, "Peter." She then looked over at Carrie and said, "I'm sorry. I don't think any of this is coming out right. It's true that you and Peter were very young when your son was conceived, and I completely agree that he did not handle things well. Or appropriately at all. I think what Peter is trying to say, though, is that he would like to help now. I know it's late. I know it's twelve years too late. He would still like to help."

Carrie's arms tightened about her waist even more, and Colt gently reached around further so that he could link his fingers with hers that were at her side.

Wading in again, Colt said, "Peter Bernstein. That name rings a bell. If I'm not mistaken, you're in the running for Maryland State Senate, aren't you?

Peter appeared surprised, and Colt knew that a man like Peter would assume a small county sheriff was little more than a bumpkin. "I assume that has something to do with your sudden desire to make monetary restitution to Ms. Beaumont."

Now, Peter's eyes flashed, his breath leaving in a rush, but he did not deny anything.

Nodding slowly, Carrie said, "Oh, I see. You're running for a state office, and you're terrified that someone will dig up that you fathered a child twelve years ago. Or maybe you were afraid that I would see your name in the paper, and I would cause a stink."

The blush on Abigail's face deepened, and Colt knew that he and Carrie had hit the nail on the head.

"Peter," she said through pinched lips, "you can be assured that there have been times I thought of you over the years. When I battled morning sickness to go to work. When I was in labor for over twenty hours. Every time my son got sick. But through it all, I realized that I was his mom, and I was giving everything I could, mostly love. And what I got out of it is an amazing child who is the heart and soul of my very being. We do not need your money. We do not want your money. You may go on about your life, as you have, and we will stay out of it and ask that you do the same."

Abigail tugged on her husband's sleeve and said, "Peter, I think we need to leave."

Peter swallowed deeply, then asked, "Does he ever wonder? Does he ever ask?"

"A smart eleven-year-old boy could hardly not know that his father's never been around," she quipped. "But I have always been honest with him. I told him that we were very young, but that his father did not want to be with me, nor did he want to have anything to do with him."

Colt watched as Carrie's words slashed across Peter's face. But she was not finished.

"My son's life has been filled with good men that he could use as examples. My father, my boss, friends, his coaches, and Colt."

Colt was proud as fuck of Carrie's backbone, but those words nearly dropped him to his knees. Peter shoved his hands in his pocket, and Colt thought he looked like a little boy himself.

"I didn't mean for this to be a payoff to keep you quiet, Carrie," Peter said. "Yes, you're right. My father wanted to know if there were any skeletons in my closet. I told him about you and the baby. He wasn't happy, as you can imagine, and wanted to know if I'd paid you off or provided any money at all. He was also not very happy when I said that I had not."

"So you decided to come down, offer me money, and that way if the press gets hold of this, I'm simply a girl from your past that you provided for."

"Carrie, I need to make this right."

She opened her mouth, but Colt jumped in. Looking down at her, he said, "Babe, take some time. Think about it." Looking at Peter, he said, "The two of you ambushed Carrie today at work, and that was not cool and not fair. You need to back off, give me your contact information, and if she wants to talk to you, she will."

He was glad that Carrie remained quiet and Peter pulled out a business card from his pocket and handed it to Colt.

Abigail's eyes spoke volumes as she said, "I'm very sorry. It was nice to meet you, and I'm truly, very sorry."

She turned to leave, but Peter glanced through the window of the diner and asked, "Is that him?"

Colt felt Carrie's body begin to shake, and he stated, "I think that's all for now." Without giving Peter a second look, he turned Carrie, and with his arms firmly banded around her guided her toward the diner door.

14

Carrie's mind was reeling as she allowed Colt to lead her inside. Seeing Jack sitting at the counter staring at her, his gaze intense, her feet stumbled. Barely whispering, she said, "What do I say to him?"

Colt leaned down and whispered, "Carrie, you've got this. You've always been honest, and he's now surrounded by people who love him."

Grateful that the restaurant was almost empty, she realized that Colt was right. George was sitting at the counter next to her mom and Jack. BettyJo and Brenda were right next to them, along with Joe and Mavis.

She glanced toward her mom, seeing fire coming from her eyes. She sucked in a fortifying breath, knowing that she needed to deal with her mom's anger toward Peter, but first and foremost was Jack. His face registered a bit of fear as he asked, "Mom, who was that man?"

Plastering what she hoped was a convincing smile on her facc, she said, "He was someone I knew a long time ago. We can talk about him later, but right now, let's get George back home."

Her normally obedient son dug his heels in and asked, "How long ago did you know him, Mom?"

Pressing her lips together, she said, "Jack, honey, please, let's—"

"Did him coming to see you have anything to do with me?"

Carrie walked toward Jack, stopping just in front of him, and looked down at his face. At almost eleven years old, he hovered in between childhood and manhood. At that moment, when he looked up at her, his chin quivered, and she hated that, knowing that he did not want to show emotion in front of everybody.

"Mom," he insisted, "you've always said that you'll be honest with me."

She nodded and felt Colt behind her, his strong hands on her shoulders, letting her know that he was supporting her however she wanted to play this.

"That man was your father, Jack. Everything I told you was true. We were very young, and we did not get married, but we cared a great deal for each other at the time. Unfortunately, when I found out that I was pregnant with you, he was not ready to accept the responsibility of fatherhood. That was his choice. My choice was to become the mom of the greatest kid in the world."

At that, Jack's lips twitched, and he breathed through his nose for a moment. She could tell he was gaining control of himself, and she smiled.

"What did he want?"

"He and his wife wanted to come by and see if I

needed financial help with you." Her mother let out a snort, and she shot her a silencing look before turning her attention back to Jack. "At this time, I told him that I did not, but Colt has his phone number in case I change my mind."

Jack's eyes jumped up to Colt before going back to his mom. "He was right here. Did he want to meet me?"

Swallowing, she said carefully, "He didn't specifically ask for a meeting, but then, I'm sure he realized that to just show up was not the smartest thing he should have done."

"Sounds like he's done a lot of not-smart things, Mom."

"I think you're probably right, Jack, but right now he's willing to accept some responsibilities."

"Are you gonna take his money?"

"No, I don't want to take his money. But Colt has advised that I should think about that. It might be wise to have him put some money in a bank account for you and then you would have it when you're older. It could help pay for college or something like that."

"I don't want his money," Jack said. "If he doesn't want to have anything to do with me, then I don't want his money."

"Jack," Colt said, gaining Jack's eyes up to his. "This is pretty heavy on you and your mom right now. Why don't we step back? Let's get George home and settled. Your grandma can come with us, and the only thing you have to worry about right now is to just keep being the great kid that you are."

Carrie sucked in her lips as she watched Jack's

thoughts churning behind his eyes. After a moment, he settled his gaze back on her. "Are you okay, Mom? I know that had to be pretty upsetting."

The fact that he was worried about her hit her right in the heart, and she reached forward, pulling him into a hug. "I've had eleven years of being the mom to the greatest kid in the world. How could I not be okay?"

He looked up at her and said, "Well, that's pretty cool because for eleven years I've had the greatest mom in the world."

She heard a sob but could not tell if it came from her mom, BettyJo, or Mavis. As she felt a tear roll down her cheek, she realized it had come from her.

That evening, Carrie sat on her front porch alone, her mind in turmoil, and her body exhausted. After the scene at the diner, Joe and Mavis boxed up food for her to take with her, and she loaded up Jack and George into her car and drove home with her mom and Colt following in their vehicles.

Once home, they helped to get George settled and made sure he had food from Joe's Place in his refrigerator. Jack had proudly carried George's box of baseball cards to him, excited as George praised him effusively for making sure they were safe.

Colt had come in with them, and she could tell he was trying to keep a pulse on her as well as Jack. He finally needed to go back to work, and as glad as she was that he had had her back, she was relieved when he left, feeling overwhelmed with the events of the day.

Her mom had been attentive to both she and Jack, but when they had a moment alone, her mom had bit out, “I can’t believe he had the nerve to show up after all this time.”

“I know, Mom,” she agreed, “I was so dumbstruck.”

“That’s part of what makes me so angry, that he just ambushed you without warning. Always so selfish! Just like when he was younger…didn’t think our family was good enough or had enough money.”

She squeezed her mom’s hand and kissed her cheek as she walked her out to the car. “I love you, Mom. We’ll be fine, we always are.” The two women hugged, and she watched her mom back out of the driveway, waving until she could not see her vehicle anymore.

Going inside the house, she noted Jack sitting on the couch, staring at the blank television. "You know, you’ll enjoy the show much more if you actually turned the TV on,” she said, hoping to draw a smile from him.

“I know you’re worried about me, Mom,” Jack said, his gaze once more penetrating. “But this really isn’t about me.”

Uncertain of his meaning, she sat down on the sofa, twisted to the side, and tucked one leg up under her ass. With her arm on the back of the sofa, she propped her head on her hand and said, “What are you thinking, Bud?”

“You know my friend, Shelley? The one you met at church when you picked me up?”

Nodding, she said, “Yeah. What about her?”

"She was in my class two years ago, and she would get really upset. I found out that her mom and dad got a divorce. Her dad just left, Mom. Can you believe that?"

"I'm sure that was hard on her," she said, observing him carefully.

"I heard her crying one day at school, and she said that after her dad left, he never came around again. I mean, think about it. Her dad had a daughter, and he was around her every day from the time she was born until she was almost nine years old. Then he moved out and doesn't see her anymore. My friend Colby's parents got divorced, but they're both in town, and he bounces between them. That kind of sucks, but he knows both of his parents still love him. But Shelby, it's like her father had her for nine years and then just walked away."

She pondered what he was saying but was still not certain the parallel he was trying to draw. He must have seen that she was not getting his meaning because he continued.

"I'm pissed that my dad never wanted to be my dad. But he's never known me. He's never seen me. So, he didn't really reject me…he just rejected the idea of being a dad. I'm more pissed for you because it sounds like the only reason he wouldn't be with you was that he didn't think your family was the right kind of family."

She gasped. "You heard grandma and me?"

Nodding, he said, "It's okay, Mom. I'd rather know." They were silent for a moment. He looked back up and held her gaze, his expression set. "But Grandma and Grandpa were perfect, and if his family didn't like them because they didn't have enough money, then they're not the kind of people I want to be around anyway."

Her heart clenched and she battled the desire to burst into big, sloppy sobs. She swallowed deeply then blew out her breath and smiled. "You know, for someone who's not quite eleven years old, you've just said a mouthful, and it was more mature than a lot of people older than you."

He grinned, gave her a hug, and bounced off the sofa to go practice pitching in the backyard, and she once again thanked the heavens for the gift of her son.

Now it was evening, George was sleeping on his living room sofa, saying he was a little afraid to take the stairs that first night back at home, and Jack had already gone to bed a little early, exhausted. Sitting all alone on her front porch, Carrie was surprised to observe headlights coming down the street and then turning into her driveway.

Seeing the Sheriff's SUV come to a stop, she smiled. As he approached, she said, "Good evening, Sheriff Hudson."

He stopped at the bottom of the porch, one booted foot up on the first step, and leaned forward toward the rail. Grinning, he said, "Now, Carrie, you've been calling me Colt today." Climbing the two steps to the porch, he stopped in front of her rocking chair, bent to place his hands on the arms of the chair, effectively trapping her, and said, "I finally made it to where you say my name. We're certainly not going to go backward now." Leaning forward, he kissed her.

This time, the kiss was not the brush of lips on lips. This time, he angled his head, taking the kiss deeper.

It had been a long time since she had been kissed like that. Actually, as the kiss hit her straight to her core, she could not remember if she had ever been kissed so thoroughly. He lifted his head, and she barely remembered to breathe.

"You okay?"

She shook her head slowly.

He lifted an eyebrow and asked, "Jack?"

She sighed and replied, "Everything."

He stood and pulled her gently from the chair, wrapped his arm around her shoulders, tugged her in tight to his side, and walked her into her house. Guiding her to her sofa, he pulled her down next to him, angling their bodies so that they were facing each other, their legs touching and his arm still around her.

"You need to break the *everything* down for me, babe," he encouraged.

She remembered he had called her 'babe' earlier when everything was going down with Peter, but she had barely had time for the endearment to register. Somehow, they had gone from Ms. Beaumont to Carrie to Babe all in one day. She had to admit, it felt nice. With Colt, it didn't feel like a throwaway. Pushing that thought to the side, she said, "Who called you from the diner?"

"It was Joe. He told me that Jack demanded his phone, declaring that if someone was going to talk to you, he wanted me at your side."

The knowledge that Jack, even at his age, had her

back warmed her heart, and she blinked away the tears she could feel forming. She pushed that thought to the side as well.

Colt continued, "So, Joe called, and I was close by, which I was glad of. I never want you to feel like you have to face anything by yourself, especially not someone trying to take advantage of you."

She nodded slowly, and he prodded, "Keep breaking it down for me, babe. What else are you thinking about?"

"Jack seems okay. We talked a lot when we got home, and he said some things that sounded very mature. He said it wasn't like a father who had been around him for years and then left. He felt like his dad really didn't reject him, he just rejected the idea of fatherhood."

Colt's eyebrows hit his hairline at that comment, and she almost smiled.

"You've got a fuckin' smart kid, Carrie. And you did that, don't ever forget that."

Her smile curved her lips. "So, for now, he's good. I think he's going to think about it a lot, and at some point, he's going to be pissed. He never once asked me for his dad's name, but he'll know it now. I'm actually okay with that. If he wants to talk to his dad at some time, he certainly can. In fact, I would encourage it."

Colt smiled and asked, "Did the steam ever stop coming out of your mom's ears?"

She giggled and realized it was the first time she had laughed all day. "I got her settled down. As you can imagine, she spent many years not caring for Peter. It wasn't that my parents wanted Peter and me to get married, but the fact that he wanted me to have an abortion and then just walked away, never having anything to do with Jack or me after that...well, let's just say that she's never forgiven him."

Colt ran his fingers through her hair and said, "So, George is settled. Your mom is settled. And Jack is in bed, and if not settled, at least doing okay for now. That only leaves you, babe. How are you doing?"

She sucked in her lips and dropped her gaze to her hands in her lap. "I guess it's just embarrassing," she said. Lifting her gaze back up to his face, she said, "I learned a long time ago to push past the embarrassment of being an unwed teen mother because I threw myself into being a mom. And ever since I first found out I was pregnant, I've loved him more than anything in the world. It's been easy being his mom, even though it hasn't been easy being a single mom. But, sometimes, I know there's judgment in other people's eyes."

"Fuck 'em, babe."

Snorting, she said, "That's easier said than done, Colt. Today I looked at the woman he did choose to marry. She could not be more different than me, and in a weird way, I guess that cuts a little bit."

"Only cut it should be is for them, Carrie."

She was quiet for a moment, and his hand drifted under her hair to her neck, his fingertips starting to massage away the tension that she had felt all day.

"What else?" he asked. "I want you to get it all out so that you're not burying it deep inside."

"It was also embarrassing with you."

His fingers flexed slightly, and she knew she surprised him. She hurried to explain, "It was so wonderful to have you at my back. It was so wonderful to show him that I had a real man, a good man, who was standing right there with me. I've got no secrets, Colt, so there was really nothing you were going to hear that was embarrassing. I guess I just felt blindsided by it all, and that made me feel vulnerable."

"Baby, it was an asshole move on his part. No doubt about it. It pissed me off and then when I realized who he was and what he was doing, that pissed me off even more," Colt growled.

She smiled and lifted her hand up to cup his cheek. "You're a good man."

"Then if you think so, Carrie, we're a good pair, because I think you're a good woman." With his arms banded around her, he pulled her so that she was sitting on his lap. She wrapped her arms around his neck, their lips meeting once again.

He slid one hand to cup the back of her head, his fingers tangling in her long tresses. Tilting her head, he took possession of the kiss, his lips moving over hers. She sighed, and not missing the opportunity, he slid his tongue into her mouth.

The feel of his tongue tangling with hers had her nipples tingling and her legs pinching together, the desire for friction overwhelming. Their heads moved back and forth, and her hands gripped his shoulders, pulling him closer. She breathed him in, memorizing the scent of spice and something uniquely Colt.

He finally pulled back, leaning his head against the

sofa, and groaned, "If I don't stop, babe, I'm afraid I'm not going to be able to."

She was breathing hard as well and leaned forward to rest her forehead against his. "I know. Jack may be crazy about you, but I don't want him coming downstairs and finding me dry humping you on the sofa."

He grinned widely and said, "Yeah, I'm not ready for Jack to see that either." They sat, breathing each other in, just reveling in the quiet of the night. He finally stood, lifting her easily and setting her feet on the floor, keeping his hands around her waist. "I want to make reservations at the Sunset Restaurant in Baytown. What night can you get your mom to watch Jack?"

Looking up at him, her hands still on his shoulders, she said, "We can do it any time."

"How about tomorrow night?"

Laughing, she said, "You don't waste any time, do you?"

He held her gaze and said, "Babe, when there's something you want, you go for it. I should've gone for you a long time ago. I held back, not because of you, but because of me. For reasons that we can get into another time when you're not tired and vulnerable, and I don't feel like kicking some certain politician's ass. But just know that I held back because I figured you wouldn't want a wreck like me. And maybe it's selfish, but I've spent five years watching you smile, and I want to claim your smile for my own now."

She leaned forward again, this time resting her forehead against his chest, hearing his strong heartbeat. He kissed the top of her head, and they walked to the front door together. Standing on the porch, they kissed like teenagers until he finally left, climbed into his vehicle, and pulled out of her driveway.

Carrie went inside, double-checked to see that the doors were locked and then crawled into bed. Her dreams were full of Colt again, but now, they were filled with the realness of his kisses.

15

This time, Carrie knew exactly what woke her up in the middle of the night. The sound of glass breaking. She threw back the covers and leaped out of bed, stumbling slightly as her brain raced to catch up with her feet. She darted across the hall, throwing the door open with such force that it banged on the wall, and Jack jumped.

Not wanting to scare him but wanting him to be prepared, she said, "Stay here. Don't come down unless I call you but have your phone with you." She grabbed the baseball bat that was next to his glove in the corner of the room and hurried to the top of the stairs.

The only noise she heard was the sound of Jack's soft feet coming up behind her. Glancing back, she shook her head sharply and brought her finger up to her lips.

She crept halfway down the stairs, and with the illumination of the night light, she could easily see that there was no one in her living room and her front window had not been disturbed. The sound she had heard came from the front of the house, so her mind flew to George. Running to her window, she peeked through the curtain and saw taillights moving down the street rapidly.

"Mom, what is it?" Jack whispered from the top of the steps.

Turning to look up at him, she said, "I heard glass breaking from the front. I want to go check on George to make sure he's okay. You stay there, just like before, and I'll let you know if you should call someone."

With her hand on the doorknob, she peeked through her security hole and saw nothing. Still, she opened the door with caution, but no one was there. As soon as she stepped outside and turned toward George's front door, it was evident that it was his house that had been attacked. His front window was broken, and light was coming from his house.

Without hesitation, she ran the few feet back into her house, looked up at Jack, and yelled, "Call 9-1-1 again." Hurrying to retrace her steps, she pounded on George's door, crying out his name. Moving to the broken window, she reached through the jagged hole in the glass, careful not to cut herself, and pulled back the curtain so that she could see in. The light she had been able to see was actually flames.

"George! George!" she continued to scream, but no answer came in return. Realizing he may have taken something to help him sleep, she turned and ran back into her side of the duplex, yelling up to Jack that there was a fire next door. She raced to her kitchen and shoved her bare feet into her rubber garden boots, grabbing her leather garden gloves at the same time. She raced back through the house, out the front door, and to the front of George's duplex. Grabbing the chair he often sat in, she slammed it through the broken window, breaking out as much of the remaining glass as she could, raking the metal chair along the bottom seal to rid it of the jagged edges.

Jerking back the curtains, she could see that George was now sitting up on his sofa, staring groggily before struggling to stand. With her hands encased in the leather gloves, she placed them on the windowsill and climbed over, her boots crunching the glass underneath the window. The flames were leaking up the wooden stairs and the walls on the back side of the living room.

Once inside, she unlocked his door and threw it open before whirling around to assist him. "Come on, George," she encouraged as he staggered slightly.

She looked up and saw Jack standing in the doorway, and as soon as she maneuvered George close, Jack nudged his way under George's other arm, allowing the older man to lean on him. They had just made it to the porch, the sound of sirens crying out once more in the night, and she looked up to see two fire trucks, two ambulances, three deputies' cars, and the now-familiar Sheriff's SUV pulling into their driveway.

Flames licked the front of the duplex, and Colt's boots pounded up the gravel drive once more, only this time behind the firemen who were already pulling out their hoses. Forgoing all semblance of maintaining his professional cool, his heart beat wildly, only able to catch his breath when he saw Carrie, Jack, and George standing to the side of the driveway near her car. *Safe! Jesus Christ, safe!*

Jack was barefoot and in his pajamas. George was wearing a white T-shirt and drawstring pajama bottoms. Carrie was in a camisole and pajama shorts with her feet in ridiculous-looking dark green rubber boots with frog eyes on them.

When he rounded her car, they did not see him coming until he swept Carrie into his embrace, capturing Jack squished in between the two of them. Burying his face in her hair, he breathed her in. The feel of Carrie in his arms was all that was keeping him standing, but the scent of smoke in her hair had his rage building.

Pulling his head back, he scanned her and Jack from head to toe as she kept saying, "Colt, we're fine. We're fine." She may have been proclaiming that they were safe, but as her body trembled, he knew she was anything but *fine*. She was half-naked, and as a paramedic came closer, he growled, "Get her a blanket." With his arm still banded around her on one side and Jack on the other, he led them to the back of one of the ambulances, grateful when a blanket was handed to him, and he could wrap it around her. Bundling Jack in another blanket, he then turned to George.

It appeared that George was physically okay, just fighting mad. "I've been attacked in my goddamn house twice this week," George groused, "and if it wasn't for Carrie and Jack, I might not be alive now!"

Colt looked over Carrie's shoulder and saw two of his deputies approaching. "What's going on?" he asked, barely keeping his voice steady.

Carrie looked up and said, "I heard a—"

"Not you, babe." He saw her brow scrunched, but he was looking past her shoulder as Deputy Mark Robbins walked up.

Mark answered, "An incendiary device was thrown through the front window of the left duplex."

The group turned to see the firemen blasting water on the first-floor fire of George's house. Looking at Mark, he ordered, "Stick with the Fire Chief. I want to know what kind of incendiary device was used. And as soon as you can get in there, keep working with him to get all the evidence we can."

As Mark walked away, another deputy stayed next to George, and Colt turned back to Carrie and said, "I'm sorry…you said you heard something?"

She nodded and said, "The sound of breaking glass woke me up. It sounded like it was near the front of the house, but not my house. I made sure Jack was awake and had the phone in case we needed to call for help and then I went downstairs. I could easily see that my front window was fine, so I went outside to check on George."

"You went outside?" Colt bit out. "You didn't call for help first?"

She shook her head slowly, appearing slightly dazed, and said, "I looked through my peephole, and there was no one there. When I checked my front window to make sure it wasn't broken, I saw taillights going down the street so I figured whoever had been there was gone."

"What then?"

"I knew George was sleeping in his living room because he took a sleeping pill and said that he thought he'd sleep on the downstairs sofa, a little afraid to traverse the stairs the first night he was back. I could see that his window was broken, and I could see the flames coming up. I ran back to tell Jack to call 9-1-1. Then I got my boots and my gardening gloves so that I could get into George's house without cutting myself on the broken glass."

Eyebrows hitting his hairline, he asked, "You went into George's house?"

She cocked her head to the side, her nose slightly scrunched, and said, "Of course. I had to get George out. I took one of the chairs and knocked the rest of the glass out so that I could crawl over the windowsill."

The idea of Carrie going into a burning house sliced through him, and he wanted to roar in frustration. He did not attempt to hide his ire but watched as Jack moved next to Carrie, slid his arm around his mom's waist, and held his stare.

"Mom's a hero," Jack declared, looking up at him as though Colt needed convincing.

Colt's sighed and scrubbed his hand over his face, nodding slowly. He bent and placed his hand on Jack's shoulder and said, "I know, bud. Looks like you were, too."

"Is our house going to be safe, Mom?"

Carrie looked down and said, "I hope so, Jack. It looks like they've taken care of the fire in George's house now, so we should be able to go back into ours soon." Turning to George, she said, "You can spend the night with us."

Colt was about to correct her when the Fire Chief walked up and obviously overheard what Carrie had just said.

"I'm afraid, ma'am, you can't do that. We're going to need to declare the entire structure safe, and while the initial flames are out, we have to go through, check for embers, and it's a crime scene as well."

"But that's on George's side…" she began.

Shaking his head, the Chief said, "The best thing you can do tonight is make alternate arrangements."

George grumbled again, and Jack looked up at his mom and said, "Are we going to have to stay in a hotel?"

Without giving it a second thought, Colt said, "You're not going to a hotel. You're all coming home with me."

Carrie looked at him as though he had sprouted another head and said, "We can't do that."

"Of course, you can. I've got lots of room. Only thing I don't have is much furniture. We'll make do for the rest of tonight and then we'll figure out what to do tomorrow."

An hour later, they arrived at Colt's house after the firemen had gone inside and collected two plastic bags of some of their belongings. On the drive over, Colt was glad that George was no longer grumbling, and Jack seemed excited about the next adventure but was quietly keeping an eye on his mom. But then, considering that Carrie appeared shell-shocked, staying very quiet, Colt worried about her as well.

Pulling into his driveway, he heard Jack exclaim, "Jeez, you have a big house! Are you the only one who lives here?"

"Yep. It was my grandparents' house. I used to spend a lot of time here when I was a kid. They left it to me when they passed away, but I'm afraid I haven't done much to it." He glanced to the side, but Carrie's tight-lipped face had not changed.

He hustled everybody inside, grabbing the items that the firemen had collected. "George, tonight, you're going to be on my sofa. I hope that's okay."

"Sheriff, I'd sleep on the floor and be thankful for your hospitality."

"Well, you're not going to have to do that. If you hang on, I'll get some sheets and a blanket." He disappeared upstairs, and when he came back, he had a folded sheet and a blanket, along with an extra pillow. Looking at George, he said, "I'm going to get Jack and Carrie settled and then I'll be back to check on you."

Carrie was standing awkwardly in the middle of the hall, the paramedic blanket still wrapped around her, and her arm tucking Jack in tightly to her side.

Walking over, Colt said, "Jack, I'm going to put you and your mom in my bedroom upstairs. I'm afraid I don't have extra furniture in my guestrooms yet, but my bed's king-size, so you and your mom will fit there fine."

Jack's face scrunched, and he protested, "I'm not a little kid, Sheriff Hudson. I don't have to sleep with my mom."

He walked over and placed his hand on Jack's shoulder, drawing him away from Carrie. "You don't have to convince me that you're not a little boy, Jack. You've been taking good care of your mom and George, and you helped to rescue him tonight. But right now, your mom is exhausted, and I think she's understandably overwhelmed about everything that's happened. I think it would be good if, for tonight, she had you with her. I think she'd sleep easier that way. Can you do that for me?"

Jack's face settled, and he nodded as Colt's words seemed to have the desired effect. "Okay, Sheriff. I can take care of mom."

Giving his shoulder a squeeze, he said, "I think, under the circumstances, you can call me Colt."

He could feel that Carrie was about to object, but they both watched as Jack's face beamed with a smile that was wider than he had ever seen, and he had seen a lot of smiles from Jack. Carrie sucked in a quick breath but remained silent, not objecting to her son now calling him 'Colt'.

"Let's get you two upstairs." Climbing the stairs, he bypassed the empty bedrooms, answering Jack's question about them by saying, "Haven't needed anything there, so I haven't bought guest room furniture yet."

Glad that he had extra sheets that were clean, the three of them quickly remade the king-size bed. While Jack was in the bathroom, he pulled Carrie to his side and wrapped his arms around her. "Honey, I know everything feels like it's out of your control, but tonight, just rest easy knowing that you, Jack, and George are safe."

She looked up, holding his gaze, and said, "I don't understand what's happening. Why is someone doing that to George?"

"I don't know, but I promise you that we're going to find out what the hell is going on. We've had some thefts, but we haven't had someone go back a second time to do anything. That has me worried. And while I'm worried, I can't concentrate if I think that you and Jack are right next door to George."

Her gaze dropped, she glanced around the room, and he knew she was taking in the large size of his master bedroom.

"Baby, stop thinking. Stop worrying. We'll talk tomorrow and figure out the next step. But for now… for a few hours…please, go to sleep with Jack here. I'm going to go downstairs and sleep on a camping air mattress and chat with George. I need you to do this for me."

His words were true, but he hoped that Carrie would feel the need as well. She continued to hold his gaze for a long time then slowly nodded. "Okay, I can't think of anything else to do right now."

"All you need to do, Carrie, is take care of yourself and Jack. Let me do the rest."

Jack came out of the bathroom, and Carrie settled her son on one side of the bed before climbing into the other. The desire to be the one sharing his bed with her was pushed down, wanting to make sure they were safe more than anything else. Closing the door, he walked downstairs.

"Sheriff, where are you going to sleep?" George asked.

"Hang on a moment, and I'll show you." He went out to the garage, pulled his air mattress and pump down off a shelf, and headed back inside. It only took a few minutes to inflate the air mattress and throw another sheet and blanket on top.

"George, I know we need to talk, but let's do that in the morning. You need your sleep, and I can rest easier knowing that you all are safe."

George nodded, lay down on the sofa, and the room quieted. After a moment, George said, "Carrie is one of the best women I've ever met in my life."

Colt agreed but said nothing, figuring George needed to get his thoughts out.

"She's a fighter, that one. She fights for the ones she cares about. She fights for what she thinks is right. I always figured it would take a special man to be able to give her what she needs while letting her give back what she's got to give."

Colt's breath halted in his lungs as he waited to see what else George would say.

"Just saying I think you're that man," George continued.

He had no idea what to say to that in return but found his lungs expanding with a deep breath of relief. But it seemed George was not finished.

"I also figure you know that I'll expect you to handle her and Jack with care."

"I wouldn't have it any other way, George."

With that, the older man settled, and Colt lay on his back for another hour, thoughts of the entire evening moving through his mind. Sleep came fitfully with thoughts of the fire and thefts, but then he found peace as he remembered the woman that was upstairs, sleeping in his bed.

16

Carrie's eyes opened slowly, and she blinked at the sunlight coming through the slits in the blinds. She remembered waking several times during the night, checking on Jack, finding him sleeping, dead to the world in his typical sprawl on the other side of the king-size bed.

Lifting her head, she eyed the empty bed and sat up quickly. Pushing her hair back from her face, she jumped up and rushed to the bathroom. Taking care of her business, she ran a brush through her long hair and pulled it up into a sloppy bun. Digging through the plastic bag, she found her bra, panties, a T-shirt, and a pair of jeans, and she dressed quickly.

The idea that a fireman had grabbed her clothes to shove them into the bag last night caused her to drop her chin to her chest, closing her eyes in mortification. Sucking in a deep breath through her nose, she let it out slowly, lifted her head, and pushed that thought to the side. It felt as though she had been pushing a lot of thoughts to the side recently, but there was nothing else she could do.

Hurrying downstairs, she could now see the house that she had barely viewed last night. Glancing into the large family room, she saw that George's sheet and blanket were folded neatly, now laying to one side. An air mattress was pushed to the far side of the room, and she realized that was where Colt must have slept.

Voices coming from down the hall captured her attention, and she walked past a study toward the kitchen. Her feet stumbled when she stepped into the large room, seeing George and Jack sitting on kitchen stools shoveling down toast and scrambled eggs that Colt was serving. Her gaze moved from her son, who seemed no worse from the previous evening's activities, to Colt, standing in his kitchen. Every time she had seen him, he had been in his Sheriff's uniform or shorts and T-shirt when coaching. He always looked good every time, but now, standing in his kitchen in a white T-shirt that stretched across his muscles and jeans that fit just right on his hips and thighs, he was drop-dead, mouth-watering gorgeous.

She pushed that thought to the side also, deciding she had no time to run upstairs and fix her hair, put on makeup, and find an evening dress to make her look more presentable. Instead, she observed three pairs of eyes looking at her and three wide smiles meeting her gaze.

"Mom! Colt made us breakfast!"

Gaining her senses, she walked over and bent to kiss the top of her son's head. "I can see that." Stepping over to George, she moved her gaze over his face and asked softly, "How are you doing today?"

His wrinkles deepened as he said, "I'm still pissed about our house, but I'm alive, we're all well, and I'm having a good breakfast. I reckon I'm doing okay."

She could not help but smile at his response and then her attention was diverted to Colt as he asked, "Coffee, babe?"

She noticed that he had slid into the endearment, now using it in front of others—including Jack—and she was uncertain how she felt about that. On the one hand, every time Colt said *babe,* a warm tingle moved through her. On the other hand, she did not want Jack to get the wrong idea. Still pondering that, she was surprised when Colt walked around the counter, sat a cup of coffee on the counter near her, placed one hand on her waist and pulled her forward slightly before bending and brushing her lips with a kiss.

Eyes wide, she jerked her head around and spied George unsuccessfully trying to hide a smile, and Jack not even pretending to hide the wide grin spreading across his face.

"Okay, here's what we need to do," Colt began, diverting her attention from the kiss. "I've already called Joe's Place and told Joe and Mavis what was happening."

Opening her mouth to protest, he said, "Carrie, honey, I need all of you to come to the station so that you can make statements about last night."

She sucked in her lips, remembering that she was a witness to a crime, and Colt was right about her needing to talk to the deputies. Nodding, she remained quiet while he continued.

"Right now, George, your side of the duplex is going to have a lot of water damage from the fire hoses as well as fire damage. I know you rent from a man in Maryland—"

"I sent him a text last night," Carrie said.

Nodding, Colt said, "Good. Carrie, I know you think that George can just live with you, but the problem with that is we don't know yet what's going on. I don't want any of you back in that duplex right now."

Jack piped up, "Are we going to keep staying here?"

Carrie shushed him and said, "No, of course, we can't—"

"Of course, you can," Colt said, and she widened her eyes at him.

"It just makes the most sense," he continued. "Do you know anyone who has spare rooms? Enough for you, Jack, and George?"

She frowned because the answer to that question was she did not. BettyJo's husband passed away years ago, and she lived in a lovely one-bedroom apartment. In fact, it was in the same complex where her mother had a one-bedroom apartment. Joe and Mavis had a two-bedroom house, and they did not have many guests since her son and grandkids lived close by, but there would be no room for all of them. She was friends with Belle and many of the women in Baytown but did not feel comfortable asking to crash at their places. And a hotel would not be in her budget. Sighing heavily, she shook her head.

"Okay, then that's settled. I've got the room, and I can provide safety. What I don't have is furniture."

His gaze intent on Colt, Jack asked, "How come you don't have furniture?"

Carrie did not even attempt to shush her son this time, knowing his youthful curiosity was no more than her own. Colt offered her son a smile, and she was glad that he did not appear offended by the question.

"My grandparents had this house built not long after they got married, and I suppose they hoped for a large family. My dad was an only child, but he wasn't...well, let's just say that he wasn't on good terms with his parents. I wasn't exactly close to him either. I used to spend a lot of time here with my grandparents and always liked the place. I was in the Army when my grandfather passed away, and my grandmother stayed here for a little while and then moved to a nice retirement home. She didn't sell the house and didn't want to leave it to my dad. She took some of the furniture with her, and at that time I told her that I didn't need any, so she sold the rest. Looking back, that wasn't the smartest thing I could've done. Because here I am, the house now left to me, and it's not fully furnished."

Carrie could tell that while Colt was giving them the gist of the story, there was a great deal left unsaid. Mostly about his father. She was very curious but decided that he would share when he wanted. She just hoped he would want to share it with her sometime.

"Why don't we bring our furniture here?" Jack asked.

At that, Carrie interrupted, "Jack, please, honey. We can't—"

"That's exactly what I was thinking," Colt said, and she whipped her head around to stare wide-eyed at him so quickly her hair started to tumble out of the hastily-made sloppy bun. His eyes were warm as they moved about her face and head.

He continued, "We can get some people to help get some of your furniture out of your duplex and in here. Jack, your furniture can go into one of the guest rooms and your mom's can go into the other."

Looking at George, he said, "If your bedroom furniture is okay, then we can get it here as well. There's something that I haven't shown you, and that's a bonus bedroom over my garage." He turned and pointed to a door in the corner of the kitchen and said, "That's how you get up to it. The space is divided into two rooms, one can be used for a bedroom and the other, a den. There's a full bathroom and a small efficiency kitchen with a small refrigerator, counter, sink, microwave, and hotplate. When my grandparents added on the garage, they decided to put a separate apartment up there in case they ever wanted to rent it to someone. George, if you're interested, it's yours."

George grinned widely, saying, "Hot damn, things are finally looking up."

Carrie's heart warmed even more toward Colt, which she thought was an impossibility considering he should have been wearing a white Stetson, declaring him one of the good guys.

He captured her gaze and asked, "Can you deal with this, Carrie?"

She sucked in her lips for a moment, her mind

racing, and almost laughed as she thought about one more thing she needed to set to the side. "I agree that Jack and I should not be at the duplex right now, and I don't have anywhere else that we can go. You and I can discuss later what kind of monetary arrangement we can make while we're here."

She watched his brows lift before he shot a quick glance to Jack. For once, he kept his mouth shut, and she smiled. Moving over to the stove, she said, "Well, let me help with breakfast and then we'll get ready and head to the station."

Two hours later, Carrie walked out of the Sheriff's Office, glad that everything had gone without a hitch. She had spoken to Deputy Lisa Perdue and essentially just repeated everything she remembered from the night before. Jack was in seventh heaven as Deputy Mark Robbins talked to him, and Deputy Trevon Harris talked to George. She knew Jack could not wait to tell his friends about the latest adventure, although she was looking forward to a day with little happening. She had not even had time to process Peter's visit, but then, she did not really want to.

While she was waiting for George to finish, she noticed Colt talked to Hunter for several minutes. Hunter began to chuckle, shaking his head in mirth, before moving back to another desk and getting on his phone.

When they were free to leave, they piled back into his SUV, and Colt drove them back to the duplex, parking near the front. "I got permission from the Fire Chief for you to be back here. George, your second story is unharmed, and I've got some friends who are going to come with trucks to get the furniture loaded."

Carrie had walked toward the duplex, stopping and staring blankly in front of her. She startled as Colt walked up behind her, put his arm around her and asked, "You, okay?

She sighed heavily and said, "I've lived here for years. I know I'll be coming back, but it just seems strange to no longer feel safe. I've always felt safe here."

Giving her a squeeze, he said, "Go on up and grab your toiletries and clothes, and we'll have some people here in a few minutes."

Moving on automatic pilot, she did as he asked, taking Jack with her. It was not long before she heard the rumble of pickup trucks, several of them pulling trailers. Looking out her bedroom window toward the drive, she recognized Hunter, Zac, Gareth, Aiden, and Brogan. She went downstairs, and each of them offered a hug to her and high-fives to Jack, saying how glad they were that everyone was uninjured.

It did not take long for that many strong men to get her, Jack's, and George's bedroom furniture loaded into the trucks and trailers. Colt suggested she get some of her kitchen items as well, and she hid a grin, having seen his poorly stocked kitchen this morning.

As Colt walked back over, she said, "They loaded up my bookcase and comfy chair as well."

He replied, "It's no big deal to move it out and then move it back in when you're ready. But while you're with me, I want everyone to be comfortable. That's why we got some more of George's furniture that wasn't water or fire damaged."

She could not argue with that logic, so she shrugged in agreement. Once everything was loaded, he locked the doors and they made their way back in the caravan to Colt's house.

Colt had been honest in wanting to get Carrie and Jack out of the duplex and safe while the thefts and George's subsequent fire were being investigated. But it was no secret to his friends that his ulterior motive was to get closer to Carrie. Pulling into his driveway, he was not surprised to see other vehicles parked out front.

Piping up from the back seat, George asked, "You got a party going on here, Sheriff?"

Carrie exclaimed when she saw Belle and some of the other women coming out onto the front porch, including her mom. Belle met Carrie in the driveway as she alighted from the SUV and said, "We figured Colt had very little food in his refrigerator, and we were right. So some of us girls all got together and went grocery shopping to tide you over. We also got a few things for you and Jack, just to make your stay feel more at home here."

Colt walked up and heard Carrie say, "That was so sweet of you, but I don't think we're going to be here very long."

Belle grinned and said, "Honey, just go with it. Colt

is like the rest of our men. They know what they want, and they'll protect it to their very last breath."

Colt winked his thanks to Belle as he walked over to the first truck to begin pulling things out. As easy as it was to load up the furniture from the duplex, it did not take long to unload it and move it into Colt's house. He had Carrie's bedroom furniture placed in the large bedroom directly across from the master bedroom. Jack's furniture was placed in a smaller bedroom that was still much larger than what he had had at the duplex.

Katelyn soon showed up with subs from Finn's pub, Trevon's wife brought boxes of pizzas, and Joe and Mavis showed up with BettyJo, their arms full of the diner's famous fried chicken. Aiden and Brogan supplied the beer, and after everything was moved in, an impromptu party on the back patio took place.

Colt stood with his hands on his hips, surveying the gathering. He remembered when his grandparents were living, they were very social and used to enjoy throwing parties in their backyard. He shook his head slightly, having not thought of those memories in many years. Casting his gaze around, he saw George flirting with BettyJo and Della, Jack excitedly hanging with the men, soaking up their stories and their wisdom, and Carrie being surrounded by good women who had her back and also knew she would have theirs if the circumstances were changed.

Carrie, used to serving others, made her way back into the kitchen to restock some of the bowls with chips and dip. He followed her in and stilled her hands as he grasped them in his own, drawing them up to his chest. Keeping her pinned there closely, he held her questioning gaze, not speaking, instead, taking the moment to kiss her lightly. She stiffened for just a few seconds and then melted in his embrace.

"Carrie, we haven't had much privacy lately, but I'm going to take this moment to say what's on my mind before we get interrupted. You've had a hellish couple of days, and I know there's a lot on your plate. But as far as I'm concerned, your days of going it alone are over. I've told you I was interested in you for a long time, but I let too much time pass. I don't want to do that anymore."

Licking her dry lips, she said, "Colt, honey, you've picked a crazy time to want to start something with me. Lately, I don't know if I'm coming or going."

"Then that just tells me that I picked the right time. You need help, and I want to give it. You need protection, and I want to give it. Give your trust to me, and I'll help you know if you're coming or going." He kissed her again, this time taking it deeper, and she moaned into his mouth. He felt her full breasts crushed against his chest, and he finally broke away, groaning, "If I don't stop, I'm gonna walk out of here with my dick leading the way."

She giggled, and he thought it was the sweetest sound he had ever heard. The door opened behind them, and he turned to see Della walk in, her eyes jumping between her daughter and him. Carrie's eyes widened as he leaned in one more time—in front of her mother—and kissed her.

Della grinned, grabbed one of the bowls on the

counter, then said, "Don't know if anyone cares, but it's been a little while since Jack had a sleepover at his grandmother's house. Thought I'd ask to see if you'd like him to have one soon." Still smiling, she moved through the sliding glass door to the patio.

"Now, that's an offer I hope you take her up on," Colt said, grabbing two more of the bowls, winking at Carrie, and following Della back to the party.

17

Three days. Three days of questioning and investigations, and the Sheriff's Department was no closer to finding who was committing the break-ins or who set the fire at George's house.

Three nights. Three nights of going to bed after having dinner sitting at a table with company he enjoyed then laying on his bed with thoughts of Carrie in her bed just across the hall.

Scrubbing his hand over his face, Colt looked up as Loretta stepped into his office and let him know that his meeting was ready to start. Nodding his thanks, he moved down the hall to one of the small conference rooms where Hunter, Elizabeth, Mark, and Trevon were sitting.

"Okay," Colt said, "what have we got?"

Elizabeth began, "We brought in Will Penland from Stuart's Pharmacy as well as going to the pharmacy to talk to the pharmacist. Will appeared genuinely concerned that the thefts were happening and were happening to some of the clients of the pharmacy. He said he had never given any information to anyone about who he made deliveries to."

"How often does he deliver?" Colt asked.

"Generally, he just delivers on Wednesdays," Elizabeth continued. "But he admitted that it can be a lot more. If one of the shut-ins in the area gets a new prescription that they have to have right away, then he'll go out whenever they need it."

"Daniel Stuart is lead pharmacist now for his grandfather's business," Hunter said. "When I talked to him, he said that in truth, they made deliveries almost twice every week now, and sometimes three times a week. It's not Will's only job at the pharmacy, but Daniel admitted that, because of the need, it was the biggest part of Will's position."

"Any similarities in the drugs that the victims are taking?" Colt asked.

Trevon replied, "I took the lists from our victims, and had Daniel take a look at them when Hunter went to question him. I've done some research into them as well. The most common denominator between them is blood pressure medication and pain medication. Other than that, many of the older people have an average of five to ten different medications that they're taking for a variety of reasons, any of which could be sold on the black market."

"Okay, do we have something else that's tying our victims together?"

"We've looked at the doctor offices, but while many

of them go to the county clinic that offers reduced fees, not all of them go there."

A knock on the door had them look up, and Loretta popped her head in to say, "I hate to interrupt, but Chief Freeman is here."

Colt said, "Send her in." He offered a chin lift to Hannah as she walked into the room and greeted everyone.

Sliding into an empty seat, she said, "I hate to interrupt, but we just had a prescription medication theft reported from inside the town limits of Easton. My people are looking into it right now, but what I can tell you is that it's an older person, they were sound asleep at night, didn't hear anything, but when they got up the next morning, their front door had been jimmied and their medication sitting on the kitchen counter had been taken."

Shaking his head, Colt said, "Same fuckin' MO."

Trevon added, "None of the victims tried to fight back or even woke up, except George. That's got to be the reason somebody went back and made an attempt on his life. Perhaps they were afraid that he could identify them."

Nodding, Colt said, "I was beginning to come to the same conclusion."

"Are we still looking at gang activity?" Hannah asked.

Trevon looked up and said, "This no longer smacks of gang activity. That tends to be more random, and this is purposeful. Gangs will have robberies as one of their initiations, but this is planned and takes a little more time. I know the Maryland Eastern Shore, and even Liam in Accawmacke has had some Bloods and others, but I just don't see this as being that type of gang activity."

"Unless we've got a different type of gang that's operating down here," Colt said, drawing their attention. "Something new. Something that's slowly organizing."

Hunter said, "We've asked for a list from Stuart's Pharmacy for the shut-ins that they deliver to. He wants to assist, but he says he needs a court order before he can give that to us."

"Go for it," Colt said. "We need to be able to warn people—without causing massive panic—that they may be at risk for robbery."

The five continued their meeting, but when Colt left for lunch, he felt no closer to stopping the robberies than when they began.

The lunch crowd was almost finished when Carrie looked up to see Colt coming through the door of the diner. Her lips curved as he made his way over to his seat at the counter.

It did not matter how many times she saw him in his uniform or which uniform he wore. Dark brown shirt and pants or khaki shirt and pants. The patch on his arm and over the chest pocket, the insignia on his collar, and the badge over his heart. She wondered what size he had to buy, considering his chest was wide and muscular. Today, she could tell there was no body armor underneath the shirt, but she had seen him when he had it on, and his chest was even larger.

For the past three nights, she had stood in the upstairs hall of Colt's house, Jack already asleep, and with her arms wrapped around Colt's neck and his arms banded tightly around her, they kissed wildly with the promise that both wanted more. Each night, they finally broke apart, her breasts tingling, her sex heavy with need, and the feel of his cock firm against his zipper.

Blowing out a breath at the memory, she moved behind the counter, walked down to the end, and leaned on her forearms toward him. "Howdy, Sheriff," she grinned.

He leaned forward, his eyes roaming over her face, and grinned in return. "Howdy, Ms. Beaumont."

"What can I get you?"

"Only one thing at Joe's Place that I'm interested in," he said.

"Is it on the menu?"

He flashed a white-toothed grin, and said, "It better not be. It better be just for me."

Glancing around and seeing no one's eyes on them, she leaned forward and quickly kissed him on the lips. "That's just a taste."

She heard the growl deep in his chest, but the bell over the door had her pulling back quickly.

"Mom! Colt!"

They both turned at the same time to see Jack bounding into the diner, his face alive with excitement.

"Colby's mom wants to know if I can come over for a sleepover tonight," Jack said, his eyes hopeful.

Nodding, Carrie said, "Of course. Give him a call and tell them that I can drop you off when I get off shift."

While Jack made his call, Carrie turned to see Colt's gaze intensely staring at her. She licked her lips, finding it hard to breathe with the air so thick between them. Leaning forward, keeping her voice low, she said, "If you're thinking what I'm thinking, then the answer is 'yes'."

This time, Colt's growl shot straight to her sex as he said, "George will be in his room over the garage. Jack will be at a friend's house. That means tonight, you and me…"

"Won't say goodnight while standing in the hall," she finished. She watched as his eyes dilated and locked her quivering knees to keep her body from becoming a puddle on the floor.

"His mom says that's fine!" Jack said, clambering up on the stool next to Colt.

Thankful for the interruption, she said, "How was camp today?" Looking over at Colt, she said, "Today was the middle school science camp."

"It was fabulous!" Jack said, his enthusiasm loud enough for anyone in the diner to hear. "We learned how to make fire."

Carrie huffed, "I would think you've had enough excitement about fires recently." Jack rolled his eyes, but it was Colt's reaction that snagged her gaze. He was always attentive to Jack, but now turned on his stool and faced him.

"What did you learn?" Colt asked.

"How to make fireballs. You can actually hold them in your hand!"

Carrie gasped, and Jack looked up at his mom. "Mom, we were perfectly safe."

His voice steady, Colt asked, "Tell me about the experiment."

Jack grinned and puffed out his chest. "I wasn't afraid at all. Some of the kids were, but not me. I figured if Mr. Jameson could do it, then I could too." He shifted slightly on his stool, and began, "We learned that fire is made up of light and heated gases from combustion. You can actually control the temperature of fire because some fuels burn with a cool flame. And if you've got the fuel on a substance that doesn't burn, you can make a fireball that you can even hold in your hand."

"Okay, keep going," Colt prodded.

"Mr. Jameson said it's best to use cotton…one hundred percent cotton fabric and thread. You make up a ball by using the cotton material and wrapping it completely with the cotton thread. He says if you use something else, then the material might melt, and that could be gross…or painful."

"I'm beginning to wonder if this science camp is a good thing," Carrie said, her hands landing on her hips at the thought that her son had spent the morning playing with fire.

"Mom, it's perfectly safe." He turned his attention

back to Colt, and said, "We learned that we needed a cool fuel. He said it could be kerosene or…um…something like napa. Something like that. Anyway, you soak the ball and then you light it. He said the fuel burns at a low temperature so you can actually hold it in your hand for a little while. Once the fuel burns out, then the cotton will actually catch on fire, and that's too hot to hold."

Carrie watched the enthusiasm on Jack's face, and while she hated the idea of him playing with fire, she knew that the camp was a great experience for him.

Joe placed plates on the pass-through and called out, "If you want to learn about fire, Jack, come on back here, and I'll show you how to cook over it!"

Carrie grabbed the plates, setting them down in front of Jack and Colt, grinning at how both loved their hamburgers and french fries. Soon the burgers were decimated, and the plates were empty.

She had been walking through the restaurant, checking on orders and refilling drinks. Seeing Colt stand, she hurried back over and said, "I'll see you tonight."

He glanced at the back of Jack's head as the boy was animatedly talking to Mavis and leaned closer, whispering, "If all goes right tonight, darlin', I'll be seeing all of you." He kissed her cheek, right by the side of her mouth, and she sucked in a quick breath. She turned and watched as he waved to Jack, Joe, and Mavis, then headed out.

Mavis sidled up to her and said, "Jack's been talking about fire, but I think tonight there's going to be some different sparks." She did not reply, and Mavis placed her hand on Carrie's arm, saying, "Are you okay about that?"

"I'm nervous." She glanced to the side and saw Mavis tilt her head to the side slightly. Explaining, she said, "It's been a long time. I've been real cautious as to who I wanted to bring into my life because of Jack. Made for a lot of lonely nights, but I'd do it all over again just to make sure I wasn't bringing someone into our lives that wasn't going to care for my son."

Mavis patted her arm. "Girl, you've done right by your boy. Not a lot of women would have sacrificed everything you have for their child, but you did, and he's turning out so good." Jerking her head in the direction of the door that Colt just left through, she continued, "If you were holding out for a man that's worth it for you and Jack, then you found it. And if Colt's been holding out for somebody worth it to him, then you and Jack are it as well." Leaning forward slightly, she said, "So, tonight, honey, you go for it."

Carrie felt Mavis squeeze her hands before letting go. Biting her lips nervously, she could not keep the grin from sliding across her face.

18

Colt drove to the middle school with Elizabeth as his detective. Having timed it almost perfectly, he watched as Tad Jameson stood outside, waving goodbye to one of the students. Parking, he and Elizabeth climbed from his SUV and walked toward the young teacher.

Tad had dark blond hair, slightly longish, with a lean runner's build. Colt knew he was in his late twenties, still with the youthful looks that the girls in his classes would probably define as cute. Tad looked up as they approached, a smile on his face.

"We met at the AL ballfield but haven't met formally," Colt said. "I'm Sheriff Hudson, and this is Detective Elizabeth Perez."

Sticking his hand out, Tad said, "Yes, I remember." After shaking Colt's hand, he turned to Elizabeth and said, "Tad Jameson." His gaze darted between the two of them, and he said, "Is there anything I can help you with?"

"We'd like to ask you a few questions about your

science camp," Elizabeth said. When out with a detective, Colt preferred to let the detective take the lead. Especially with Elizabeth—it seemed to put people at ease to talk to a woman, giving him the opportunity to observe closely.

Tad's face registered surprise, but he smiled widely. "I can't imagine what you'd want to know about our camp, but I'd love to talk to you about it." Chuckling, he added, "I know it might seem geeky, but I love working with the kids and getting them to love science as much as I do." He looked back toward the building and said, "Would you like to step inside where it's cooler?"

Nodding their agreement, they followed him through a side door of the middle school, down a hall, and into a science classroom. Colt noticed the large room with all the desks in the front and the lab tables in the back. It had been many years since he had been in middle school, but like most people entering schools, it always brought back memories.

"I think I was actually in this classroom many years ago," he said.

Eyes wide, Tad exclaimed, "You're from here? That's cool!"

With a slight nod toward Elizabeth, he leaned against the counter and watched as she began her questions.

"Can you tell us about this camp?"

Tad's gaze jumped between the two of them, and he said, "Sure. My goal is to try to get students excited about the world they live in, and science is all around us. When I decided to come to the Eastern Shore to teach, I knew it was an economically depressed area. And unfortunately, many students from this background don't realize that there's a world of opportunity out there for them. But if we wait until high school we may have lost them. I petitioned the school board to offer a science camp for a month in the summer to see if I can capture some of the enthusiasm that the younger students would have, plus give them something constructive to do in the summer. Because I also mentor some teens in high school, this gives me a chance to scope out some potentially needy students."

Nodding, Elizabeth smiled with enthusiasm and continued, "What are some of the experiments and projects that you teach them?"

His face scrunched in thought, and he said, "Well, last week we did water purifying with charcoal and a simple experiment on whether color affects memory. We also did something really cool with eggs and how sugary drinks can affect the teeth. Eggshells are made of calcium, so we were able to use eggs soaked in various drinks to see how it affected them." His hands began to wave, and his eyes were bright as he described the experiment.

Colt could see why Jack caught on to Tad's enthusiasm. He continued to watch him carefully as Elizabeth prodded him more.

"Today it was really exciting because I was teaching them about fire. Most of us never think about what fire is, what makes fire, and how fire can burn at different temperatures."

"Was this the first fire experiment that you've done?"

Shaking his head, he said, "No. We did a fire experiment last week as well. Plus, that's always something that's in our curriculum during the school year." They were quiet for a moment, and Tad tilted his head to the side, and asked, "Can I ask what this is in reference to? I'll be honest, I've never been questioned by the police before."

"We've had some suspicious behavior recently, and it came to our attention that some students were learning about fire from this camp. We have no connection, but we're just trying to follow up on any line of inquiry."

Tad nodded, less enthusiastically than before, but still with a great deal of interest.

Standing, Colt asked, "Have you had any student this summer or before that you found to have a particular fascination with fire?"

Shoving his hands into his pockets, Tad said, "Sheriff, I have to tell you that most kids have a fascination with fire. I mean, sure, some kids are afraid of it. I have some that are scared to get near a Bunsen burner. But most students get really excited when we have some kind of an experiment dealing with flame."

"Anyone in particular?"

Eyes shifting slightly, Tad shook his head slowly. "Not anyone that I noticed. Not anyone that sent off alarms in my head."

Elizabeth pulled out her card and handed it to Tad. "If you think of anything, please, give me a call."

He took the card from her, his smile now back firmly on his face, "Sure thing! And if you're ever in the area on one of the mornings we have our camp, please drop in. The kids would love to get a chance to talk to the Sheriff or a detective!"

Walking back out to their SUV, neither Elizabeth nor Colt said anything until they were driving back to the office. Finally, Elizabeth began to chuckle, and she looked over at Colt and said, "Jesus, was I ever that young?"

Unable to hold his own chuckle in, Colt said, "Not that young or that geeky." Feeling as though he had not moved the investigation forward at all, he settled his mind toward the evening.

Carrie stared into the bathroom mirror, nervously analyzing everything about her appearance. Her hair was down, unadorned while falling over her shoulders and down her back in soft waves. She had her mother's dark brown hair, but her father had blessed her with an auburn sheen from his own red hair. Her makeup was slightly heavier than what she wore to work, highlighting her blue eyes and dusting her cheeks with a rosy glow.

She had very few clothes for going out to a nice restaurant; any extra money was spent on Jack or going into savings. But the dress she was wearing was one she had bought several years ago when a friend was getting married. It was deep blue, tight across the bust with a squared neckline that showed a hint of cleavage. The dress continued to be tight down to her waistline where it flared into a flirty skirt that came to mid-thigh. She had bought it knowing that she was going to be dancing at the wedding and was afraid a skintight dress all the way down might be too confining. She discovered the dress had been perfect, loving the way it flounced as she moved.

She heard a noise across the hall and wondered if Colt was ready. He had come home earlier, gone straight into the shower, and she figured it took him a lot less time to get ready than her. She turned back and forth, satisfied with how she looked, and stepped out of the bathroom into the hall.

Colt had just stepped out of his bedroom, and she sucked in a quick breath, taking him all in from bottom to top. Boots. Black dress pants. Midnight blue dress shirt and a matching tie hanging around his neck. As her gaze moved to his clean-shaven, square-jawed face, she jolted seeing his eyes burning straight onto her. She watched in fascination as he also did a head-to-toe scan, and before she knew it, he closed the steps between them, banded his arm around her waist, and jerked her to him.

She squeaked as her body was pressed up against his, but he angled his head, slammed his lips down, and kissed her as though the world was ending in a moment and this was how he wanted to spend his last few seconds.

Wearing heels, she gained a few inches but still felt dwarfed by his size. She clung to his shoulders, feeling the kiss down to her knees, hoping they would continue to hold her up. But then, as tightly as he was crushing her body to his, she did not need to worry about her legs supporting her. The light kisses that he had been giving her had sent tingles throughout, but this kiss was nothing like those. This was giving and taking, asking and demanding, begging and promising.

His tongue thrust into her mouth, and she reveled in the minty taste as he licked and explored every crevice. *God, this man can kiss.* Inadequacy passed through her mind, knowing that she had never been kissed like this, but with his dominance, she quickly learned what he liked. Dragging her tongue around his, she swallowed his groan, knowing she was doing it exactly right.

Suddenly he pulled his head back, roughly dragging air into his lungs as his eyes lifted to the ceiling as though looking for heavenly guidance. His arms had not released her at all so her breasts continued to move against his chest with every pant.

Dropping his gaze to hers, he said, "I don't think I can do this."

She blinked. Twice. Inadequacy shot back through her as well as uncertainty. His arms still had not loosened, so when she spoke, it came out as a mere whisper. "Sorry?"

His tortured gaze moved around her face before dropping to her cleavage, which was now threatening to spill out over the top of her dress, before moving back up to her eyes. "I know we have dinner plans. I wanted to take you out. I wanted to take you out, give you a good meal, show you off. But now all I want to do is drag you into my bedroom, strip this dress off, leave those fuck-me shoes on, and keep you there all night."

"Okay," she managed to say, the one word still breathy.

She watched his eyes widen, his pupils dilated with lust, and he groaned, "Don't say it if you don't mean it, babe."

She had got dressed up for dinner and was looking forward to a nice meal on the arm of this man. But right now, after the kiss he just gave her, her nipples tingling, her panties wet, all she wanted was him. "I mean it."

19

Colt's arms barely loosened, only enough for him to shift down a few inches, bend them tightly around Carrie's middle again, and lift. With another squeak, she clasped her hands around his neck as her feet dangled above the floor.

Executing a quick about-face, he stalked straight into his bedroom, not stopping until the backs of her legs were touching his bed. He slowly lowered her feet to the floor, his hands now moving to the zipper in the back of her dress. Taking his time, he lowered the zipper, each click of the teeth sounding out in the room. When it reached her ass, he stepped back, and his gaze followed the movement of the material as it slid off her shoulders, snagging slightly on her breasts, then dropping all the way to the floor. Now clad in a demi-bra, her full breasts spilling out of the top, and tiny panties, she kept her arms on his biceps as he drank her in.

With a deft move of his fingers at her back, her

demi-bra was unsnapped and dropped to the floor as well.

His hands moved to her breasts, full and heavy, and he lifted each one, his thumb swiping over her taut nipples. "I've been admiring your figure for a long time, babe," he confessed, "but your tits are more beautiful than I could've ever imagined." He bent and latched his lips around one of her nipples, sucking hard, and heard her gasp. He moved from one to the other and back again until she shifted forward and began rubbing her front on his hard erection as though desperately seeking ease to the friction that she so needed.

Feeling as though he might come in his pants like an untried teenager, Colt lifted his head away from her luscious breasts and dragged in a ragged breath. Her fingers immediately went to the buttons on his shirt, and he was glad she had more dexterity than he because he might have just ripped the buttons straight off. Her breasts touched his chest again as she leaned forward to pull the shirt off of his shoulders. He quickly tossed the shirt onto the floor while her hands were unbuckling his belt.

She worked with the same desperation that he felt, and soon his cock was free, bobbing outward, a drop of pre-cum on its tip. He had wanted their first time to be slow and gentle, full of finesse and care. But she dropped to her knees, pulling his pants down about his ankles, and took him in her mouth. He threw his head back as his hands clutched in her hair, her head moving up and down as her mouth licked and sucked and tongued his erection.

Taking him almost to the breaking point, he reached down and pulled her back and pushed her gently onto the bed. Kicking off his boots, he stepped out of his pants and boxers, fisting his aching cock. He leaned over and grabbed a condom from the nightstand and rolled it on. Looming over her, he grabbed her panties and pulled them off, leaving her heels on. With her ass at the edge of the bed, he lifted her legs, exposing her slick sex to him, the scent of her arousal filling his nostrils.

It had been a long time, and he had a feeling it had been even longer for her. Wanting to make it special, she reached her hands up toward him and moaned, "Please, just take me."

Bending over her, he lifted one of her legs to his shoulder, placed his cock at her entrance, and plunged. Her tight walls sheathed him, and once he was seated, he had to catch his breath, uncertain how long he could hold off. "Can you take it? This first time may be hard and fast."

Her blue eyes held his gaze, and a slow smile curved her lips. "I can take whatever you want to give."

He dragged his cock back out before plunging it in again, over and over. Her breasts bounced with each movement, and he reached up, palming their fullness before tweaking her dark nipples.

She came hard, her inner muscles grabbing him, and he felt his balls tighten and the burn shoot through him as he came right along with her. Letting go of her breasts, he planted his hands on the mattress right by her hips and continued to thrust until every drop was drained.

His legs, suddenly weak, were about to give out, and he regretfully pulled out of her body as he sucked in great gulps of air. Feeling as though he had run a marathon, his chest heaved with the effort of breathing. Finally dropping his chin so that he could stare at her, he found her gaze on him, her lips still curving into a gentle smile.

"Wow."

Hearing that one word from her and a chuckle erupt from deep in his chest, he nodded. "Fuck yeah, wow." He stalked into the master bathroom, took care of the condom, and washed his hands while letting the water get warm. Wetting a washcloth, he came back out and saw her sitting on the edge of the bed. "Uh-uh," he grunted, adding, "lay back down."

She obeyed easily, and he gently cleaned between her legs then tossed the cloth onto his nightstand. Kneeling, he slid her shoes off her feet and climbed onto the bed, dragging her body completely onto the mattress.

"I take it we're not going to dinner," she said, her smile piercing his heart.

"Babe, now that I've had a taste, I think you're the only thing I want."

Laughing, she said, "Then take your fill."

He rolled her under him, kissing her until his cock was aching once again. Sliding down between her legs, he kissed her inner thighs before latching onto her clit, sucking it deeply. With his fingers and his tongue, he fucked her again until she came hard against his face.

"Oh, God, I didn't think I could come again," she moaned.

He moved back up onto the mattress, rolled to his back, and settled her body on top of his. "Do you have enough energy to ride me, babe?"

Licking her lips, she said, "Well, I can get us started, and if I get tired..."

He rolled on a condom and said, "Then I'll carry us across the finish line."

With that, she lifted on her knees and settled her body over his cock, once again sheathing him. With her hands on his shoulders and her breasts bouncing with every movement, she rode him. When she finally tired, he grasped her full hips in his large hands, lifted her slightly and then began pumping his hips up and down.

She was so close, it only took a moment for her to throw her head back and cry out once more, her inner muscles clenching around him. With one last upward thrust, he poured himself into her once again.

This time, she crashed down upon his stomach, eliciting an 'umph' as the air was forced from his lungs. Wrapping his arms around her, they slowly allowed their bodies to cool and their breathing to even before he gently laid her to the side. Once more dealing with the condom, he cleaned her again.

"I feel bad about dinner," he said. Catching her lifted eyebrow, he laughed and added, "I didn't say I feel bad about what we did to miss dinner...just that I feel bad that I haven't fed you yet."

"Let me get dressed, and I'll fix us something," she suggested.

Scowling, he replied, "What kind of man would I be to make you fix dinner after promising to take you out?"

He was still standing by the bed, and she got up on her knees, moving directly to him. Pressing her naked body against his, she wrapped her arms around his neck. "Colt, we can go out to eat at any time. I don't feel slighted in the least." Giggling, she glanced down at his half-erect cock and added, "Believe me, I don't feel slighted!"

He chuckled, but she was not finished. Continuing, she said, "Seriously, we can go to dinner anytime. We've got plenty of food in the refrigerator that I can heat up quickly. Jack is gone. George is gone. So we can take advantage of getting to know each other better while we have the house to ourselves."

Her gaze was trusting and open, something he had grown to love about her. He knew her words were true…she did not need a fancy restaurant or an expensive meal. She just wanted to be around people that she cared for, and the realization that he was one of those struck him deep.

He reached his hands up to cup her cheeks, his thumbs running over her soft skin. Bending, he kissed her again, this time lighter and softer, but with just as much promise as any of his other kisses. "Okay, babe. Let's get dressed and we'll heat up something together. We'll make the most of tonight, and how about I take you to breakfast tomorrow?"

"You're on," she said, her eyes bright. "But it has to be somewhere other than The Diner!"

Laughing, he swatted her ass as she climbed off the bed. A few minutes later, they were both dressed in comfortable clothes, heading downstairs to the kitchen.

It did not take long for Carrie to serve some of the cold fried chicken that she had brought home, finding left-over potato salad and baked beans as well. Steaming green beans in the microwave, she soon plated a simple meal. Colt grabbed a couple of beers from the refrigerator.

They sat at the dining room table, and she glanced around the large room, noting that the walls had fresh paint but no pictures hanging on them.

"What are you thinking?" he asked.

She sucked in her lips as she stared at her plate for a few seconds, then lifted her gaze to him. "Can you tell me about your grandparents? When you mentioned them to Jack, I could tell that you cared a great deal for them. I was just wondering about this house. It's so big and so beautiful, and I can tell that you have kept it up, but it seems to lack...um, personality."

Chuckling, he said, "Babe, I think you can say it doesn't just lack personality. It has zero personality."

She waited, not wanting to pepper him with questions but hoping that he felt as though he could share with her. He did not make her wait long.

Leaning back in his chair, he said, "From what they

told me, my grandparents built this house right after they first got married. They wanted to have a house that they could live in their whole lives and hoped to have a large family, so they built a big house. My grandmother had trouble conceiving, several miscarriages and then, finally, she had my father. He was an only child, but from what I can tell, they lavished love on him."

"And yet you said they weren't close…"

Nodding, he said, "My father was a teenager in the seventies and fell into a bad crowd. He experimented with drugs and drank to excess. He ran around, and while he never got into serious trouble, he always seemed to be right where others were when trouble was happening. From what I understand, the sheriff brought my dad home several times. He was never arrested, just always with the people who were causing trouble. There came a point where my grandparents had to enforce tough love, but in his case, he basically told them to go fuck themselves, and he refused to have anything to do with them."

"Oh, honey, I'm so sorry." She thought of her own loving father and could not imagine him ever behaving that way. "I assume that's why you said you weren't close to him either."

"My dad married my mom, who at the time liked the same things he did. They partied a lot, from what I was told. But she matured, they had me, and for the most part, she was a pretty good mom. She gave up partying, joined the PTA, started doing all the things that she should."

Snorting, he continued, "My dad was a hard man, a

big man. On the outside, he said and did all the right things. He came to all of my ball games, but God help me if I didn't play as well as he thought I should. Behind closed doors, he was demanding and demeaning, and it got worse if he had been drinking."

"I wasn't expecting that," she admitted. "I guess I expected him to be aloof and lackadaisical."

"My dad wasn't an alcoholic, but when he drank, he got mean. He wasn't physical, but his words were harsh, and they could hurt."

"And your mom?"

"She mostly wanted me to toe the line so that Dad wouldn't take things out on her."

Blinking, Carrie was stunned. Gasping, she said, "I can't imagine any mom who would not throw herself in front of a train for their child!"

He stared at her, his gaze warm, and said, "And that's why Jack is lucky. You're the best kind of mom there is."

His words touched her heart, but she remained silent, giving him more time to finish his story.

"My dad was a hard man to understand, but I think he realized he pissed away his youth, pissed away his young manhood, and pissed away all the things that were now open as possibilities to me. So he began to live vicariously through me. He wanted me to get a baseball scholarship. He wanted me to be the best on the team." Looking at her, his lips curved slightly as he asked, "Did you know I went to high school with Mitch, Grant, Aiden, Brogan, Callan, and Zac? I was part of the Baytown Boys baseball team. Hell, there were a lot of us, and many of us are still in the area. My dad appeared very supportive at every game, but I knew if I wasn't playing the way he wanted me to, there was hell to pay at home."

Grasping his hand, she asked, "Did he hurt you?"

Shaking his head, Colt replied, "Mostly he was just demeaning. Not only to me but to Mom, too."

"So you escaped to your grandparents' house…here."

This time, his smile widened, and she could tell the memories were better. "I loved them and loved this place. My grandfather was thrilled when I had a great game and supportive when I didn't. I don't think I ever walked into this house when my grandmother didn't have cookies, a pie, or cake ready for us to dive into. I know it pissed my dad off that I was so close to his parents, but I didn't care. Honestly, by the time I was sixteen, I was as big as my dad and certainly stronger. I think he understood that I was getting to a point where I was no longer going to take his abuse."

"How did he feel about you joining the Army?"

"He felt that I joined the military as an ultimate 'fuck you' to him, but I wasn't ready to go to college and had no interest in trying to play college ball. I turned eighteen right as I graduated from high school and joined the Army the next month. It pissed him off, and we never talked again. The fact that I had gone into the military police made him even madder, according to my mom."

"What happened to your parents?"

"My mom died of ovarian cancer a couple of years after I left home, and my dad just deteriorated. I think he began to drink more, and he ended up having a car accident, which killed him. I was always thankful it was only him and that he did not injure anyone else.

"I re-enlisted a couple of times before getting out and coming here to take the sheriff's job. I was in the military for twelve years, and during that time, my mom and dad died, my grandfather died, and I was married and divorced."

At that last tidbit of information, she jolted, eyes wide and mouth open. "Married?"

20

As soon as Colt saw Carrie's stunned face, he realized that the information he had just blurted required more finesse than he had offered. Sighing, he squeezed her hand as she was trying to pull it back, not wanting to lose their connection. "I'm sorry, Carrie. That didn't come out the way I meant. I should never have just said that without preparing you first."

"I…I was just not expecting that."

She held his gaze, and he took it as a positive that she was no longer trying to pull her hand away from his. "I'm afraid that it's a tale that's not much better than what I've been telling you."

She bit her lip, her head tilted slightly to the side, but remained quiet.

Hoping he was reading her right, he said, "I met her when I was at my first station. I was barely twenty years old, but careful to avoid the bars around the base that we had been warned about. Some of them were full of women hoping to snag a soldier. Instead, I met her one day at a beach. She was gorgeous, smart, we talked and laughed, and for the next couple of months, we were inseparable. She had a job at an advertising agency, and we talked about getting married. I was upfront with her, letting her know that being married to a soldier was going to be hard. She would be alone a lot of times, and we would definitely have to move. But she swore she was ready, all for it, so we got married. The first four months were great, but slowly, I began to see the handwriting on the wall. My hours were long, and she complained. I'd want us to hang out with some of my buddies and their women on the weekends, but she said they were common. My paycheck came in every two weeks, and she said she had no idea how little soldiers made."

Carrie was watching his face, her expression serious, but he had no idea where her head was at with what he was telling her. Wanting to know, he asked, "What are you thinking, babe?"

"It's kind of weird, Colt. It's a little bit like jealousy, but that's ridiculous because this was a long time ago. I think maybe I'm just envious that this other woman had your heart in her hand, but she wasn't taking care of it."

He did not think it was possible to care more for Carrie than he already did, but at her words, he felt his heart open up, wanting to take all of her in. Squeezing her hand, he admitted, "I think that's the nicest thing anyone's ever said to me." Gaining her sweet smile, he wanted to finish his story so that she would know all about them and they could lay it to rest.

"I got deployed and was gone for a year. When I

came home, everything was different. She had fallen in love with someone from her office…someone who made good money and was home every evening by five o'clock. The crazy thing was that it didn't suck horribly. By the end, I had realized that the marriage was a mistake. I was too young to truly understand what kind of woman I wanted to be with and was just glad that we had not had any children together."

"So, you spent another ten years in the Army?"

Nodding, he said, "Just about. I got my Police Science Degree while I served overseas for a couple of tours and then was tired of it. My grandmother was still living but not doing well, and I found myself homesick for the Eastern Shore. I came home, ready to become a detective, but the sheriff's position came open. I decided to run and ended up running unopposed, so here I am."

She grinned and admitted, "I remember the first time you came into Joe's Place. You were so handsome, my knees felt weak."

At that, he chuckled and asked, "How come you never made a move on me?"

"Me make a move on you? I was just a small-town waitress in a diner, an unwed mother who had little to offer any man, especially not a man like you." Before giving him a chance to respond, she added, "But what about you? Why didn't you make a move on me?"

"Honestly? I didn't think I had a chance with you, Carrie. I noticed you right away. Not a lie, honey. You've got a figure that would make any man hard just looking at you. But besides your great fuckin' figure, you have the prettiest smile I've ever seen in my life. I was about to make my move when Jack came in one day. I realized that you had a son, and at first, I assumed you were married. Later, when I found out that you weren't...well, I didn't feel like I was in a position to become someone's father figure."

He observed her holding her breath and was uncertain if she even realized it. Leaning forward, he said, "Breathe, babc, 'cause I'm definitely ready to be a father figure to Jack."

The air in her lungs left her body audibly in a loud whoosh, and he leaned in for a kiss. It soon flamed, emotions and confessions all tied up into passion.

Standing, he drew her to her feet, pulled her close, and said, "Let's go back to bed."

Her lips slowly curved, and she murmured, "Sleepy, already?"

"Not until we've worn each other out making love."

She softly repeated, "Making love. I like the sound of that."

"Make no mistake, Carrie. That's exactly what we will be doing."

Carrie had only been in Jillian's Coffee Shop one other time and was entranced by its character. The dark paneled walls, brass sconces, beautiful artwork, and glass cases holding knickknacks from bygone times, along with the scent of roasting coffee beans made her decide to come back more often. Jillian had greeted them warmly and seated them at a corner table near the front. She and Colt were both enjoying a full Belgian waffle breakfast, accompanied with egg, bacon, and coffee.

The night before had been exactly as Colt promised. They had gone back to bed where he made love to her, slow and easy and worshipful. When he finally tucked her back into his front, wrapping his arms around her, tangling his legs with hers, she found sleep came easily. Her body was sated, and while they had covered a great deal of territory with their dinner conversation, what remained was that he wanted to be a father figure to Jack and she knew that he cared for her.

She woke this morning with his cock nudging her ass and discovered she was not too tired for another round of sex. In fact, she would have continued to stay in bed, but Colt was insistent that he take her to breakfast.

So, now, ensconced in a delightful restaurant, she enjoyed her breakfast. Her phone vibrated a message, and she pulled it from her purse, took a look, and grimaced.

"What's up?"

She sighed and replied, "It was from our landlord. He's letting me and George know that he's redoing George's side of the duplex. He'll make some upgrades at the same time and has decided to go ahead and do upgrades to my side as well. That's all very nice, but that means that George and I can't go back right away."

"I don't see that that's a problem, babe. George is settled in his apartment at my house. You and Jack are settled with me also."

Holding his gaze, she bit her lip and said, "But it was only supposed to be very temporary."

His brow shot down, and he asked, "Are you feeling temporary with me?"

"Course not. You know that."

Shrugging his large shoulders, he said, "Then keep staying with me, and we'll see what we feel like doing by the time the duplexes are ready."

Leaning back, she huffed. "Doesn't that seem like we're moving fast?"

"Carrie, we've known each other for five years and just admitted that for all five years we both thought about each other. I don't think that's the definition of moving fast."

A giggle slipped out, and she admitted, "I suppose you're right." Sighing, she added, "I just need to figure out what to do about Jack's birthday party. I didn't cancel anything because I thought I would be back into our house—"

"Have it in my house," Colt interrupted.

Wide-eyed, she said, "Colt, do you seriously want to have fifteen or more eleven-year-olds running around your yard and in and out of your kitchen?"

He laid his fork down and leaned closer. "Carrie, babe, this is us. I've been alone, but that house was never meant for a single person. I hadn't found what I was looking for, but now I have. I don't want to rush you. I don't want to rush us. But right now, it's your home. It's Jack's home. And we're going to have a fuckin' birthday party there for him."

Another giggle slipped out, and she nodded. "Is it okay if I tell you that I think you're awesome?"

Picking up his fork, he said, "You can absolutely tell me I'm awesome. But only if you let me tell you that I think you're even more so."

She hated to bring it up, but said, "We still haven't decided what to do about Peter."

"Has Jack talked about him?"

Shaking her head, she said, "No, not really. When I've mentioned him, he just says that he doesn't want to talk to him."

"Well, considering at this point Peter wasn't requesting to talk to him either, I think that's fine."

"What about the money?" As soon as the word money left her mouth, she saw a dark cloud pass over Colt's face. Not understanding it, she remained quiet, hoping that she was not ruining their perfect morning.

He sighed heavily, then said, "I want to take care of you and Jack. When I said I was ready to be a father figure, I meant in all ways. And that includes financially. But that doesn't mean the fucker shouldn't pay. If Jack doesn't want it now, then it can go into a fund that he can either use or give away when he's an adult and ready to make that decision."

She was quiet for a moment and then held his gaze, seeing his concern, and offered a little smile. "This is nice. A little scary, but nice."

His thumb ran over her knuckles as he held her hand and asked, "What is, babe?"

"This. Our talking. It's nice to have someone besides

my mom to talk over decisions that I'm making about Jack."

A slow smile spread over his face, and she was mesmerized by the warm look in his eyes. "I'm serious, Carrie. This is you, and me, and Jack."

They finished their breakfast, still enjoying the ambiance of the coffeehouse and their company while sipping their coffee. She looked over and said, "Oh, there are two of Jack's camp leaders together. I guess they must be friends."

Jack looked over his shoulder and watched as Tad and Will walked in with Tom Pearl and another man he did not know. Curious and more than a little bit suspicious, he asked, "I recognize Tad from the middle school and two of the other men, one working at the pharmacy and one working at a pawn shop. Who was the other man you recognize?"

"The one in the blue shirt is Brian Jeter. He works with Pastor Hackett at the church where Jack is doing camp."

"He works with youth?"

"Yes, but not just middle school. He also works with teenagers. Jack says that they're separated for part of their activities and then they all come together. I was a little nervous about having an eleven-year-old with high schoolers, but the church seems to have it well in hand."

21

Colt stood in his kitchen watching Jack excitedly talk about the sleepover and the scary movies they had sat up and watched. Carrie was smiling, enjoying every story, the love she had for her son obvious in every action. The house had come alive, reminding him of when his grandparents lived there.

Once Jack wound down, Colt moved over to the counter, leaned forward, placed his weight on his forearms, and said, "Jack, I've got a couple questions I want to ask you. Is that okay, bud?"

Jack was shoveling down a bowl of cereal even though he had eaten breakfast at the sleepover. He looked up at Colt, nodded, and replied, "Sure. Ask away."

Grinning, Colt said, "I'm just curious about your church camp and science camp. I'm interested in the men that lead them."

His face scrunched, Jack asked, "Pastor Hackett?"

Shaking his head, Colt clarified, "No, Brian Jeter and Tad Jameson." Seeing Jack nod slowly, he added, "I just wonder what you can tell me about them, and your impressions of how the camps are run." Jack was a smart boy, and Colt hoped he was not catching onto the fact that he was being questioned, although one glance at a wide-eyed, glaring Carrie let him know that Jack's mom certainly knew.

Jack's nose scrunched again, and this time it appeared he was thinking. "Of the two camps, I'd have to say that I like the science camp at the middle school the best. Mr. Jameson is really cool, kind of funny. You know, the kind of teacher that you hope you get because they love what they do, and they make it exciting. It's also nice because there's no stuff we have to memorize or be tested on. It's just learning cool stuff, and I like the experiments."

"Good," Colt said, realizing that he meant the sentiment. He was glad that Jack was having a good summer and enjoying himself.

"Of course, the girls really like Mr. Jameson. They think he's cute. It's funny because sometimes high school kids come over to meet with him, and if you didn't know he was the teacher you might think that he was one of them."

Carrie interrupted, "I thought the camp was for all middle school. You didn't tell me that high schoolers came also."

"Oh, the camp is for middle school, but he told us he runs a high school science mentor program. I think that means he talks to the high school kids about science stuff to do. So, sometimes, near the end of our camp when we're cleaning up, a few of them will come over and talk to him."

"Do you know any of them?" Colt asked.

Shaking his head, Jack said, "Nah. Not really, because they don't play on the AL team. But I've seen a few of them at the church camp too."

"Speaking about the church camp, what you think about it and Brian Jeter?"

"It's pretty cool, too, although, as I told mom, it's a little weird because I get the feeling that sometimes they get real personal."

"Personal?" Colt asked.

Shifting on the stool at the counter, Jack thought for a moment, then said, "I know kids are always going to hang in cliques, right? You know…rich kids, poor kids, popular kids. So, you'd kind of expect church camp to make sure everybody mingles together. But sometimes I get the feeling that they're not only allowing everybody to separate, they almost encourage it. I don't know, maybe Mr. Jeter's just trying to find out who the needy kids are in case the church needs to step in and help." Shrugging, he added, "I seem to fit in with just about everybody, so I don't mind it too much."

Colt smiled and said, "That's a great trait to have, Jack. The ability to be friends with all kinds of people. So, tell me a little bit more about Mr. Jeter." Ignoring Carrie's huff, he kept his gaze on Jack.

"In some ways, he's kind of like Mr. Jameson. The girls think Mr. Jeter's super cute, but the guys seem to like him, too. He gets to do the cool stuff. Pastor

Hackett is the one that does the Bible stories and prayers, and Mr. Jeter is the one who has us divide up and do activities. There's a couple of helpers that work more with us middle school kids, and he seems to hang around the high school kids the most."

Colt nodded, taking all the information in, then asked, "In either of these camps, have you ever heard any of the kids talking about doing things outside of camp? Things that you know would not be good. Maybe bragging about things they've done that they shouldn't have. Any talk of drugs, drinking, stealing—"

At that, Carrie gasped, and Jack looked at Colt in surprise, asking, "What's going on?"

"Colt, we need to talk in private!" Carrie said.

Before he had a chance to respond, Jack looked up at his mom and shook his head. "No, Mom. If Colt needs information to help solve crimes, then I want to help."

Colt shook his head and said, "Jack, this is not an interrogation. But there are some things going on in the county, and we've wondered if perhaps there were not some young people involved."

"Like George's break-in, right?" Jack asked.

Filtering through what he wanted to say, Colt finally responded. "There are some thefts that are taking place that seem organized and yet…not professional."

Jack watched him carefully, and Colt could tell that Jack was filtering through the information, so he waited quietly.

Finally, Jack said, "I haven't heard anything at all. That doesn't mean that it's not happening, I just haven't heard anybody say anything that made me think they were up to no good."

"Then that's all I needed to hear," Colt said, standing up straight with just his hip leaning against the counter now. Smiling, he said, "And hopefully you won't hear anything, and we'll find out that it had nothing to do with young people at all."

Jack seemed completely satisfied with that and went back to finishing his second breakfast before bounding out of the kitchen saying, "I'm going to go check in with George to see if his sleepover with his son was as much fun as I had."

Glancing to the side, Colt could see that Carrie was fuming, so he turned and walked the few steps to her. Pulling her into his arms, he felt her body stiffen, and he nuzzled the side of her face and tried to rub the tension out of her back and shoulders.

"Babe, listen to me," he said, lifting her chin with his knuckle so that her eyes met his. "Jack's a smart boy, but my conversation with him might keep him safer than if he was ignorant of some of the things that are going on. He wants to do the right thing, and this information will help assure that he does not fall into a group of kids who might influence him the wrong way."

She held his gaze for a long moment, then tilted her head slightly to the side and asked, "Like your dad?"

Nodding slowly, he said, "There are a lot of kids out there from good families who get with the wrong crowd and make wrong choices. You've done a fuckin' phenomenal job with him, and now that I'm part of the equation, I want to kick in and help with that too."

"I don't want him to be used for getting information—"

"I get that, Carrie. Chances are when other kids see that I'm in his life, the ones who might be into shit won't want to be around him. But if he happens to overhear something or see something that could stop crimes from happening, then I want him to have that power as well."

She sucked in her lips, and he could see her mind working behind her eyes. He gave that to her for a moment, then asked, "Talk to me, babe. I don't want to be flying solo here."

Shaking her head, she said, "You're not flying solo. I guess it's just been that I have flown solo for his entire life. I had my parents, and Joe and Mavis, but as far as parenting, it was just me. I just need to get used to it, that's all."

They stood in the kitchen, embracing for several more minutes before she asked, "Do you really think it's kids that are breaking into places?"

He sighed, saying, "I don't know, babe. Right now, the investigation is wide open, and we're looking at everything."

She lifted on her toes, kissed the underside of his jaw, and murmured, "Well if anyone can find out what's going on, it's you."

She slid from his arms and moved over to Jack's empty cereal bowl, taking it to the sink. He watched her performing such a simple task with ease in his kitchen and smiled. The house no longer felt like an empty tomb.

George and Della, along with Joe and Mavis, were standing at the long table in Colt's backyard, making sure the hot dogs, hamburgers, potato chip bowls, and fruit platters were kept well-stocked.

Hunter, Trevon, Mitch, Grant, and Lance were off to the side, beers in hands and eyes on the kids playing. With the party at his house and room not being an obstacle, he insisted on Jack inviting kids from the AL ball team as well, prompting many of the other coaches to show up, too. Considering these men brought their wives, he saw Carrie standing with her new friends, beaming.

Most importantly, Jack was in the middle of an impromptu show of his pitching skills using the new pitching net that Colt had given him. Carrie had insisted that the other kids not bring presents to the party, not wanting any child to feel as though they had to bring a gift. Instead, her invitation simply asked for the gift of their presence. He liked her play on words, and Jack was thrilled with the number of kids who came.

Making his way over to the men, Colt smiled as he approached. Clapping him on the back, Mitch said, "I haven't been out to your house many times, but I've got to tell you, I've never seen it so alive."

He chuckled and admitted, "I had a party out here one time when my grandparents lived here. I thought it was the greatest place in the world to have a big party. Glad I could give it to Jack."

They stood watching the kids for a few minutes, then Grant asked, "Anything new on the robberies?"

Shaking his head, he said, "No. I think somebody's figured out that we're looking hard, and they're laying low right now."

Mitch said, "Hunter said you're thinking of possible teens."

"I was going to bring this up at our next group meeting," he said, "I'm not coming up with anything definitive, but considering that it's organized, and yet not appearing professional, that's definitely a way we're thinking."

"I've known Stuart for a long time, and if somebody's gaining information from his pharmacy about who's getting home deliveries, he's going to be seriously unhappy."

Nodding, Colt said, "I get that. I've never heard anything negative about him at all, or the pharmacy. I know they do good work, especially with the elderly."

Hannah had walked over to the group of law enforcers, and he asked her, "Have you ever had to deal with Tom Pearl?"

"Other than I know he runs the Pearl Pawn Shop with his dad and happens to live in Easton, no. Why?"

"I saw him with some people that are on my list to keep an eye on." Seeing everyone stare at him, he shook his head, and said, "Right now, everybody's a fuckin' suspect. It's driving me crazy."

They all chuckled, each understanding what he meant.

Mitch looked over at Trevon and said, "I hear you're about to go detective?"

Trevon grinned and said, "Colt's been real good letting me work this case with Hunter. I'll take my exam soon and then we'll see."

Shouts from the kids drew their attention, and they watched as Jack continued pitching, his skills well above what most eleven-year-olds could do.

"Are you ready for a ready-made family?" Mitch asked, gaining everyone's attention.

"Abso-fucking-lutely," Colt said, his eyes moving from Jack back over to Carrie. As happy as he was, his only regret was that his grandparents never had a chance to meet them.

At the end of the day, when everyone had gone and the party had been cleaned up, he, Carrie, George, and Jack sat in the living room looking at the gifts the adults had given to Jack. There were several envelopes from friends, each with some money inside.

Jack sat and added up his money, then looked at his mom and grinned. "I've got enough."

"Enough for what, boy?" George asked.

Jack, staring at George, said, "Enough to buy tickets for you and me to go see a Baltimore Orioles game."

George sucked in a breath, blinking in disbelief. His voice raspy, he said, "Jack, boy, don't you be spending your money on me."

"I told Mom a long time ago that I wanted to have enough money so that you and I can go see a game together."

He threw his arms around George's neck, even at the

age of eleven not too old to express his feelings. Colt looked over at Carrie, tears shining in her eyes as she stared at her son in pride. Feeling the lump in his own throat, Colt said, "We'll pick a game, and we'll all go together."

As the evening drew to a close, he realized how much he liked the sound of that…*together*. He got another dose of it when he walked upstairs and heard Carrie sitting in Jack's room, talking. Not ashamed to eavesdrop, he listened.

"So, Colt and I discussed it, and we're willing to consider having Peter put money in an account for you. I don't need his money, but he is your biological father, and it can be set aside for college or when you're a grown-up or whatever you want to do with it."

"You and Colt discussed it?" Jack asked.

"Yes. I know I usually make all decisions about you by myself, but I felt like I needed someone else's perspective so that I was making a good decision, and not one just based on emotion. Is that okay?"

"I like thinking about you and Colt together," Jack admitted. "I don't really want Peter's money since he never wanted to have anything to do with me. But it makes sense, so I'm okay if it goes into the bank and sits there."

Leaning slightly forward, he could see Carrie pulling Jack into a hug, his boy-man arms going around his mother's neck.

"I loved my party today, Mom. But the best thing of all was having it here."

"I know, it was great having all the extra room," Carrie began.

"No, Mom. What I mean was having it *here*. Here where Colt is. Like we're a real family."

At that, Colt felt the lump reappearing in his throat, and he could swear he saw his grandmother smile in his mind.

22

The day had dawned sunny and fair, but Carrie was not sad to see the large, white fluffy clouds sometimes breaking up the bright sunshine. It kept the temperatures cooler as she stood under the canopy tents near the Baytown pier. The colorful tents dotted the grassy area near the dunes, close to the opening of the pier.

Baytown's public beach was beautiful, and the only public beach in the area. The wide expanse of white sand leading into the Chesapeake Bay gave families plenty of space for their umbrellas, towels, and beach chairs.

She had only walked out on the pier once before, several years earlier when Jack had heard about it from some friends at school. He had been excited then with the promise of fishing off of it one day, and that had not happened until now. Today, Baytown was hosting a fishing tournament off the pier for children and senior citizens. Jack and George were thrilled to be paired together. George assured Jack that he had spent his childhood fishing and would teach Jack everything he knew.

At the invitation of Belle and her new friends, she was in the process of joining the American Legion Auxiliary since her father had served in the military. She was glad her mother had joined as well, giving Della the chance to meet other women close to her own age. The Auxiliary often held bake sales to raise money for the various activities the American Legion supported.

Having Saturday off, she decided to help out and had spent the previous evening baking cookies and brownies for the bake sale. Jack had begged her to make rice crispy treats, but she was afraid in the warm sun they would turn into a sticky, gooey mess. Of course, Jack had not seen the problem with that, declaring that licking the melted marshmallow off his fingers was one of the best parts. Common sense prevailed, and she stuck with making what she felt like would be best… oatmeal raisin cookies and deep, double chocolate brownies.

She and Della had only been to one auxiliary meeting so far, and she was trying to remember so many new names and faces. Glancing to the side, she saw her mom manning a table with Mitch's and Jillian's moms, Nancy and Claire Evans. Corine McFarlane was in the process of balancing little Finn on her hip when she called out to her husband. "Eric! Get over here and take Finn! He'll be fine in the stroller on the pier." Katelyn kissed her son before thanking her dad and waved to little Finn as he was strolled away. Slicking her dark hair away from her face, she said, "Love my boy, but it's nice to have an extra pair of hands around!"

Carrie remembered the days when Jack was very small and knew exactly what Katelyn was referring to. As hard as it was to not have his father around, having her parents to lean on made all the difference in the world. She looked up and caught her mother's eyes on her, a small smile playing about Della's lips, and she knew her mother was having similar remembrances.

Sophie and her mom, Tonya, were at another table slicing the cakes and pies, selling them per piece. Business was steady, and she was glad that some of the women from the auxiliary were baking that morning, bringing fresh goodies to restore their quickly-depleting stock.

"This is going to be ridiculous in a few months when a bunch of us have babies," Rose said, tucking her hair behind her ears and wiping the sweat from her brow with the back of her hand.

Smiling, Carrie tilted her head to the side and said, "Who else besides you is pregnant?"

Rose's blue eyes widened, and she gasped, "Oh, goodness! Did we not tell you? We were all at a party about two months ago when Jillian said she was pregnant. Then Lia and Jade chimed in to say that they were also. So that makes four of us who are going to have babies next fall and winter."

Shaking her head, Carrie said, "I had no idea! No one is showing yet."

Tori walked by, looked at her mother-in-law, Nancy, and said, "Where is Grandpa Ed?"

Nancy slid little Eddie out of Tori's arms, kissed her grandson, and said, "I just texted him and he says he's on his way."

"Well, Mitch has the morning shift and then he can help out as well," Tori replied, pulling a stuffed giraffe out of her large bag and handing it to her son.

Carrie laughed and said, "Oh, I remember those days. You feel like you drag your life around in a diaper bag when they're babies and then, when they're toddlers, everywhere you go has to involve their very special toys."

Jillian tossed her long braid over her shoulder and asked, "Is it hard to believe how fast the time has gone? I mean, does it seem like the last eleven years have gone quickly?"

Carrie let out a rueful chuckle and said, "I was just thinking about that the other day. I can't believe that Jack is eleven. I still remember every stage he went through."

She realized she had the attention of their group of friends and added, "I loved every stage that he was in but wasn't sorry to see him leave that stage. I loved him as a baby but was excited when he was toddling. Then, when he started preschool and elementary school, I loved those ages as well. I admit, now, it's a little worrisome to think about him going to middle school, but I love the fact that he's becoming a young man."

Belle sighed, "Well, if you and Colt have children, then at least you will have been through this once."

At those words, Carrie blinked, both at the thought that she and Colt would stay together and have children, and at the thought of how adorable Colt's children would be. Nibbling on her lips, she wondered if she was brave enough to become a mom again.

Looking around, she realized the others had grown quiet, all staring at her.

"You're a great mom, Carrie," Belle said. "If it does happen again for you, you'll be even more amazing the second time around."

Giving her head a little shake, she said, "Let's not get ahead of ourselves. I have no idea what the future holds in any way. Especially with me and Colt."

Katelyn laughed and said, "Just remember…these men don't waste their time once they find the right woman. And I can't imagine anyone better for Colt than you."

Their conversation was interrupted when a cheer arose from the crowd, and she looked toward the pier. From her place under the tent she was unable to see clearly, but it sounded as though the first team had brought in their fish. "I hope Jack and George catch something today or he'll be so disappointed."

"Which one? Jack or George?" Jade asked.

Laughing, she replied, "Both of them!"

Colt wandered through the throngs of people filling the Baytown beach. The fishing competition had brought in townspeople, others living on the Eastern Shore, and vacationers. Baytown only had Mitch and four police officers, so Colt's Sheriff's Department always assisted when there was a large event happening in the county. He had several deputies on duty, handling everything from parking, traffic, and assisting with the Baytown Police.

He had passed by the food trucks earlier, the scent of grilled meat and vegetables and spices filling the air, already making him hungry. But it was the tents containing the baked goods that truly captured his attention. Or rather, the one beautiful woman standing behind the table selling cookies to a group of children, a wide smile on her face, that had him grinning.

He had helped at many of the events in the county over the last five years but had never looked forward to one as much as he had this one. Jack and George's enthusiasm had been infectious, and he was looking forward to checking on them later in the day to see what they had caught.

The American Legion had grown to mean a lot to him since his return a couple of years ago in Baytown. When Carrie had mentioned that Belle had invited her to a meeting the prior week of the auxiliary, he was happy for her. He recognized that her world had mostly been the diner and Jack, and he wanted to encourage her new friendships. Plus, with her caring personality, she would fit right into the Auxiliary's activities.

A cheer arose from the fishing pier, and he assumed the first catch of the day had occurred. As he turned to take a walk near the beach, he observed Grant and Ginny rushing in that direction. Moving quickly through the crowds as he listened to the codes through his earpiece, he headed to assist. A fight had broken out between two teenage boys, and it was quickly subdued. It appeared they were fighting over the same girl who was standing off to the side in tears.

Seeing that it was handled by Grant and Ginny, he continued through the beach crowd and back to the sidewalk on Beach Road near the food trucks. Hearing his name called, he turned around and lifted his chin in greeting as Mitch walked up to him.

"All okay?" Mitch asked.

Giving him the rundown, they laughed about the teenagers and Mitch said, "It's hard to believe we were ever that young and that dumb."

Colt agreed, then admitted, "I'd like to think I wasn't that dumb, but I probably was."

"I don't know if you even remember Tori since she didn't go to Baytown High School. Her grandmother owned the Sea Glass Inn in town, and Tori would spend her summers here. I fell for her when we were kids, and we actually dated in high school even though she lived in Virginia Beach."

Shaking his head, he said, "I had no idea until she moved back here as an adult that you two had known each other before."

"She was married for a little while before coming back," Mitch said.

Colt admitted, "Yeah, me too. I got married early when I was just as young and dumb as we were talking earlier. I suppose we have to live life before we learn how to be smart."

"Well, you being with Carrie is smart," Mitch said. "I'm real happy for you."

Just then, Mitch's dad, Ed, strolled by with little Eddie, and Mitch plucked his son out of the stroller, giving him a kiss. Gareth walked up, his son in his arms as well. Colt admired them before tossing a wave goodbye, continuing to make his way through the crowd.

As he neared the bake sale tents again, he saw Carrie reaching her hands out to hold a baby while a young mother was digging in her purse for money to pay for the baked goods her toddler was holding onto. He jolted, seeing Carrie holding the baby. She had always appeared so natural in the role of Jack's mom, but he never thought about how she would have looked when Jack was a baby. In that instant, he knew that if her arms were filled with his child, she would not be more beautiful. Sucking in a quick breath, he waited to see if thoughts of children would make him feel panicked or trapped. Instead, it sent a warm surge of longing through him.

A few hours later, both he and Carrie were off duty and walking along the beach. Something caught his eye as it sparkled on the sand and he bent to scoop up a piece of green sea glass. "Hold out your hand," he said.

She did as he requested and watched as he placed the sea glass on her uplifted palm. Tilting her head to the side, she asked, "Is that sea glass?" Grinning widely, she said, "I've never had a chance to look for sea glass. It's beautiful!"

"It reminds me of you," he said, closing her fingers around the smooth surface. "The broken glass is tossed and tumbled by the water and sand, making it smooth and beautiful. Just like you."

Her top teeth captured her bottom lip as she sucked in a quick breath. He turned so that they were facing each other, no space between their bodies. Bending, he kissed her lips, soothing the place she had nibbled.

Shouts erupted from the fishing pier and he knew the tournament was near the end. Hating to separate, he held her gaze, his thumbs sweeping over her cheeks. "Guess we better go see how they did."

She nodded and snuggled into his side as he wrapped his arm around her shoulders, tucking her in tightly as they walked along the fishing pier, admiring the view. The tournament was over, and Jack and George had won second place. Colt was not sure who was more excited…George, Jack, or Carrie. If he was honest, his name was in there as well because he had clapped and cheered as loud as anyone when their names had been called.

Townspeople smiled and nodded their greetings, their acceptance of he and Carrie together evident. He looked down at her face, and asked, "Happy?"

She stopped, turned to face him, placed her hands flat against his chest and looked up into his eyes. "There's been a lot of times in my life that I've been incredibly happy. When Jack was born. Celebrating all his milestones. Having fun at Joe's Place. Knowing that even though my dad is gone, my mom is still around to enjoy her grandson." She sucked in her lips for a second, her eyes cutting away from his as though she were pondering her next words. He waited patiently and then she rewarded him when she looked up at him again, a wide smile spreading across her face. "But right now, with my son so excited to have spent the day with George, my mom working alongside of me and our new friends, and you standing right here with your arms around me…I've never been happier."

Heedless of the people around, he bent and kissed her, knowing he could say the same and vowing to spend his life making her happy.

23

Colt did not often sit in on his detectives' meetings, but being personally interested in this investigation, he wanted to know where they were with their cases. Trevon had joined Hunter and Elizabeth, and Hannah and Liam were in attendance as well since they had also had elderly people robbed of their medication.

Trevon said, "One of our problems is that unlike a city where people are close together, in the county we're so spread out. Many of our elderly live in homes that are along country lanes with neighbors far apart."

"We're considering getting notice out to the elderly in our county to make sure they lock their doors at night and maybe go so far as to lock up their medication," Elizabeth said. "If so, I'll make sure that it's in Spanish as well as English."

Hunter groused, "If Will is not directly giving the names of who he delivers to, how else are they getting them? Is someone following him? Is someone hacking into the pharmacy to get the list?"

"Following him would be easy," Elizabeth said, "because he has set delivery times."

"He also has that bright blue pickup truck that's not too hard to disguise," Trevon added. "If someone wants to follow him, it's pretty easy."

"Each of us has elderly assistance," Colt said, looking at Hannah and Liam. "We need to tell our deputies and officers to increase their watch when they do their elder checks."

"What about the phone calls when they check in?" Elizabeth asked. "Should we be asking where the medications are kept? And then advising that they should keep them locked up?"

Colt rubbed his chin, feeling the tension in his jaw. "My fear is that we'll end up with more victims like George. When the robberies occur at night and the older person is asleep, whoever is getting in has no resistance and can make it a quick and easy theft. George heard them and went to confront them…or at least see who was there in his house. Then the robbery became an assault. And then it became arson and attempted murder."

"So, you're concerned that if we make the drugs more difficult for someone to steal, it could become more dangerous for the victims?" Trevon asked.

Shrugging, he sighed. "It's a concern and a consideration that we need to think about."

They continued to brainstorm for several minutes about making the elderly residents safer without putting them in more danger.

Trevon added, "Hunter has had me checking, but I

see no tie into the organized gang activity that's coming from the north or even from Virginia Beach."

"So what's happening with the medication that's being stolen? There's got to be a central person that it's going to…someone who has the links to get paid for it."

"Is there any tie into Tom Pearl?" Colt asked.

Shaking his head, Hunter replied, "None that we can see. Other than he and Will are friends."

"Because we have identified the thefts occurring at houses where medications are delivered, I want to get hold of Will's phone records and emails. We've got enough probable cause, so make that happen."

Elizabeth nodded and said, "I'll work on getting the warrant."

"Let me know as soon as you have anything," Colt said, pushing himself up. With a chin lift goodbye, he headed back to his office.

Carrie placed the plates filled with chicken fried steak and french fries onto the table, checking to see if her customers needed drink refills. The lunch crowd was thinning, but she could not deny that the tips had been good.

She jumped every time she looked toward the door, and Mavis finally asked, "Girl, what's wrong with you? You're as nervous as a cat sleeping under a rocking chair."

"I talked to Peter yesterday and told him that we were ready with a decision. He's going to come by. I said we could just talk on the phone, but he seems to want to visit in person."

"Are you sure you're ready for this?" BettyJo asked.

Nodding, she said, "Yeah. The other day I was caught off guard, but I'm ready now." Making her way around the diner again, refilling drinks and getting dessert orders put in, she looked up as the bell over the door rang.

Peter walked in, and she offered a small wave in greeting. Moving toward him, she ushered him to a booth in the corner and nodded toward BettyJo to indicate that she was taking her break.

"Carrie," he greeted, his hands nervously clutched together on the old tabletop.

She had noticed his dress pants were ironed with a crease when he walked in and could not help but compare them to the perfectly creased, dark brown pants that made up Colt's uniform. The two men could not be more different, but every comparison between the two only made her think more of Colt.

Blinking, trying to clear her mind, she focused on Peter. "I feel bad about you driving all this way," she said. "We really could have talked over the phone."

He nodded jerkily and said, "I realize that, but I felt like this was important enough to speak in person." He sucked in a breath through his nose, and let it out slowly, his gaze on his hands for a moment before lifting his chin and holding her eyes. "I admit that Abigail read me the riot act after our last visit. And she was right. I do owe you an apology." Sighing, he said, "I owe you a lot more than an apology."

"You know, Peter, it makes me feel good to hear you say that, but we really don't need to dwell on the past. We were young. I was in love and thought you were, too. But here we are, years later, and I can truly say that I'm happy."

His gaze drifted out toward the diner, and she battled her ire, not wanting to fight with him. "I can see that you don't understand how this job would make me feel happy. Quite frankly, sometimes it doesn't. But I've found friends here. True friends. Friends who stepped in when I was sick or Jack was sick. I had my mom with me, and we were accepted here. It might not be the country club atmosphere that you're used to, but it's a life that I made for myself."

Giving a quick shake, he said, "Please, I didn't mean to imply that this was not a good life. I have no right to judge anyone's life, considering that I've typically done whatever my father wanted me to do, including joining his law firm. I'm often not happy there, but I didn't have the strength of character that you have to strike out on my own."

Those words surprised her, and she leaned back against her seat, waiting to see what else he would say.

"I know that Jack probably doesn't want to have anything to do with me," he said, shaking his head slowly, "and I can't blame him. If he ever does want to meet me, please know that I'm completely open to that."

She licked her bottom lip, thinking of how she had practiced what she was going to say to him, and now it was time. Her stomach twisted slightly, but she forged ahead. "Right now, Jack says he does not want to meet you. But I have no doubt that he's curious. I'm going to leave that decision up to him. I will also let you know that he said that he did not want any of your money, but he's old enough to understand the meaning of child support and that we have never had that." Ignoring the wince that crossed Peter's face, she continued, "I am uncertain what all of your motives are. You never sought us out until you decided to run for office and then you realized you had what could be considered a skeleton in your closet." She leaned forward, gaining and holding his attention as she said, "Don't you see, Peter? Jack is anything but a skeleton. He's not something to be ashamed of or something that you need to pay off. He's a living, breathing, fabulous, intelligent, caring, wonderful, funny, inventive, light of my life boy."

Peter's eyes closed for a moment before opening again, nodding slowly. "I know that you're right. My choice of words last time was unpardonable, and believe me, that was part of what Abigail blasted me about. In truth, what started out as what could be considered a payoff to make sure that you don't speak to the press against me has now made me realize that I fucked up twelve years ago when you told me you were pregnant and I didn't man up then, and I haven't manned up since then. If the press comes asking questions when I announce my candidacy, you are completely free to give them your unflattering opinion of me, of which I realize I deserve."

Shaking her head, she said, "Peter, I may have been furious with you at various times during the past twelve years, but I'm not out to ruin your life. And I don't need child support. I am completely able to take care of all of Jack's needs myself. What I have decided is that it would be foolish for me to refuse you if you would like to open up a bank account for Jack to use when he's an adult. Whether for college, travel, whatever he would like."

He appeared relieved, whether because he truly wanted to help Jack or just felt like this was one more box to check off for his political aspirations. But she found that she did not care. Whatever his motivation, as long as it would make Jack's life easier to pursue his dreams, then she was fine with it. She may have gone through all the difficult times with Jack, but of his two parents, she was the lucky one. She got the love of her son, and that was worth more than any of Peter's money.

They slid out of the booth at the same time, and Peter tentatively reached his hand out. She did not hesitate, but clasped it in her own, smiling at the thought that only Colt's touch sent shivers through her. She watched as he walked out of the diner and then turned around to see Joe, Mavis, and BettyJo observing her carefully.

Smiling, she walked over to them and said, "Stop worrying. The time when I give any thoughts to Peter and what I didn't have is over. Now, I just focus on Jack and Colt and the future. It's our time."

Jack was waiting at the church, most of the other kids

already picked up by their parents or rides. Today, his grandmother was picking him up, but his mom had let him know that she was running a little late. That was okay with him since it gave him a chance to hang with Shelley until her dad picked her up. Now, with most of the kids gone, he walked back toward the door to wait in the shade, where he could still keep an eye on the parking lot so he would not miss his grandmother.

The sound of low voices caught his attention, and while he knew it was rude to eavesdrop, the temptation was great. Turning around, he could see his friend, Colby, standing just inside. He was about to throw open the door and say hello when he heard harsh words.

"You don't got no choice. You stick your nose where it don't belong, then that puts you in with the rest of us. Your job right now is to shut the fuck up, say nothing to no one, and when we need you, you're ours. Ours to control, ours to demand, ours to tell you what the fuck to do."

Shocked at the tone of the words as much as the cursing, Jack stood in indecision…throw open the door and confront whoever was speaking or run away. Before he had a chance to decide, the door slammed open, almost hitting him. The two older boys who walked out never noticed him in the shadows of the building. Not seeing anyone else around, he darted through the doorway, observing Colby standing to the side. His friend's face was pale, and tears shimmered in his eyes.

"Colby," he called out, rushing over.

His friend looked up in surprise, then his eyes jerked

open wide as he shot his gaze around as though looking to see if someone else was nearby.

Rushing to assure him, Jack said, "Nobody's here. They all left."

Eyes even wider, Colby asked, "You saw them?"

"I heard part of it. What was going on?"

Continuing to shake his head back and forth, Colby said, "You shouldn't have heard. I can't tell you."

Jack stepped closer, carefully observing his friend, paying attention to things he never noticed. A sheen of sweat covered Colby's face. The skin underneath his eyes appeared darker, something he knew his mom used makeup to cover up when she did not have a good night's sleep. Colby's eyes continued to dart around as though searching for someone or searching to see if they were alone.

"Colby, if there's something going on, you can tell me. You can talk to me."

His voice hoarse, Colby replied, "I can't, Jack."

"Are they being mean to you? Are they picking on you?"

Colby jerked his head back and forth. "No. They're friends of mine."

"Friends?" Jack asked, his voice rising. "You and *I* are friends. Since when are you friends with Billy Neiman and John Roster? And since when do friends talk to other friends that way?"

Walking back a step, Colby asked, "You heard?"

Stepping forward, lowering his voice, Jack replied, "I heard enough to know that they were telling you to keep your mouth shut. What I want to know is if you're in trouble, why won't you talk to me?"

Colby's eyes glazed over as he looked to the side. His voice barely above a whisper, he said, "Jack, you don't know. You don't know what it's like to be scared."

"You do know who my dad is, right? Well, sorta like my dad. Sheriff Hudson? If anyone can help you, it's him. If you want to talk to him, we can give him a call right now. If those guys are trying to get you in trouble, you need to tell someone."

A car pulled into the parking lot, and both boys turned to look out the window in the door. Jack noticed it was Colby's mom. Putting his hand on his friend's arm, he said, "Please, let me help."

Colby's gaze dropped to the hand on his arm, then pulled away. "Nothing's going on, Jack. You don't need to be sticking your nose where it doesn't belong either." With that, he darted to the door and ran to his mom's car, climbing in before she drove away.

Sighing heavily, he wondered what to do when Brian Jeter turned the corner and smiled as he moved closer.

"Jack, do you need a ride home?"

Jack stared at the man for a moment, his mind in turmoil over everything he had just witnessed with Colby. Brian moved closer, but another car pulled into the parking lot, and Jack smiled in relief as he saw his ride. "Got to go," he shouted out. "Grandma's here."

Without saying another goodbye, he shot through the door, ran across the parking lot, and climbed into Della's car.

24

Colt had made it plain that he did not expect Carrie to be his live-in housekeeper, but even though she worked in a diner, she enjoyed cooking, especially in a kitchen like Colt's that was large and bright with windows.

Ever since she had gotten home, she had noticed Jack was much quieter than normal. When she tried to question him, she received short, curt answers. So, she left him to watch TV, moving back into the kitchen. She had already defrosted thick pork chops, mixed boxed stuffing, and filled the pork chops after slitting them in the middle.

George came down from his apartment, and the two of them chatted in the kitchen while she continued to fix dinner.

"Somethin' going on with Jack?" George asked.

Glancing over her shoulder at the wizened older man sitting at the counter, she said, "I just get the feeling that something happened at camp today, and he won't talk about it."

"He's a good boy," George said. "Maybe he's just ruminating on things for a bit. He'll let you know when he's ready to talk."

Nodding, she said, "I think sometimes it's getting harder."

"Harder?" George leaned forward and snagged a carrot, munching on it as he watched her carefully.

She stopped slicing the carrots, laid the knife down, and leaned across the counter, her weight resting on her forearms. "I sometimes think it was easier when he was younger. His problems were skinned knees, something that I could kiss and make better. The older he gets, it'll be harder and harder."

George leaned across the counter, patted her hand, and said, "Well, if you don't need me in here, I think I'll mosey into the den and watch some TV with Jack. Never know what the two of us might decide to talk about."

Grinning, she mouthed a *thank you* and watched as George walked down the hall toward the front room.

With the pork chops in the oven, several minutes later, Colt walked through the back door. Just like every day, as soon as his eyes hit her, he grinned widely, and she felt it right through her heart. And as always, she met that grin with one of her own.

Walking around the counter, Colt stepped right in her space, wrapped his arms around her, and tucked her face next to his heartbeat. He kissed the top of her head, she then squeezed him around his waist and leaned her head back. He had never missed the opportunity and did not start now. Dropping his head, he kissed her, hard and fast , but ever so sweet.

"Where are George and Jack?" he asked when he separated from her.

She sighed and said, "Jack's been out of sorts since he's been home from camp today. George is in the den with him, just hanging."

She could tell he was watching her carefully before he asked, "You worried?"

She bit her lip, pondering his question, then said, "Yeah, sort of. I mean, I wanted him to have space to think things through, and certainly, as he continues to become a young man, he's going to have things he needs to think about. But at the same time, I don't want him worried about something."

"Well, if he doesn't snap out of it soon, I'll talk to him." He let her go and walked to the refrigerator to get a beer.

She sighed again, this time heavily, looking back down at the carrots as she continued to chop.

Colt walked back over in her space, and said, "Hey, babe, if you don't want me to talk to him, I won't."

"No, no," she rushed to say. "It's just that…that…"

"Babe, say whatever's on your mind, please."

She held his gaze and said, "I just can't get over feeling badly that you've gone from having a house to yourself, with all your privacy, to walking in at night and being faced with your house filled with a woman, a boy, an older man, and all the problems we bring."

Setting his beer down on the counter, he walked to

her, pulled the chopping knife out of her hand and laid it down next to his beer. Leaning his hips back against the counter, he spread his legs and drew her forward so that she was standing close to him, touching from hip to chest.

With his arms banded around her, he said, "For the first time in longer than I can ever remember, I *want* to come home at the end of the day. I don't walk into a house that's empty, void of people and conversation. Now, when I leave work, I'm excited on the drive home, knowing that when I get here, there will be people I care about, allowing my life to intertwine with theirs."

Sucking in a quick breath, she stared into his eyes and said, "Colt, that's beautiful."

"I mean every word, Carrie. And you've got to know that it's not just because there are people in the house. It's because the people in the house are you, and Jack, and George."

Jack remained quiet during dinner, the three adults aware but not saying anything to make him feel uncomfortable. George had whispered to Carrie and Colt that Jack had not confided anything to him.

As the dinner came to a close, Colt said, "Jack, let's go out into the backyard and toss the ball. We can work on your pitches."

For the first time since coming home that day, Jack perked up, his eyes lighting with interest. He ran to grab his glove and ball while Colt kissed Carrie's cheek, whispering, "I'll talk to him, babe."

Breathing a sigh of relief, she thanked God that Colt was becoming the father to Jack that he had never had.

For almost half an hour, Colt and Jack tossed the baseball back and forth, and Jack used his practice net for his pitches.

"You know, Jack, I hope you don't just see me as the Sheriff or your coach. I care a great deal about you and your mom. If there's ever anything you need to tell me or just want to talk about, I'm here.

Jack stood, his glove in one hand, pounding it with his other fist before turning his face up toward Colt. He hesitated for another moment, then finally asked, "Do you ever wonder what the right thing to do is? I mean, you're the sheriff, so do you just memorize all the laws and then that's what you do?"

Colt led Jack toward the Adirondacks that were in the backyard, and they settled into the seats. The sun had not set, but it had passed over the trees, engulfing them in cool shadows. One of the reasons Colt loved the property besides the house was the yard, expansive, surrounded with tall, mature trees.

He sucked in a breath of fresh air, letting it out slowly as he pulled his thoughts together. Looking at Jack's anxious face, he answered, "A lot of what I do, yes, is determined by the law. I have to be aware of what is legal and not legal for people to do. If they're doing something that's not legal, then I have to consider the laws that are being broken. Sometimes a person can get off with a warning. Other times, especially if it's a more serious crime or they've been in trouble before, then they can get arrested. But even that process is guided by the law."

He observed Jack nodding slowly, seeming to take in what he said. Not wanting to rush Jack, he leaned back in the chair and added, "Of course, a lot of times in life, we are guided by other things besides the law. Things that are just right and wrong. We always want to try to do what's right, and sometimes we don't. Sometimes we mess up."

"What if you think maybe someone else is doing something wrong and you don't say anything about it? Does that make you wrong? Or what if you're afraid to tell anyone?"

Colt had wondered if Jack was questioning about a possible mistake he had made, but his new question made him wonder if he was a witness to something. Realizing that Jack was struggling with what to divulge, Colt said without hesitation, "If you know that someone is doing something they shouldn't, you don't want them to get hurt or others to be hurt. I understand that it's a heavy burden for anyone your age, but I think you're mature enough to be able to handle telling someone who can help you."

Jack looked up and held his gaze for a long moment before saying, "I think one of my friends might be in trouble. But I'm not sure what to do about it."

"Jack, you know my job is to help people, so do you want to tell me about it?"

Shoulders slumping, Jack said, "I don't think he wants anyone to know. He told me to stay out of it, but honestly, I think he did that because he's afraid."

Unease snaked through Colt, and he asked, "Do you know what he's afraid of?"

"I think he's afraid of the other boys. The ones that I heard threatening him."

At those words, Colt forced his body to remain relaxed on the outside while carefully considering how best to handle the situation with Jack. "I'm concerned that someone is threatening your friend," he said. "I can't make you tell me what's going on, but if you think your friend is in trouble, wouldn't you want to do everything you could to help them?"

Nodding, Jack said, "Yeah. That's all I can think about ever since I've gotten home from church camp."

The unease that he felt earlier increased, and he encouraged, "I'd like you to tell me what you know and then trust me to do the right thing."

Sitting up straighter, Jack nodded. "I know I can trust you, Colt. Absolutely."

Glancing beyond Jack's shoulder, he observed Carrie standing at the sliding glass door. Making a slight motion with his hand, he indicated to her that she should not come out yet. She nodded, blew him a kiss, then turned and walked back into the kitchen.

Focusing his attention on Jack, he said, "Just tell me what happened. You don't have to analyze it or embellish it. Just tell me what you saw and heard."

Jack began hesitantly at first, but then his voice grew stronger as he continued telling his story to Colt. "Most of the time at the church camp, it's a lot of fun. But sometimes there are high school kids that seem to be real cliquish. I mean, I get it, and that's okay, but some of them seem like bullies. I noticed they've been hanging around my friend Colby, and ever since they have, Colby has gotten a lot quieter. And then today, I was just outside of the door when I heard a couple of them threatening him to keep his mouth shut and not say anything to anybody."

"And you tried to talk to him?"

"They left, and he was waiting on his mom, so I went inside to talk to him. He was real upset and then told me it was none of my business."

Colt asked, "Do you know who the boys were?"

"Billy Neiman and John Roster were the two that were threatening Colby today. They seem the meanest to me. And they're always hanging around Mr. Jeter, the camp leader. I figured, him being a church person, he was trying to get them to be less mean, but sometimes I just wonder if he's not very good at his job because they don't get any nicer."

Colt fought the urge to immediately confront Brian Jeter but simply said, "Jack, I'll tell you what I'll do. I'm going to look into a couple of things behind the scenes. I won't talk to Colby unless I have to, but what you've told me makes me a little suspicious about what some of the kids might be doing." He observed Jack's eyes widening, and he rushed to say, "Jack, do you trust me?"

Again, Jack held his gaze, then slowly nodded. "Yeah, Colt I trust you."

"Okay. Then my job is not only to take care of this county as sheriff, and take care of the players on the AL baseball team, but my job now includes taking care of you, and your mom, and George."

"Kind of like a family?" Jack asked, his gaze piercing and steady.

Colt could see the hopefulness on the boy's face, and his own heart warmed. "Absolutely, Jack. Like a family."

He watched as the tension left Jack's shoulders, and he stood, placing his hand on Jack's shoulder as they walked back toward the house.

Jack said, "I know Mom could tell I was upset about something."

Giving his shoulder a squeeze, Colt said, "I think it would be a good idea to let her know that everything is going to be okay. We don't want her to worry."

He smiled as Jack rushed in, hugged his mom and then said, "I'm going to finish watching the game with George."

He moved over next to Carrie, and they watched as Jack headed down the hall toward the den. She looked up at him and said, "Is everything okay?"

"He's worried about one of his friends. Colby. I told him I was going to check out a few things at the church group, especially Brian Jeter." Leaning against the counter again with her in his arms, he asked, "What can you tell me about Colby?"

"He is a sweet kid. His mom is a single mom, like me. His parents divorced when he was about four years old. She was on medical disability for a while, and I know money has been really tight. I think the church has been helping them out." Sucking in her lips, her brow furrowed as she asked, "Is there something that I need to be worried about?"

"Babe, the time that you can stop worrying is now,

and it's certainly the time that Jack can stop as well. I'll take a look into things." Shifting her to his side, he led her toward the den where Jack and George were watching TV.

Smiling, she asked, "Have I told you recently that I think you're awesome?"

Stopping in the hall before they got to the den, he backed her up against the wall, nuzzled her neck, and whispered, "You can never tell me enough how awesome I am."

Throwing her arms around his neck, she plastered her front to his and said, "Well, you are."

Kissing her again, she mumbled against his lips. "And you're pretty awesome kisser as well."

Chuckling, they headed into the den and settled in, watching the game as a family.

25

Carrie slipped out of her bedroom, walked to Jack's door, and peeked in. Her son was fast asleep, and she quietly pulled his door closed and padded across the hall. Stepping through the doorway of the master bedroom, she was immediately engulfed in Colt's arms.

"He's asleep," she said.

Colt grinned. "Didn't figure you'd be over here if he wasn't."

She lifted her arms and placed her hands behind his neck, her body pressed tightly against his. Their lips met in a slow, languorous exploration. He caught her by surprise when he bent and slid one arm behind her knees and scooped her up into his arms, stalking toward the bed.

Each night, after Jack was asleep, she had slipped into Colt's room. Jack knew that she and Colt were in a relationship, but she was not ready to discuss with him how far the relationship had progressed. Lately, life had been so unpredictable, she wanted to make sure that Jack was in a good place and not confused.

It was hard to leave Colt's warm embrace, but she had been so thankful he understood. That was one of the things she loved about him…he cared greatly for Jack.

Now, all thoughts flew from her mind as Colt lay her on the bed. Looming over her, he dragged her sleep shorts down her legs, snagging her panties as he went. Tossing them to the side, he bent and kissed each calf, slowly working his way up her legs.

"Jesus, Carrie, I smell your need, and it's like fuckin' nectar."

She could not stop the giggle from erupting and said, "I swear, only a man would think arousal would smell as good as flowers."

He nipped the inside of her thighs, grazing the skin with his teeth, and said, "Better than flowers, babe."

She leaned up on the mattress, propping her upper body up on her elbows as she watched his dark head disappear between her legs. More butterfly kisses landed on her inner thighs, and she fought the urge to press her hips upward.

He lifted his head, speared her with his glance, and gently ordered, "Relax."

She flopped back onto the bed, allowing her legs to open widely, giving him full access. With the flat of his tongue, he licked her slit, and she gasped as shivers of delight moved through her. He worked his way toward her clit and inserted a finger into her channel, finding just the right spot to create the friction her inner core craved. She closed her eyes tightly, giving herself over to the physical sensations as her fingers clutched the bedcovers.

He continued to suck and lick until she thought she would go mad with wanting as her sex quivered under his ministrations. Just when she thought she could take it no more, she felt her body tighten, and she cried out, succumbing to the spasms of pleasure moving through her.

Her legs flopped open, and she barely felt the soft kisses as he moved over her mound, upward over her abdomen, circling around her belly button, before pushing her camisole upward. The material passed over her breasts, and he latched onto one engorged nipple, sucking hard.

As he took his time, she reached down and ran her fingers through his thick, black hair. She watched as he moved between both breasts, giving equal attention to them.

He lifted his head, and with a twinkle in his eye said, "You know, you've got the best pair of tits I've ever seen."

Barking out a laugh, she slapped her hand over her mouth to still her mirth. As he lowered his head and continued to suckle, she closed her eyes, once more giving over to the sensations he was drawing from her.

Unable to wait another moment, she begged, "Please, Colt. I need you. I need you inside now."

He crawled over her body further, dragging her

camisole over her head and tossing it onto the floor. Looming above, he shucked off his boxers, shifting his body so that he could pull them all the way off, and they landed close to her clothes. He grabbed the condom from his nightstand, but looking down at her, asked, "Are you on the pill?"

She nodded and said, "Yes. I've been on the pill for years."

"I know I'm the first man you've been with in a long time, and I get tested for my job, so I know I'm clean. And to be honest, it's been a while for me, too, and I've never gone ungloved. But I want you to be able to trust that, so we can get tested—"

"Colt, I trust you now. I couldn't be here in this house—with my son, in your bed—if I didn't trust you." He hesitated, and she watched as his dark eyes worked, thoughts moving behind them.

"What are you saying, babe?" he asked, his voice rough his gravel.

She reached her hands upward, clutching his shoulder, her fingers digging into his flesh. Her lips curved into a slow smile, and she said, "I'm saying I trust you to take care of me. And that includes trusting you to take care of my body. If you want nothing between us, that's fine with me."

He growled as he tossed the condom back to his side, moved his hand between her legs, spreading her arousal over her folds. With the tip of his cock at her entrance, he slowly entered, inch by inch.

She felt his fullness, but this time, it was different.

Flesh on flesh, his cock dragged along her inner core, and she gasped at the sense of fullness.

Looking up, she watched as his face appeared tortured, his eyes closed, his jaw tight. "Please, look at me, Colt."

His eyes jerked open and the air rushed from his lungs as he admitted, "I want to remember this moment. I want to remember how you look spread out on my bed, taking my body into yours. I never want to forget the gift you're giving me, and how I always want to strive to deserve it."

His words rushed over her, filling each deep and dark crevice. As he continued to push his cock deeper until he was fully seated, she clung to him, a tear sliding from her eye. When he was fully seated, she urged him to move, but he held steady. "Not going to rush this, Carrie."

Slowly, he pulled his cock out before gliding it back in again. Finding the rhythm she craved, he thrust, alternating between fast and slow until she was mad with longing. Lifting her legs higher, she dug her heels into his ass, clinging to his shoulders with her hands. The play of muscles underneath her fingertips gave proof to the magnificent body and power he held.

Her inner core tightened, and she urged him on, thrilled when he acquiesced. Suddenly, before she could have imagined, she came, her muscles quivering. He threw his head back, coming at the same time. She was fascinated, watching his face as he pulsed into her. The force of their climax took her breath away, and he gasped loudly, still pumping as though wringing every last drop from his body.

He finally dropped his chin, pierced her with his intense gaze, and said, "I love you, Carrie. Jesus, I never thought I could love anyone the way I love you." He rolled to the side, pulling her with him so that her body was still partially laying on his.

His words rang in her ears, but she hesitated. *Do confessions of love count if they were wrung from the depths of an orgasm?*

"Stop overthinking," he encouraged, giving her a squeeze. Tucking her closely, he said, "My words aren't because we had sex. Incredibly good sex, which blew my mind—"

She giggled at that but quieted as he continued.

"I think I began to fall for you the first time I saw you in Joe's Place. You got a rockin', smokin' hot body, but swear to God, it was your smile that knocked me on my ass."

Her grin still on her face, she admitted, "I noticed you, too. I thought you were the most handsome man I had ever seen. Tall, dark, kind of broody—"

"Broody?"

"Yeah… You know, the *'don't mess with me'* vibe that just made me want to take you home and take care of you."

He chuckled and shook his head, then shifted out of bed, stalking to the bathroom. Coming back a moment later with a warm, wet cloth, he gently cleaned between her legs. She climbed from the bed and snagged her panties, top, and sleep shorts. Once dressed, she turned toward him, and he wrapped her in his embrace.

"Lay here with me a while."

"I don't want to fall asleep," she said, her voice full of longing.

"Let's just enjoy each other for a little while longer. Jack always sleeps late." He held her gaze, and she slowly acquiesced. Climbing back into the bed, he added, "Sometime soon, you know, he's going to know we're in a serious relationship."

She snuggled closely as he curled his front around her back, tucking her in tightly to him. Her sated body relaxed, and she said, "Maybe, just maybe, I can let myself snooze here for a little while." After a moment, she whispered, "I love you, too, Colt."

A knock on the door caused Carrie to jolt awake, uncertain where she was. Sitting up quickly, she elbowed Colt in the chest, and he grunted as he jerked upward as well.

"Mom?" Jack's voice came from outside the master bedroom door.

"Oh, my God!" she whispered. "I can't believe I slept so late!"

Shoving the covers down, she hopped up, wishing she had her robe instead of just her t-shirt and sleep shorts as Colt said, "It's only three a.m., babe."

Realizing it was way earlier than Jack normally arose, all thoughts of a robe left her mind, and she rushed to the door, throwing it open. "What's wrong?" As the words left her mouth, she spied his pale face.

"Sorry to wake you, Mom, but I threw up."

Before he had a chance to say anything else, her hand snapped to his forehead, checking to see if he had a fever.

Shaking his head, he said, "I don't think I'm sick, because as soon as I threw up, I felt better."

"Well, you did have a lot of junk food tonight when we were watching the game." She suddenly stiffened, feeling Colt's presence right behind her back. He had one of his flannel shirts in his hand and slid it up her arms and over her shoulders. It hung to her thighs, and for a second she luxuriated in the soft feel and scent of his shirt on her.

"Hey, Buddy," Colt said, resting his hand on Carrie's shoulder. "I've got some Gatorade in the fridge if you think that would help. I don't have ginger ale, but it'd only take me a few minutes to run to the all-night mart and get some."

"You don't need to do that, Colt," Jack said. "I'm sure Gatorade would be good."

With a chin lift, Colt slid past them and into the hall, heading down toward the kitchen. She quickly buttoned the top of the shirt while watching her son carefully. He did not seem shocked or upset that she had been in Colt's room in the middle of the night. Nonetheless, she felt the need to say something. "Honey, I'm sorry that you had to go looking for me when you felt sick—"

Jack's brows lowered, and he said, "Why would I go looking for you? I figured you'd be here."

Now it was her turn to lower her brows, but before she had a chance to ask what he meant, he continued. "Mom, I'm practically a teenager, not some little kid. I know you and Colt are together, and couples sleep together."

Carrie was flabbergasted, unsure of what to address first. Finally blinking, she snapped, "You're eleven years old…that's not a teenager."

Colt had made it back to them, handing Jack the bottle of Gatorade. He placed his hand on Carrie's stomach and gently moved her backward into the master bedroom, clamping his other hand around the back of Jack's neck, and said, "Come on in, buddy. You can sip on the Gatorade, and we'll talk for a few minutes before we all go back to bed."

Carrie's eyes bugged out, but Colt simply leaned in, kissed her forehead, and said, "It's time. Trust me?"

She knew that the answer to that simple question was 'yes', but she also knew that he was not a parent. As her feet moved back toward the bed where she perched on the side, she also knew that Colt would never do anything to hurt them. And, since he had once been a boy, he might have more insight than she.

"Babe, take a breath and relax," Colt ordered gently.

She rolled her eyes, but Jack echoed, "Yeah, Mom. It's all cool."

"Jack," Colt began, "You're eleven years old, and you're right, that's not a little boy anymore. But then, you're also not a full-grown man yet. What you are is at the age where you're learning to become the kind of man you want to be, and the fact that your mom trusts me enough to help with that is a bigger honor than I ever thought I would have."

Just with his opening sentence, Carrie felt tears hit the back of her eyes and her shoulders relaxed, knowing that Colt would never do anything, or say anything, to hurt them.

Continuing, Colt said, "I would never disrespect your mom, and that includes taking advantage of her. A good man would never do that. When we talked earlier, we said we were like a family. You're not just extra. You don't just come along with the woman that I've fallen for. My feelings for you are strong, just on their own. Do you understand what I'm saying?"

Carrie's gaze shot over toward Jack, her heart clenching as she watched the easy smile on her son's face as he nodded.

"Good," Colt said. "So, just to make sure there're no misunderstandings, we're not just *like* a family. As far as I'm concerned, we *are* a family."

Jack sat up straighter, his shoulders back, his head held high. Twisting slightly, he looked at Carrie and said, "Mom, you're the greatest mom in the world. And I'm sorry that Peter was too chicken to take responsibility for you and me, but I don't want you to take that on. That's on him. But if I could pick the kind of dad I'd like to have and the kind of man I think you deserve, it would be Colt."

Unable to hold back, she wrapped her arms around her son and held him tightly as tears slid down her cheeks. Opening her eyes, she looked over Jack's head at Colt, seeing him swallow deeply, blinking as though to keep the moisture back as well.

After a moment, Jack squirmed and said, "You're squishing me."

Letting him go, she lifted her hands and swiped her tears away from her cheeks and said, "Moms are allowed to squish their eleven-year-old, almost a teenager, learning to be a man, kid who got sick in the middle of the night."

Wading in, Colt said, "On that note, I'd suggest you keep sipping the Gatorade and head back to bed."

Standing, Jack walked straight to Colt and threw his arms around Colt's waist. Colt did not hesitate, encircling Jack in a hug as well.

"Good night, Colt."

"Good night, buddy," Colt replied.

Carrie walked Jack back to his bedroom, twisted the cap on the Gatorade, and set it next to his nightstand. Looking down at him, she said, "You're probably too old for me to tuck you in, but can I just say that I think you're the greatest kid?"

He grinned up at her and said, "Yeah, you can tell me I'm great anytime you want to!"

She bent and kissed the top of his head and said, "I hope you can go back to sleep. If you get sick again, come find me."

Turning, she walked out of the room and flipped off his light, not hesitating to walk straight back to the master bedroom. Eyes on Colt, she walked straight into his arms, snuggling against his chest as he held her tightly.

"Family, huh?" she mumbled.

With his lips pressed against the top of her head, he asked, "Yeah. Is that okay?"

She leaned her head back and held his gaze, saying, "I think it's perfect."

Bending, he took her lips, the kiss soft and sweet and full of promise. He led her back to bed, tucking her carefully into his arms, and they both fell asleep once again.

26

At the end of the briefing, Colt told the team that they would be driving to the church to talk to the pastor and Brian Jeter.

Trevon shook his head and said, "Colt, this may be nothing more than some kids acting like badasses, thinking they're cool."

"It's not like we're going in guns blazing, Trevon," Colt said. Staring at his deputy who seemed to be dragging his feet, he wondered what Trevon was thinking.

Deciding to talk to him later, he turned to Hunter and said, "You're with me." Leaving the others to their assignments, he and Hunter headed down the road.

"What do you know about this church?" Colt asked.

"Not much. Being new here, there's a lot of this area that I'm still learning," Hunter said. "You grew up here… any thoughts?"

Shaking his head slowly, Colt said, "My father was the kind of man who liked his family in the pew every Sunday, but I can't say that he practiced what he heard preached. Plus, this church wasn't around back then. It's newer."

On the Eastern Shore, there were quite a few churches around, some of them older and others more modern, not affiliated with a particular denomination. They soon pulled into the almost empty parking lot of the one-story brick building that housed the church offices and a large industrial size building that held the sanctuary. Entering the door leading to the church offices, they encountered a round, pleasant-faced woman who asked, "Hello. May I help you?"

"We were hoping to speak to Pastor Hackett. Is he here today?"

Her smile remained on her face as she nodded and said, "Please, follow me." She walked over to a door, knocked on it, and stuck her head in, saying, "Allen, the Sheriff is here to speak to you."

She opened the door wider, her smile beaming as she allowed Colt and Hunter to enter.

The office had carpet, but it was not plush. The desk was wooden but not opulent. The chairs appeared comfortable and slightly worn.

Alan Hackett stood, his smile wide as he greeted them. "It's good to see you," he said. "Sit, please. How can I help you?"

Colt observed the pastor's clear eyes focused on him and Hunter.

"We'd like to get some information about the youth camp," Hunter began.

Nodding, Pastor Hackett said, "I don't know if you ever went to church as a child, but many churches used to have something for a week or two for the children, calling it Vacation Bible School. It was a great way to give the kids a chance to have games and activities during the summer, and it gave churches an outreach to a lot of families who might not normally come to church. But it was only for the younger kids. Brian suggested this year that we have something for the middle and high schoolers as well. I confess, I liked the idea, but couldn't figure out how I could put anything else on my plate. But when he suggested that he handle it, I was more than happy for him to do so." Tilting his head to the side, he asked, "Is there a problem?"

Shaking his head, Colt said, "Not a problem, per se, but we're doing some investigations and wanted to cover all of our bases as to what some of the youth in the county are doing the summer."

Hunter asked, "What can you tell us about Brian?"

Pastor Hackett's brows lowered slightly, and he replied, "Well, he's fairly new to our church and does not serve in an official capacity, although I suppose for the summer he's almost like an intern."

"Did he come with references? A background check?"

Shaking his head slowly, Pastor Hackett said, "He did come with references, and I called two of them. I didn't do a background check. I know that's something that a lot of churches are doing, but I just haven't started checking up on the people who want to offer their services to God."

Colt kept a poker face while Hunter visibly startled. "You do listen to the news, right? There are a lot of people who are working with children in churches who should never be."

Eyes wide, Pastor Hackett asked, "Oh, my…is that what this is about?"

Holding up his hand toward the pastor while shooting Hunter a glare, Colt said, "No. We have an ongoing investigation, and we're gathering information. But no, that is not what this is about."

Shoulders slumping in obvious relief, the pastor said, "Thank God."

"What else can you tell us about Brian?" Colt prodded.

"He's incredibly enthusiastic and has run the whole program," Pastor Hackett said, seemingly more relaxed. "Obviously, I'm here. I enjoy having the youth in our church, and it gives us an opportunity to grow our membership. As you know, many people are leaving some of the traditional churches, preferring more independent churches that are not mired down in the politics that can occur with a national denomination. I feel like we've been able to reach many of the youth in this county who might not otherwise have come to church."

"Is he working as a paid employee of the church?" Colt asked.

Shaking his head, Pastor Hackett replied, "No. There is a small stipend for helping run the camp, but he's not paid a salary." The pastor shifted in his seat, and said, "I understand about ongoing investigations, and I'm sure there are things you can't tell me, but you have to realize your line of questioning is giving me concern."

Colt weighed how much to say, then decided to give

the pastor a little bit of information. "I'm sure you've read in the news that we have had a string of robberies in the county. They seem to be drug-related, and we are simply following a line of investigation that they could be perpetrated by young people. Right now, we're looking at any particular gatherings of young people where we might be able to get some information."

Nodding, Pastor Hackett said, "Well, I'm sure Brian would be more than happy to talk to you."

"One more thing," Colt said. "How much do you know about Billy Neiman and John Roster?"

Pastor Hackett's affable face changed, and he sighed heavily. "As I told you, I was very excited when Brian wanted to encourage a middle school and high school program for the summer. Some of our high school youth work part-time jobs, but many of them don't. I've got nothing against those two young men, but I've had to talk to them several times about the way they speak to others. I wouldn't go so far as to say they are bullies, but certainly, they have had some bullying tactics."

"Have you talked to Brian about your concerns?" Hunter asked.

Continuing to nod, Pastor Hackett said, "Yes, I have. He seems to think that by befriending the boys, they'll learn by example." Sighing heavily again with his shoulders slumping, he said, "I hope so."

The three men stood, the officers thanking him and then the pastor encouraged them to go into the sanctuary where he knew Brian was working on an activity for the next camp day.

As they left, he said, "Be sure to tell Trevon hello for me."

Colt looked at him, and the pastor explained, "He's one of our regular members."

Colt and Hunter walked out of the brick building and headed toward the larger industrial building that housed the sanctuary.

"Did you know Trevon went to this church?" Hunter asked.

Shaking his head, Colt said, "No. He didn't mention anything. Of course, where a man chooses to worship is not my concern, but it's strange he didn't mention it, considering I asked him to do some investigation."

Walking into the sanctuary, they found Brian with his poster boards spread out and a paintbrush in his hand. He looked up and smiled and said, "Sheriff, nice to see you."

Colt introduced Hunter and said, "We were just talking to Pastor Hackett and would like to ask you a few questions in regards to an ongoing investigation."

Brian nodded, his smile firmly in place. "Well, I'm not sure how I can help, but I'd be more than willing to try."

"I'm curious as to the interest you had in running this camp, considering it's not a paid position."

Brian's eyes widened at the question but said, "I grew up in Southwest Virginia in a very rural, depressed county, similar to this. The church was really important to me growing up because I have to say that my home life was not great. After high school, I had a job at a YMCA where I was able to work with young people and discovered that I really liked it. I came to the Eastern Shore with a friend one time for a fishing trip and fell in love with the area. I have an application in at the YMCA in Accawmacke, but they don't anticipate having a position for me until the fall when they have someone transferring." Shrugging, he said, "I met Pastor Hackett, really liked this church, and thought that maybe during the summer I could work with the youth here."

Nodding, Colt said, "We're investigating some crimes in the area that we suspect might be perpetrated by young people. What can you tell us about Billy Neiman and John Roster?"

Unlike Pastor Hackett's sigh of resignation at the sound of those two names, Brian appeared to brighten. "I know that they can be very off-putting, and I do have to watch them when they're talking to the younger ones. But they're the kind of youth I feel like I can make a difference with. Neither comes from a good home, and both have built-in anger issues. But I truly feel like by befriending them and being a mentor to them, I can make a difference in their lives."

"What kind of difference are you hoping to make?" Hunter asked.

"The kind where they can have goals that lead them out of the poverty they been brought up in."

Colt asked, "What kind of goals?"

Brian's face scrunched in thought as he said, "Nothing that you probably haven't heard before, but perhaps they haven't. Things like short-term goals leading to long-term goals. Deciding that they want to have a life that's different than the one they were brought up in. The kind of life where people don't look down on them just because they're poor. But I want them to have a work ethic to know that if they work hard, they can move ahead."

After talking for several more minutes, they took their leave of Brian and walked back out to the SUV. Climbing inside, Hunter said, "I've got to tell you, I don't know what to think about him."

"I know what you mean," Colt agreed. "Brian's words match up, but they can be interpreted in different ways. He could either be of great benefit to those young men, or he's leading them toward financial goals with illegal activities."

27

Jack had enjoyed the science experiments that Tad had them work on that day, but thoughts of Colby continued to run through his mind. His friend had not come to camp, and it was the first day that he had missed it. As the other students left, Jack dragged his feet, knowing that his mom was going to be a few minutes late picking him up.

"Jack, what's got you looking so down in the dumps?" Tad asked, walking over to him.

Looking up at the young teacher, he smiled and shrugged. "Just got a lot on my mind, I guess."

Sitting on the stool next to Jack, Tad asked, "Anything I can help with?"

Shaking his head at first, he then asked, "Do you know where Colby is today?"

"He was here first thing this morning but said he didn't feel good. His mom was at work and couldn't come pick him up, so I had Billy take him home."

"Billy?"

"Yes, he's already eighteen and a good driver." Hurrying to add, Tad said, "I got permission from his mom first."

Jack was quiet for a moment, and Tad asked, "I take it you don't care for Billy?"

"I just don't like him very much," Jack admitted. "Yesterday, I even overheard he and Johnny saying mean stuff to Colby."

Eyes wide, Tad gasped and said, "Mean stuff? Like what?"

"Oh, you know, just bully stuff. Like they always do."

Shaking his head, Tad looked off into the distance and said, "I'm sure that must have been upsetting."

"Colby didn't want me to say anything, but I can't just sit back and let something happen to a friend of mine. I want to stay after him until he lets me know what's going on."

Nodding, Tad said, "I think that makes you a good friend. Tell you what, I'll call Colby in just a few minutes once you're picked up and make sure that he's okay. I'll also let him know that he can talk to me anytime he needs to."

"Thanks, Mr. Jameson," Jack said. Waving goodbye, he walked down the hall to the main front doors of the school to wait for his mom.

The front of the building was hot, the summer sun beaming down directly, sending heat waves rising from the asphalt. Jack walked over toward the side, where some trees cast a bit of shade. As he turned the corner of the building, he heard voices and instinctively stayed in the shadows.

He could see Colby standing near a black pickup truck with Billy leaning over him. Even from a distance, he could see Colby's pale face, shaking his head back and forth. Billy's face held anger, and just as Jack was about to go into the building to get help, he heard a door from the side open and Mr. Jameson call out, "Get going! Get him out of here!"

The door slammed shut, and Jack tried to make sense of what he was hearing and seeing. *If Mr. Jameson was supposed to check on Colby, why was he yelling at Billy to get him out of there?*

"Get in the Goddamn truck!" Billy yelled. Jack watched John Roster climb out of the passenger door of the pickup truck, grab Colby's arm and drag him around, forcing Colby up into the truck. Billy and John stood to the side, seeming to be in deep discussion.

Still staying within the shadows of the building, Jack moved closer, his hand in his pocket on his cell phone. As he came up onto the side of the truck, he could see an old tarp in the back. Uncertainty filled him, but he knew he could not let Colby down. *What would Colt do?* He knew the answer to that… Colt would jump into action, ready to save the day.

Without giving the situation any more thought, he scrambled into the bed of the pickup truck, covered himself with the tarp, then called his mom, just as Billy and John got back into the truck.

Carrie was close to the middle school, having left the

diner late when one of the seasonal servers had not come into work on time. That was one of the reasons that Joe and Mavis employed her, BettyJo, and Brenda full-time, even paying them extra so they could afford healthcare. Seasonal help was a necessity but often unreliable with some of the people they hired.

Her phone rang, and she saw that it was from Jack. Connecting, she answered, "Hey, sweetie. I'm on my way, almost there."

"Mom!"

His voice sounded excited but muffled. "Jack? I can barely hear you."

"Mom, listen! I'm in the back of the truck because Billy was forcing Colby into it."

Not understanding what he was talking about, she said, "Jack, slow down. I don't know what you're trying to tell me. Can't it wait till I get there?"

"No, Mom! Billy Neiman was forcing Colby to get into his truck, and Mr. Jameson told him to. He was threatening him! I climbed into the back of the truck because I don't want them to get away!"

Still trying to figure out what Jack was telling her, her heart began to pound as she realized whatever was happening, her son was upset. "Jack, are you telling me you're in the back of a moving pickup truck?"

"Yes, Mom, I'm hiding."

"Where are you?"

"I don't know. We just pulled out of the middle school parking lot and turned to the right."

"Okay, Jack, I'm going to call Colt, but first, tell me exactly what happened."

Jack said, "I talked to Colt last night about Colby being threatened by Billy Neiman. I don't know what's going on, but something's not right. Then today, I saw Billy and John grab Colby and force him into the pickup truck. Then I heard Mr. Jameson yell for them to take him away. I didn't have time to call, and I didn't want them to get away, so I jumped into the back of the pickup truck, and I'm hiding under a tarp."

"What does the truck look like?"

He rattled off the license number and said, "It's a black Ford pickup truck. It looks kind of new."

"Jack, you stay hidden and stay low. I'm calling Colt right now and then I'll call you back."

Disconnecting, she had made it to the middle school parking lot and quickly turned around before turning back to the right. Hitting speed dial for Colt's number, she prayed he would pick up.

"Hey, babe—"

"Jack is in trouble. I need your help!"

"I'm putting you on speaker. What's going on?"

"He said something was going on with Colby and Billy Neiman. I don't know what's happening, but he said Billy was forcing Colby to get into his truck and they drove off."

"Okay, babe, I'm on it—"

"That's not all, Colt! Jack told me he didn't want Colby to be alone, so he climbed into the back of Billy's pickup truck and is hiding under a tarp. Colt, they're driving down the road and Jack's in the back of the truck!" As she said the words, the gravity of the situation finally hit in her heart pounded in fear.

"Fuck! We're on our way, I'm calling it in."

"He said that they just left the middle school and turned right, so they must be going south on Highway Thirteen," she added, before giving him the license number of Billy's truck that Jack had given to her. "I was on my way to pick him up, so I'm trying to find them now."

"Carrie, just stop and let us handle it."

"No fucking way. You do what you've got to do, but my child could be in danger. I've got to call him back." Heart racing, Carrie pressed her luck and sped down the road, her eyes scanning for a big black pickup truck. Unfortunately, in rural areas, there were lots of big black pickup trucks, even though the road was not overly crowded.

Dialing Jack again, her heart leaped when he answered. "Baby, are you okay?"

"Yeah, Mom. I'm fine. I'm beginning to think that I didn't think this through all the way. I don't know what I'll do when we get somewhere, but honestly, Mom, I couldn't let Colby hang out there by himself."

"Colt is on his way, and he's called it in. Do you think you're still on Highway Thirteen?"

"Yeah. We haven't turned off anywhere yet. Oh, wait a minute, he's slowing down. We're turning, Mom. We're turning to the right again. Let me see if I can tell where we are."

"Jack, stay down. Please, stay down."

At first, all she could hear was rustling and then after a moment, he said, "Mom, I peeked up. We turned at the gas station that Joe always complains has the prices too high. The Gas and More."

"Okay, now stay down. I'm calling that into Colt."

Wishing she had two phones and more than two hands, she knew she was breaking laws trying to call and drive at the same time. Not giving Colt a chance to answer, as soon as the phone connected, she said, "Colt—"

"Carrie, you've got Hunter. I'm putting you on speaker."

"Jack said that they just turned right by the Gas and More."

"Carrie, I've got you in my sight. I want you to pull off at the gas station and let me pass you. I've got other units responding, and I don't want you in the middle of this."

She agreed, but only because she did not want to do anything to hinder Colt getting to Jack. Seeing the Sheriff's SUV in her rearview mirror, she flipped on her blinker and pulled off at the Gas and More, watching as Colt and Hunter turned on the street right next to it.

She hesitated, uncertain what to do. Two more sheriff's vehicles turned and followed Colt, and she waited, anxiously, surprised after a moment that two more came as well. Dialing Jack, her breath was shallow as she waited for him to answer, but the call went to voicemail.

28

The pickup truck came to a stop, and Jack lay still, listening. His heart was pounding, and he wondered, not for the first time, about the choice he had made to climb into the back of the truck. Before he had a chance to ponder the situation further, he heard a door open, and Billy said, "The old lady's gone. Found that out at the church. She's off visiting somebody for a few days."

Jack could hear sniffling and wondered if it came from Colby. His suspicion was verified when he heard Colby's shaky voice say, "I don't want to do this. I don't want to be here."

"Well, you're here, so suck it up," John retorted.

Jack heard multiple footsteps walk away from the truck and leaned up, ever so slightly, peeking out from underneath the tarp to see that the truck was parked outside a single house on a small road. Billy and Johnny were moving toward the front door, each with their hands around Colby's upper arms, dragging him forward. Billy pulled something from his pocket, jammed it into the doorframe, and with a quick pop, the front door swung open.

Gasping, he realized he was watching a robbery taking place...*just like at George's house!* Billy disappeared inside, still dragging Colby along with him, while John turned and leaned his back against the front of the house. With his arms crossed in front of him, John kept watch.

Darn! He's watching so I can't get out! Pulling out his phone, he sent a text to both Colt and his mom. **At yellow house. Number fourteen. Billy took Colby inside.**

His phone vibrated, and he looked down as his mom texted in return. **Colt on his way.** Just as he read that, his phone vibrated again, Colt replying. **Stay out of sight. On my way.**

Breathing a sigh of relief, he startled when he heard footsteps coming back toward the truck.

"Did you get it?" he heard John ask.

"Easy," Billy replied. "Wasn't it, kid?"

He could hear Colby crying, "This isn't right. You shouldn't take that."

"Jesus, this is easy," Billy replied. "Quit crying. The old lady isn't out of anything. The pharmacy will send her new pills, so she'll be fine. Hell, if she doesn't lock her house any better than that, we might make a return visit."

Jack heard the truck doors opening and slamming again and prayed that Colt was nearby. The engine started, and they pulled out of the driveway, bouncing him as Billy hit potholes. Once on the road, he could tell they were not speeding. At first, surprised that Billy was not gunning the truck away, he realized that Billy was probably trying to not draw any undue attention to himself.

The truck made a few turns, but he had no idea where they were, hating that he could not alert Colt to their location. He had not been able to discern any conversation from the cab of the truck, but suddenly could hear John shout, "Shit!"

Wondering what was happening, his heart pounded, fear and uncertainty tearing through him.

Colt's heart was beating harder than he ever remembered, horrific scenarios running through his mind. *The truck crashing with Jack unprotected in the back. Billy discovering Jack and needing to keep him quiet. Billy and John turning on the two younger boys.*

"Hold on, man," Hunter said. "Just remember, we gotta do everything by the book."

Hunter's words bounced off Colt, and he wondered if he would be able to keep from wringing Billy and John's necks when he finally got to them.

Hunter was in contact with the other deputies that were following, and Colt knew he was putting roadblocks in place at either end of the road. When patrolling the county, they had a large, spread out, rural area, but he knew that he was a helluva lot better off than other rural law enforcers. For Colt, east and west were the Atlantic Ocean and the Chesapeake Bay. South was the Chesapeake Bay Bridge Tunnel, and Hunter had already alerted the Tunnel Authority so that the black truck would not be able to get onto the bridge. Liam had been notified to the north, so that meant Billy had very few places to run.

Hunter called out, "Over there. Dead ahead," just as Colt's gaze landed on a black pickup truck driving slowly toward them. Colt glanced in the rearview mirror, seeing another deputy's car pulling behind him. As Hunter signaled, they moved beside him, creating a roadblock. With flat farmland on either side of the road, he prayed that Billy would slow down and come to a stop, not attempting anything stupid that could harm Jack in the back of the pickup.

Heart in his throat, he finally breathed a sigh of relief as the black pickup truck slowed to a halt. Jumping from the SUV, he stalked toward the truck with Hunter right on his tail. Deputies had come behind Billy's truck, completely cutting off his escape route.

As Billy climbed from the driver seat, he shouted, "What's the problem? We were just giving Colby a ride to church."

As Colt approached, he watched Colby's wide-eyed, pale face as Billy continued to question why he was being harassed.

With a sardonic edge to his voice, Hunter asked, "Is that right? Just a little drive in the country? Being a good Samaritan and giving a ride to a kid?"

Colby looked between Hunter and Colt, his mouth opening, but shutting quickly as Billy growled, "Shut it, kid."

Suddenly, just as Colt reached the truck, the tarp shifted to the side, and Jack popped his head up from the bed. Colt felt as though his knees would hit the concrete. Until he had taken Carrie and Jack into his heart, he had never been afraid to do his job, but now knew what true fear was.

Jack bolted from the back bed of the truck, his feet hitting the asphalt road, a shaky grin on his face.

Billy turned around, stammering, "Wh…what the hell? Where…where did you come from?"

Jack looked up at Colt and said, "You don't know how glad I am to see you!"

Colt felt relief pouring off Jack as much as himself. He grabbed Jack up in a bear hug, not caring if it embarrassed him or not.

Jack immediately said, "I saw Billy and John force Colby into the truck. And then they went to some lady's house and broke in. They said they stole her pills."

By that time, the other deputies had gotten Colby and John out of the cab of the truck, frisking each of them, finding the pill bottles in John's pockets. They began putting handcuffs on the two older boys.

Jack looked up and said, "Colby wasn't doing anything, Colt. He was forced to go with them."

"I understand that, Jack," he said. "We're going to have to take everyone into the station where we can get statements from each of you. That includes you too, okay?"

Jack nodded but startled when he suddenly said, "Mom?"

"We're going to call her right now, buddy."

Jack walked over to Colt's SUV, greeted Hunter, and climbed into the backseat, buckling his seatbelt. Colt slid behind the steering wheel, already having Carrie on the phone. "I've got them, babe. He's good. He's fine. We're heading back to the station, and you can meet us there."

As soon as Colt disconnected with Carrie, Jack began telling what had happened. Colt stopped him and said, "Hang on, buddy. Once we get to the station, then you're going to need to go over all of this. And I'll be listening, but I can't be taking charge since you and I are involved."

Colt glanced into the rearview mirror, seeing Jack nod. It did not take long to drive back to Easton, and Colt spied Carrie's car in the front of the parking lot. "Looks like we've got a welcome party," he said.

By the time Jack climbed out of the backseat, Carrie was already running over. Dropping to her knees, she pulled her son into a hug. After a moment, her eyes snapped open, and she stood, her hands on Jack's shoulders and said, "Don't you ever scare me like that again!"

Jack looked up and said, "Mom, I'm sorry I scared you, but I had to do something. I just couldn't let them take Colby away."

Colt stepped up, knowing that Carrie, Jack, and he had a lot to talk about later, but for now, he said, "We need to head inside so we can get everyone's statements."

They walked up the steps and into the reception area, both Carrie and Jack's eyes darting around. Hunter took the lead, and they followed through several security doors and back into a large room with many desks inside.

Colt turned to Jack and explained, "Hunter is the lead detective in this investigation. He and Detective Perez are going to have you give a statement of what you know. Then they're going to talk to Colby. They're also going to be interviewing Billy and John separately."

As he looked at Jack, he had to fight a grin, seeing the excitement on the boy's face. Bending slightly so that he could look into Jack's eyes without appearing to treat him like a little boy, he added, "Jack, just know that I'm very proud of you. Right now, make sure you keep to the facts and tell them exactly what happened."

Nodding, Jack said, "I get it, Colt. I can do that." A few minutes later, Hunter walked into the room, his eyes moving past Colt and Carrie. They landed on Jack, and he smiled slightly. "Okay, Jack. Follow me."

Colt watched as Carrie's gaze followed Jack's every step he took until he disappeared behind a door. Wrapping his arms around her, he pulled her in close, kissing her forehead. "Babe, I know you're freaked. Take a deep breath. He's fine. He's with us. And he is a fuckin' hero."

Carrie's head jerked back as her eyes sought his and said, "Colt! He put himself at risk. In danger. I mean, anything could've happened—"

"I know, babe," he said. "And I'm going to talk to him, man to man, about what to do when faced with a dangerous situation in the future. But honestly, he did really good. He was worried about his friend and not willing to let his friend hang out there by himself."

Carrie did not reply but burrowed in closer to him.

Finally, she sighed heavily and asked, "What happens now?"

"For Jack, Hunter needs to ask him questions and get his official statement. Basically, Jack will explain what he heard, what he saw, and what he did."

"And Colby?"

"Colby's mom is being called and should be here soon. If what Jack is saying is true, that Colby was forced into the truck and was being forced to go along with what happened, then he'll be released to his mom."

"Colt, when he called me, he said something about Mr. Jameson," she said. He did not reply, and Carrie continued to hold his gaze. "Do you think he knew what the boys were going to do?"

"I can't talk about an active investigation, sweetheart, but I will say that my detectives will find out from Billy and John exactly what's going on."

"Oh," she said, and he smiled as her soft voice hit him in the gut like it always did.

Trevon signaled for him, and he said, "Babe, stay here for a while. If you need anything, then let someone know. I'm going to be in the observation room. They'll bring Jack out to you as soon as he's finished and then the two of you can go on home."

"You'll be late?" she asked, her face already resigned.

Nodding, he sighed. "Yeah, I want to see this one out, so I'll be home whenever I can get finished."

She lifted up on her toes and kissed him lightly. "Okay, honey." As her heels lowered back to the floor, she gave him a squeeze and said, "Thank you for bringing my son back to me."

With her soft kiss and sweet voice wrapping around him, he headed toward Trevon but looked forward to when he could get back home to them.

A few minutes later, Carrie observed Colby's mom, Janice, being ushered in. Her face was pale, and her hands clutched her purse as the officer escorted her through the back hallway.

"Can I get you anything?"

Carrie jolted at the voice next to her, having focused on the door Jack had gone through, and looked around to see one of the officers.

"Oh, I'm sorry. I didn't even hear you come up. Thank you, but no, I'm fine."

"I'm Deputy Lisa Purdue," she said, sticking her hand out in greeting.

"I'm Carrie Beaumont."

Smiling widely, Lisa said, "I know. I hope I'm not speaking out of turn when I say that we have all been rooting for you and Colt. He's a good man, and we're really happy he's with you."

Surprised, Carrie smiled in return. "I agree he's a good man. I'm very lucky."

With her head tilted slightly to the side, Lisa replied, "I'd say you're both lucky."

Just then, the door in the back of the room opened, and she watched as Jack was escorted toward her, Hunter at his side. Her gaze scanned her son's face, searching to get a hold of what emotion was coming from him. He did not appear upset, but somewhat more…contemplative. This was not his typical expression, and her concern was heightened. She forced her hands to stay at her sides instead of reaching out to him the way she needed but knew he would not want.

Before she had a chance to speak, Hunter said, "We're all done, Carrie. Jack did really great. You should be proud of him."

Smiling down at Jack, she said, "I am."

"Of course, Jack can talk to you," Hunter instructed. "But this is an active investigation, so we have impressed upon him the importance of not talking about everything at this time to anyone other than family."

She nodded her agreement, her mind full of questions but deciding to ask Jack when they were alone. She stuck out her hand toward Hunter, and he shook it firmly.

"Don't worry, Carrie. It's all going to be fine."

"I know that Colt is going to be late, but can you let him know that we're on our way home now?"

"Will do," Hunter replied.

She nodded her goodbye toward Lisa as well and was about to turn toward the door when Jack halted. He faced Hunter and stuck out his hand, giving it a firm shake. "Thank you, Detective Simmons," Jack said.

Carrie observed the two, struck by how mature Jack appeared at that moment. Wondering if her heart could take in anything else that day, she said softly, "Let's go home, Jack."

He smiled, and the two of them walked outside,

climbing into her car. Once behind the wheel, she felt her hands begin to shake, emotions crashing into her.

Jack reached over and placed his smaller hand on one of hers that was resting on the steering wheel. "Mom, it's okay. We are all fine, and we're going home."

Her trembling lips curved into a smile, and she asked, "How did you get so smart?"

"Because I've got you for a mom," he replied. "Because you always gave me good people in my life to help me be smart."

A snort slipped out, and she shook her head. "Okay, I guess with that answer, we'll have dessert before dinner tonight."

With an excited yelp and a fist pump from him, she laughed, watching her son bounce between youth and manhood.

29

Colt walked out of the sheriff's building and climbed into the passenger seat of the SUV. Hunter, behind the wheel, turned and looked at him, asking, "Are you sure you want to do this?"

"I'm not going to fuck anything up," Colt said. "And it's not that I don't trust you and the others to do the right thing. But yeah, I'm going to be there."

He had watched as Colby gave his statement before being released to his mom. Then he went to the observation room and watched as Hunter and Elizabeth grilled Billy first, then John. John was still seventeen years old, and when his dad showed up, he was furious with his son. Billy, on the other hand, had just turned eighteen, which meant they dealt with him as an adult.

With the information from Jack and Colby, Hunter had turned up the heat on both of the others. Billy clammed up until faced with the reality that John was giving it all up. With the offer of a possible deal, Billy confessed as well, giving them what they needed.

Afraid their prey might be getting away, they headed to one of the neighborhoods outside of Baytown along with several deputy's cars. Colt was impressed with the properties in the neighborhood, each backing onto inlet waters.

Hunter said, "We knew he lived here from already checking into him, but these houses are impressive for someone on a teaching salary."

Seeing their destination, Colt saw a car parked outside in the driveway and hoped that their suspect was still inside. Following behind his detectives and deputies, he allowed them to take the lead, knowing he needed to keep himself in check. Two of the deputies headed around to the back of the house while Hunter and Elizabeth knocked on the front door, announcing who they were.

Shouts were soon heard from the back, and leaving two more deputies in the front, Hunter, Elizabeth, and Colt raced around the house. The deputies had their guns drawn on Tad. A quick glance from Colt showed that Tad had a boat tied up on his own personal dock, and with a suitcase at his feet, it was not too difficult to assume the young teacher was making a water escape.

Tad's hands were up, his eyes narrowed as he looked around at the law enforcement circling him. As Elizabeth read him his rights, he sneered and said, "I want my lawyer."

Colt walked nearer, feeling Hunter's heat at his back. "You play it smart, don't you fuckin' try to play us."

"I've got nothing to say to you, Sheriff."

Leaning in, keeping his voice steady, Colt said, "You put my son in danger. I'm going to fuckin' see you buried." Turning, he stalked away, calling out, "Search everything he's got. House, possessions, boat, accounts…everything. Finish tying up this case with a big fuckin' bow."

Two deputies loaded Tad into the back of their vehicle, taking him to the jail in Easton. Colt entered the house but stayed out of the way, allowing his detectives and deputies to do their job.

Several hours later, he and Hunter drove back to the station. By late evening, Colt sat next to Hunter across the table from Tad and his lawyer. Hunter had laid out the evidence they had gathered, and he fought to keep the grin off his face is it was obvious Tad slowly realized his freedom was slipping away.

"You won't get out of going to prison," Colt said, "and the District Attorney is looking at the drug charges, but also contributing to the delinquency of a minor and gang activity, as well as accessories to arson, kidnapping, assault, murder and whatever else we can throw at you. You give us the names so we know where you sent the drugs, you might be able to work some kind of deal." Looking at the attorney, he added, "I would strongly advise you talk to your client."

The attorney sighed and looked over at Tad before turning back to Colt and Hunter, saying, "I have done so, Sheriff. My client is ready to talk."

It was the middle of the night before Colt got home. Just like in years past, the house was quiet, seemingly empty when he first walked in. But immediately, he was struck with the difference now. Jack's baseball glove and shoes were near the back door. George's jacket was hanging on the back of one of the kitchen chairs. Carrie's purse was sitting on the kitchen counter, a note next to it.

Walking over, his eyes scanned the note, and following its instructions, he moved to the refrigerator. Opening the door, he spied that it was no longer empty as it used to be, but was filled with food. There, wrapped in cellophane, was some cold fried chicken and a beer setting near the front, just for him.

He pulled out a couple of pieces of chicken, quickly eating them and washing them down with the beer, not sure when he had last eaten. With a quick clean-up, he headed up the stairs. Jack's door was closed, but he opened it quietly, peeking inside. The room was dark, but with the light coming in from behind him in the hall, he could see that Jack was sprawled across the bed, sound asleep. He hated that he had not had a chance to talk to Jack more today but was glad that he was not awake and worrying.

Moving across the hall, he walked into the master bedroom, his gaze landing on Carrie in his bed. Unlike Jack, she was not asleep, but her eyes focused on his.

"I heard you come in but thought you might need a few minutes of quiet to yourself," she said softly, tossing back the sheet, climbing from the bed. She walked straight to him, encircling his waist with her arms, laying her cheek next to his heartbeat.

He inhaled deeply, breathing her in, knowing she was giving him exactly what he needed. "Appreciate it, baby," he mumbled against her hair.

"Are you okay? Is there anything I can do for you?"

He thought back to what he told her about falling in love with her smile. But it finally became clear to him that it wasn't just her smile but the way she wanted to take care of those in her life. She was not peppering him with questions about the case but wanted to know if there was anything he needed.

"Right here, Carrie, this is all I need." He stood with his arms wrapped around her for several more minutes, then asked, "I know Jack is sleeping now, but did he have trouble finding it?"

She leaned back and held his gaze, saying, "George was waiting on us when we got home, and we let Jack talk to us while we had dinner. I think it was good for him to just talk. He was upset about what had happened but was more worried about Colby. I let him know that Colby's mom was with him, and he seemed glad about that. After dinner, he was kind of quiet, but he went outside and pitched into his net for a while. I figured the physical activity was good for him."

Nodding, he agreed. "I'll talk to him tomorrow, just to make sure he understands what's happening. For now, I'll just let you know that Tad confessed to leading some teens to perpetrate the medication robberies."

She sucked her lips in, and he pressed her face back against his chest, feeling her arms tighten about his waist even more.

"Go on back to bed, baby, and I'll be there soon. I

want to take a quick shower, then the only thing I want to do is curl around you as I fall asleep."

She squeezed him again, then let go. Lifting on her toes, she placed a kiss on the underside of his jaw before turning and moving back to the bed. Taking a quick shower, he knew the best thing about coming home to a house that was full of life was crawling into bed next to Carrie.

The next morning, Colt met with the other law enforcement leaders. Mitch, Hannah, Liam, Dylan, and Wyatt drove to Easton and were now ensconced in one of the small conference rooms.

"Tad Jameson has been cultivating a few young, needy kids to break into houses and steal medication. Once the bottles were disposed of, the medication couldn't be traced back to the victims."

"Who was his next-in-line contact for the drugs?" Mitch asked.

"Right now, he hasn't given up a name," Colt replied, shooting a glance toward Liam. "But he's indicated that it's in Accawmacke County."

Jaw tight, dropping his chin to his chest, Liam shook his head. "Fuckin' hell. As soon as that asshole gives up a name—"

"You'll be the first to know," Colt assured.

"So, none of this had anything to do with the pawn shop thefts?" Hannah asked.

"Turns out that one of the teens, Billy, was stupid

and took a few items besides the medication. He didn't tell Tad but had another friend take them to the pawn shop. He got scared and decided to try to get them back. It was a friend of his sister's that worked at Pearl's, and he convinced her to put the items in the front and walk away one night without lowering the security screen. As soon as she left, he broke through the window and grabbed the items. So, Jonas and Tom Pearl weren't involved."

"What about the pharmacy delivery driver? Will Penland?" Dylan asked.

"Seems he was not involved either. He and Tad are not close, but they know each other. That was actually how Tad got the idea. Will was describing his job, and Tad realized how easy it would be to steal from older people and shut-ins. They generally have a lot of prescription drugs but little home security."

"You also suspected the youth group leader from the church," Wyatt said.

Nodding, Colt replied, "It seems that Tad was good at using his contacts. He was also friends with Brian Jeter. He encouraged the teens that were working for him to join the youth group. Brian, not realizing he was being quizzed, was giving information about some of the older members of the church that might be away visiting relatives, alerting them to the possible targets of empty houses."

"And George? The fire?" Mitch asked. "Was that just an attempt to deal with him since he had awoken and could possibly identify someone?"

Continuing to nod, Colt said, "In all the other

robberies, they were able to get in and out without the person waking. In George's case, he came out of the bedroom and startled them. They hit him and then ran, escaping. Later, they were afraid that he might be able to identify them."

Hannah, her eyes scanning the report in front of her, asked, "And Colby?"

"With Billy already being eighteen years old, Tad wanted to recruit someone younger. Using the information from Brian about Colby's family, he knew there was a financial need, and if he could get Colby involved in a few of the thefts, he could frighten him into continuing to work for him."

"He didn't count on Colby's best friend being Jack," Wyatt grinned.

Chuckling, Colt shook his head. "You got that right. Jack wasn't about to let his best friend have a problem without him being ready to jump in."

"You ready to take that on permanently?" Mitch asked, one eyebrow lifted.

Colt leaned back in his seat, rubbing his hand over his chin, nodding, he grinned. "I can't think of a better son to claim than Jack. I can't think of a better woman to have at my back than Carrie."

The group stood, scooting their chairs back, and Colt said, "And speaking of that, who's ready to have lunch at The Diner?"

Ten minutes later, with his friends behind him, Colt pushed through the door of Joe's Place, ringing the bell above. As always, his gaze scanned the room until they landed on Carrie. And per usual, her gaze was searching him out as well. Her smile lit her face, and he knew he wanted to come home to that every night for the rest of his life.

Two weeks later, Carrie waited in the kitchen for Colt to come home from work. As soon as he walked in the door, she tried to hide her nerves but knew she was unsuccessful when he took one look at her, stalked straight over, and wrapped her in his embrace.

"What's up, babe?" he asked.

She had spent most of the afternoon trying to figure out how to word what she wanted to say, but all of that jumped out of her mind when she blurted, "My landlord sent me a note that said the duplex is ready for George and me to move back into."

Without skipping a beat, Colt walked to the door leading to George's apartment over the garage and shouted up, "George! Can you come down to talk?"

"Be right there," George shouted his reply.

Still without saying anything else in reply to her statement, Colt moved to the back door, threw it open, and shouted, "Jack! Need you to come in, buddy. We got something to talk about."

As he moved back toward her, Carrie placed her fists on her hips and said, "Colt! I wanted us to talk about this privately first."

Holding her gaze, he shook his head, and just as

George and Jack came into the room, he said, "This involves all of us, so we're going to have a family meeting."

Her eyes bugged out of her head as he turned to George and Jack, saying, "Let's settle around the table." The others moved without question, and Colt excused himself, going upstairs. He returned a moment later, sat down, and linked his fingers with hers.

Turning to all of them, Colt said, "Carrie has just informed me that your former landlord has finished with his repairs on the duplex and is ready for you all to move back."

Jack gasped, and George's brows lowered, but Colt was not finished. "As far as I'm concerned, that would be a waste of time."

Jerking her head around toward Colt, she wondered what he meant.

"We can stay?" Jack asked, his voice near a whisper.

Now, jerking her gaze back to her son, she began, "Jack, honey, we can't—"

"As far as I'm concerned, we're a family," Colt declared, "and families belong together." Before anyone had a chance to speak, he continued, "George, you need to make whatever decision is best for you, but I want you to know that that apartment over the garage is yours if you want it."

Slapping his hand on the table, George grinned. "Colt, I absolutely would like to have that apartment. We can discuss rent because I won't be a freeloader, but it's plenty big for me, gives me privacy, but still makes me feel like I'm part of a family."

Carrie, heart pounding, stared at her son, seeing the hope in his eyes. Not knowing what Colt had planned, she swallowed audibly before turning to hold his gaze.

He twisted in his seat to face her, capturing her legs between his knees, taking both of her hands in his, he said, "Carrie, this isn't exactly the setting I pictured, but now that I think about it, it seems perfect. I've been in love with you for a while now, knowing that I want to spend my life with you. I love having you in this house and would like you to stay." He shifted slightly in his seat, sticking his hand into his pocket. Colt pulled out a ring, holding it up for her to see. It was a diamond solitaire, the white gold band encrusted with smaller diamonds.

She gasped once more, and he held her left hand and said, "Will you do me the honor of becoming my wife?"

Her mouth dropped open as tears hit her eyes. Before she had a chance to speak, Jack prodded, "Mom!"

Nodding her head up and down in jerks, she said, "Yes, yes, I'll marry you."

Colt slid the ring onto her finger, leaned forward and kissed her gently, then turned toward Jack and asked, "You, your mom, and I can talk about it more, but I'd like to become your dad. I'd like to officially adopt you. But if that's not what you want, then I'm just honored to have you in my life."

Carrie looked over at Jack's face, tears shimmering in his own eyes, as he nodded. "There's nothing to talk about, Colt. I'd give anything to have you be my dad."

Jack jumped up from his chair and raced toward his mom, and Colt wrapped his arms around both of them.

Grinning, George said, "Woowee, looks like we got ourselves a family!"

30

ONE MONTH LATER

The sky was blue, dotted with white clouds that floated by, occasionally giving respite from the hot sun. The background was filled with the beautiful skyline of modern buildings. Closer in, toward the right, was the eight-stories tall, long brick warehouse, dotted with windows that overlooked the Oriole Park at Camden Yards in Baltimore.

Their seats were halfway up behind the dugout, her mom to her right, Colt to her left, and Jack in between Colt and George. Her son could barely stay in his seat, cheering for each player that came to bat, groaning if they struck out.

Glancing down the row, she spied the expression on George's face. The boyish excitement on the older man's face caused her own lips to curl into a smile.

Her lap was filled with the remnants of a hot dog, popcorn bag, and soda. Colt had made sure they were well supplied with food, and she hesitated to imagine how much Jack had already eaten that day.

Looking around at the other spectators, she could tell that most were riveted to the game on the field, but her mind was filled with thoughts of the changes in her life. She and George had turned in a notice to their former landlord that they would not be returning to the duplex. Their friends had helped them move the rest of their furniture into Colt's house. George set up his apartment over Colt's garage, and while he had a small kitchen, he ate dinner with them most evenings.

Her furniture blended well with what Colt already had, his rooms now filled. Her mom kept her small apartment, but if she happened to stay over, Carrie's old room was now used as a guestroom.

Colt wanted her to have the wedding of her dreams, but with her ready-made family, her dreams had already come true. They planned for the wedding in the backyard of their home in another month, surrounded by family and friends. Joe and Mavis had even decided to close the diner down for the day.

Jack and George jumped to their feet, cheers screamed out, and Carrie startled, her gaze shooting back toward the field. While her mind had been drifting like the clouds above, the bases were loaded, and a home run was just hit. As the Orioles score climbed up by four, she watched her son's glee as he shouted and clapped.

Colt's arms slid around her shoulders, giving her a squeeze, and her eyes moved to his handsome face.

"You happy, babe?"

Her smile widened, and she replied, "How could I not be? My son is happier than he's ever been. George looks more youthful than I've ever seen him. My mom is relaxed and content, knowing we're not struggling. And I've got you. There's nothing else in the world that can make me happier."

As another batter walked onto the field, he was ignored by Colt and Carrie, who at that moment only had eyes for each other.

He leaned forward to kiss her but stopped a whisper away from her lips. One hand glided up to her face, his thumb smoothing over her cheeks. "Your time for struggling is over. My time for being alone is over. This, right now, is our time." His lips lowered to meet hers and, ignoring the game around them, she celebrated in his kiss.

Seven Years Later

It was another glorious, blue sky, white-fluffy-cloud spring day. The Baytown High School stadium was crowded, almost every seat taken. Men, once boys who loved baseball, now filled the bleachers with their wives and children. Tori and Mitch Evans. Jillian and Grant Wilder. Katelyn and Gareth Harrison. Ginny and Brogan McFarlane. Jade and Lance Greene. Maddie and Zac Hamilton. Belle and Hunter Simmons. Lea and Aiden McFarlane. Callan and Sophie Ward. Rose and Jason Boswell. Many other of their friends, relatives, and coworkers sat near them, all enjoying the game.

But front and center were Carrie and Colt Hudson. And all eyes were on the pitcher for the Baytown High School baseball team, affectionately known as the Baytown Boys. The pitcher was a senior, already signed with a full-ride college scholarship to play baseball the next year.

Tall, strong, lean muscles, his face was a mask of concentration. With his final pitch, the batter struck out, and the crowd cheered wildly.

Carrie's heart beat sure and strong in her chest as she watched the Baytown Boys lift Jack up in their arms, carrying him off the field. In the midst of the revelry, he looked up, his eyes pinned on her, and he grinned. For a flash, she saw the little boy that had been her heart and soul since the day he was born. Then she could tell his eyes drifted to the side, his grin even wider as he took in Colt and the other two children with them. Colt was holding their almost six-year-old son, Carson, in his arms, so that he could see over the crowd down toward his adored older brother.

"Mama, mama!" She glanced down at the three-year-old, dark-haired, blue-eyed little girl in her arms.

"Did you see? Jack's silly!"

Kissing her daughter's forehead, she gave her a bounce and said, "Oh, Beth, he's not silly. His friends just are excited, so they picked him up to bounce him around like you."

Colt set their son back on his feet and turned to pull Beth from her arms, blowing raspberries on her neck as she giggled. Looking down at the dark head and dark eyes of Carson, she felt the air rush from her lungs, realizing how fast the years had flown. It seemed like yesterday that Jack was that age.

The crowd began to disperse, George taking Carson by the hand and Della carrying Beth. Colt wrapped his arm around her and said, “What’s the matter, babe?”

Sighing, she admitted, “I know I should be thrilled, but all I can think of is how fast time is flying. I want to capture it and hold onto our time.”

Colt stopped and turned toward her, drawing her into his arms. Holding her gaze, he leaned down and kissed her lightly. “You’ve given me everything, Carrie. A family. A home. And these things aren’t going anywhere. It will only get better…graduations, marriages, grandchildren. No matter how many years pass, as long as you and I are together, we’ll always be in our time.”

Wrapping her arms around his neck, she pulled him tighter, their hearts pressed together, and she kissed him once more. Settling back on her heels with a smile, they linked fingers and walked with the rest of their friends and family to the fence to greet the Baytown Boys champions.

Don’t miss the next Baytown Boys!
Count On Me

Scott Redding was determined to live his life and not be defined as an amputee.

Meeting Beau Weston was to help the older man settle his affairs… not change Scott's life.

Farmer Lizzie Weston was as independent as she was hardworking. Accepting help from Scott would never work… afterall, what could he know about farming?

As Scott and Lizzie worked to save Weston farm, animosity grew into understanding… and then to love.

But someone is out to force Lizzie to sell, and it's up to Scott to save the farm… and her.

Please take the time to leave a review of this book. Feel free to contact me, especially if you enjoyed my book. I love to hear from readers!
Facebook
Email
Website

ALSO BY MARYANN JORDAN

Don't miss other Maryann Jordan books!

Lots more Baytown stories to enjoy and more to come!

Baytown Boys (small town, military romantic suspense)

Coming Home

Just One More Chance

Clues of the Heart

Finding Peace

Picking Up the Pieces

Sunset Flames

Waiting for Sunrise

Hear My Heart

Guarding Your Heart

Sweet Rose

Our Time

Count On Me

Shielding You

To Love Someone

For all of Miss Ethel's boys:

Heroes at Heart (Military Romance)

Zander

Rafe

Cael

Jaxon

Jayden

Asher

Zeke

Cas

Lighthouse Security Investigations

Mace

Rank

Walker

Drew

Blake

Tate

Hope City (romantic suspense series co-developed with Kris Michaels

Brock book 1

Sean book 2

Carter book 3

Brody book 4

Kyle book 5

Ryker book 6

Rory book 7

Killian book 8

Saints Protection & Investigations

(an elite group, assigned to the cases no one else wants…or can solve)

Serial Love

Healing Love

Revealing Love

Seeing Love

Honor Love

Sacrifice Love

Protecting Love

Remember Love

Discover Love

Surviving Love

Celebrating Love

Follow the exciting spin-off series:

Alvarez Security (military romantic suspense)

Gabe

Tony

Vinny

Jobe

SEALs

Thin Ice (Sleeper SEAL)

SEAL Together (Silver SEAL)

Letters From Home (military romance)

Class of Love

Freedom of Love

Bond of Love

The Love's Series (detectives)

Love's Taming

Love's Tempting

Love's Trusting

The Fairfield Series (small town detectives)

Emma's Home

Laurie's Time

Carol's Image

Fireworks Over Fairfield

Please take the time to leave a review of this book. Feel free to contact me, especially if you enjoyed my book. I love to hear from readers!

Facebook

Email

Website

I am an avid reader of romance novels, often joking that I cut my teeth on the historical romances. I have been reading and reviewing for years. In 2013, I finally gave into the characters in my head, screaming for their story to be told. From these musings, my first novel, Emma's Home, The Fairfield Series was born.

I was a high school counselor having worked in education for thirty years. I live in Virginia, having also lived in four states and two foreign countries. I have been married to a wonderfully patient man for thirty-five years. When writing, my dog or one of my four cats can generally be found in the same room if not on my lap.

Please take the time to leave a review of this book. Feel free to contact me, especially if you enjoyed my book. I love to hear from readers!

Facebook

Email

Website

Made in United States
Troutdale, OR
09/05/2023

12653949R00200